Praise for Facing the Mind Trap

*"Teresa Devine's debut novel weaves a story of
love that overcomes the winds of change.
Masterful writing!"*
- DiAnn Mills, Lethal Standoff - Tyndale Publishing 2024

FACING

THE

MIND TRAP

TERESA DEVINE

24/7 Purpose® Publishing

Contents

CHAPTER 1

The Fall

My car rolls toward the faded stop sign, and I'm reminded of another crossroad ahead of me. Can a weekend at the lake cottage revive a twenty-year marriage on life support, or is it too late?

I stare at the stop sign with hopeless dread about thoughts of divorce. My brain sizzles. The annoying sound of the turn signal intensifies and jolts me back to the present. I wipe my brow, grip the steering wheel with both hands, and check the rearview mirror to see if I'm holding up traffic. Slowly turning to the right, I sigh. Why do I take on so much? Cramming in new proposals didn't help with back-to-back calls with my sales team.

Another forty-five minutes before arriving at the lake cottage should give me enough breathing room to unwind. Plus, I'll have a few hours alone before Jacob arrives—or longer, considering Atlanta traffic on a Friday evening. It's bumper-to-bumper madness. After a deep breath, I settle into the supple leather. The winding roads hypnotize me as thoughts return to Jacob.

Imagining life without my husband makes me queasy and afraid. But something must change. It's foolish to ignore our separate lives, chilly conversations, and silent dinners. Tensions are thickening. We used to laugh until we cried, yell at the TV umpires during baseball games, and take long walks in the park eating chocolate fudge ice cream. His favorite. He called me his ginger spice, referring to my auburn hair and fiery spirit. Still love that nickname. Since he towers over me, I loved reaching up so he could wrap his arms around my waist and lift me up for a kiss. He laughed through his big wide smile, deep ocean-blue eyes, and sandy-brown hair while twirling us around. What happened? We were so great together.

Early in our marriage, being with Jacob was my favorite pastime. But today, I search for ways to be apart and avoid the pain by masquerading as an overly busy, happy couple. Meanwhile, the deceptive charade widens the hole of separation.

I'm thankful Jacob's not having an affair, but I need a better reason than two people allowing busyness to wipe out a love story like ours. How pathetic. Is it naïve to expect a few quiet days at the lake cottage could be the magic remedy for our fading marriage? As I inhaled deeply once more, I released it all.

Years of memories invade my thoughts, trying to pinpoint the precise moment we detached. The distance happened so gradually, like ocean waves eroding the seashore. Since the children were born, our marriage began weakening and the distinction of us as a couple became a family frenzy. As empty nesters, we face a massive void once filled by our two remarkable children. I yearn for a renewal of the love that once bound us together, but I'm clueless on how to revive it. Is this our permanent reality with no way back?

I'd like to blame Jacob for our disconnected relationship, but we're both guilty contributors to the downfall. Juggling demanding careers, school activities, and ambitious kids, our lives were hectic. We had minimal private time together. He spent many days traveling, yet some-how, he created special moments with our children. They spent lots of time with me, but more *quality* time with Jacob. I admit being envious and even resenting him for it. Raising the kids was amazing, and we still adore them as young adults. However, I wish we had united more often versus parenting as isolated role models.

Ahead, I spot the faded bass fish mailbox on the right, which means I'm nearing the cottage entrance. My stomach churns thinking about the outcome of this weekend. At the driveway entrance, I notice the large stone columns and the massive cedars lining the drive welcoming my arrival. I lower the window to inhale the pungent aroma of fresh-cut grass, fall leaves, and damp trees. The birds sing loudly as if they're welcoming my homecoming. I swear this property was larger as a kid.

Fond memories of cousins playing volleyball and diving off the boat dock fill my thoughts. Summer gatherings were an annual family tradition. However, this place symbolizes more than just cookouts and fireworks. It's part of my heritage. My life is built on unforgettable experiences with memories I hold close—and skeletons even closer.

I tap the brake, close my eyes, and squeeze the steering wheel.

God, if You're listening, please restore my marriage and heal the pain from my past. I beg You. The weight of this lingering sorrow is killing me. If our marriage is over, please give me strength to move on without Jacob. Amen.

Head on the wheel, tears stream down my face. I release the brake and creep toward the ivy-covered carport and park. I shut the car off and sit quietly, taking in the surroundings. Why should God answer my prayers? Even though we attend church occasionally, I don't feel close to Him. Seems like I only cry out to God when I need something.

Back to more pressing matters. The pressure of this weekend's outcome is sinking in. With a quick glance in the visor mirror, I notice puffy bags under my eyes. I pat my cheeks and fluff my hair. I need to prepare the cottage before Jacob arrives. We like it cozy. I rub my sweaty palms together and realize my desire to please him hasn't faded. I better get moving. It may take some time to unpack the luggage and stock the kitchen.

I step out of the car, peering at the spider webs covering the windows. Can't see through them—sorta like our marriage. As I scan the property further, I stop and stare at the ground. The overwhelming loss of our family gatherings brings back the queasy stomach. Then it hit me. The last summer reunion was the year of the family incident. My knees buckle, so I reach for the car door handle to catch my balance. I shake my head. Instead of unloading my packed car, I keep revisiting the past and wasting time.

One would think I'm staying two weeks. I can barely maneuver the luggage. If Jacob was here, he would lovingly tease me about the size of my makeup bag and the amount of sunscreen I use for my pale, freckled skin. Did I remember to pack my facial cream for those pesky wrinkles? I prefer to call them grooves of wisdom. I bet Jacob misses the perky, petite Isabelle with longer ginger hair. More likely, he sees an aging, boring woman with nothing left in common. The woman he tries to avoid.

I try to keep my balance walking toward the front door, pulling a large roller bag and two bags flung over my left shoulder. There it is. The coveted leprechaun statue sits in the same spot since my earliest memory. Paint chips lay on the ground from the weathered concrete, and his nose has deteriorated. I plop the bags down and lean the statue over to capture the front door key. I grin, recalling how Grandma Millie loved that statue, and to her, Irish traditions were more sacred than home security. With rare antiques and valuables, Aunt Maggie wanted an alarm system installed, but Grandma refused. Feisty Irish confidence was her trademark. I miss her.

As I open the door and step in, I'm hit with the harsh odor of musty pine and mothballs mixed with a slight hint of Grandma's cinnamon apple cobbler. I gather my luggage outside the door and place the bags on racks in the master bedroom. The cottage is dark. I rush to the sliding patio doors facing the mountains and pull back the curtains to gaze at the colorful view. I gasp, looking at the stunning hills showing off their cornucopia of colors. A dim, overcast sky hovers over the land-scape, whispering a gentle reminder of the slow death of another fall season. Still, it's my favorite time of year. I love witnessing the transfor-mative power of discarding the old and embracing the new. Especially now.

On my left, Mr. Merriweather shuffles down the narrow path toward the old church cemetery, carrying a red rose. Rosemary's favorite. As usual, he's dressed in his long wool coat and tweed Gatsby cap. His cane wobbles more since our last visit. Is his health worsening? His dedication to his lovely wife Rosemary goes beyond this earthly understanding, and I yearn to reignite the romance in my marriage if we still can.

My phone rings, and glancing at the screen, I see Jacob's picture. I smile.

"Hi, there. I made it to the lake cottage."

"Hey, I bet traffic was awful with the leaf-watchers heading out of the city. I'm still at the office, and unless there's an emergency, I expect to arrive on time."

"Sounds good. Traffic wasn't that bad. Fall colors are spectacular, and guess who's taking a rose to the love of his life?"

"Must be our favorite neighbor. How is Mr. Merriweather?"

"We haven't spoken yet, but I'll stop over tomorrow. I can't believe it's been six years since Rosemary passed. I miss her and her delicious peach pies. Remember her hugs? Like plunging into a super-sized bean bag chair with vice grips. Imagine having a marriage like theirs?"

"Whatever. You're never happy, Isabelle." The hint of frustration didn't escape me.

"You took it the wrong way. You can't deny they had a rare, unmistakable love, and I'd kill for an ounce of Rosemary's warm charm. That's all I meant." I sigh.

He huffs. "Why be so hard on yourself? Rosemary was special in her unique way, and so are you."

"Thanks. You've always been my biggest fan, I think." Did I force him to give me a compliment?

"I've told you countless times you are amazing. A little overbearing, yes."

I smirk. "Whatever."

"Listen, we raised two amazing kids, and you're a top-ranking sales executive. Give yourself some well-deserved credit."

"I suppose. Can the law firm survive without you for three days?"

"Sure, they can."

While being distracted by the vivid colors blanketing the mountains, I continue listening to Jacob and step out on the weathered deck to keep a watchful eye on Mr. Merriweather. I press my foot on a rotting board. Looks like my marriage isn't the only thing being neglected. Still listening to Jacob, he runs through the set-up list for the cabin and offers to help when he arrives. A loud crackle and pop startle me.

"Is that the big cedar? Oh, my goodness, Jacob. It's starting to fall."

"What's happening? Isabelle . . . Isabelle?"

I drop my phone and race to Mr. Merriweather, but piles of dead leaves slow me down. The old tree is breaking, and my elderly fragile neighbor is right in its path. Can he hear it? I wave my arms in the air, but he keeps walking.

"Watch out. Get out of the way. The cedar is falling, Mr. Merriweather."

"Isabelle, are you there?"

CHAPTER 2

The Nightmare

JACOB

After a loud thug, Isabelle's phone is silent, sending a shock wave through my blood vessels. I hang up and call back, but I get her voicemail. Fear becomes panic and burns the pit in my stomach. Wait, I bet she's assisting Mr. Merriweather. If he's hurt, she may be taking him back to his house. It could take a while before she returns my call. No need to overreact. My hand struggles to hold the phone steady while I call 911. The dispatcher asks for my emergency.

"I'm not sure what is happening, but my wife dropped her phone after screaming about a tree falling in our backyard. She said our elderly neighbor was walking nearby so he might be hurt or even Isabelle, my wife. Please hurry. I'm heading there now." I give her the address and grab my keys and laptop.

My assistant, Beth, overheard my call, and offers to cancel my meetings. I nod and ask her to lock up my office. Darting into the elevator and riding five floors down seems like an eternity. Once the door opens, I sprint through the parking garage to my car.

With my warning lights flashing, zigzagging through traffic, I speed to the lake cottage. I'll be there in under an hour if I drive without getting arrested, and my hands stop shaking. At least I have a half tank of gas. I'm dizzy, envisioning Isabelle or Mr. Merriweather being harmed.

Lord, please protect them from harm and help me stay calm.

I plug in the phone charger and call Isabelle's phone again. No answer. I'm gaining speed. A semi-truck hauling farm tractors pulls in front of me in the passing lane and slows me down. I call her again but still no answer. Mr. Merriweather doesn't have a mobile phone, so I ring his house. No one answers.

The semi-truck merges toward the middle lane, and I'm free to speed up again. I approach the fast lane and press the pedal to the floor. The thought of my wife hurt or worse and my inability to help makes me crazy. Hearing a helicopter whizzing overhead, I peer up through the windshield. Is it rushing to rescue Isabelle? I can't shake the sick feeling in my gut.

Just minutes from the cottage, I spot flashing lights on the horizon. Could it be from firetrucks and ambulances? Please, no.

My car skids into the cottage driveway. I leave the door open and sprint to the backyard and spot the big cedar lying like a giant fortress. My pulse races. Where is Isabelle? So many people rushing around it's difficult to see what's happening.

Mr. Merriweather sits near the fallen tree with a paramedic, seemingly unscathed. At least he's moving his arms and talking. I rush to him and kneel so he can hear me.

"Are you okay? Where is Isabelle?"

"Oh, Jacob, I'm so glad to see you." He weeps uncontrollably and can't speak clearly. "I'm fine, but poor Isabelle. It's all my fault."

My eyes tear up as I clutch his shoulders. "Where is she?"

He points toward the massive tree. I whirl around and spot a female medic standing near the timber with her arms crossed, observing those working around the fallen cedar. I race to her.

"Hi. I'm Jacob Beckham. Isabelle's husband." I lean forward, putting my hands on my knees, and breathe. My lungs fill with air, while fear pounds in my heart. "Is she here?"

She stares back at me with widened eyes that sends a panic surge up my spine.

"Yes, your wife is here. I'm Pamela, from the Somerset medical unit. Your neighbor shared Isabelle's information with us. I'm so sorry."

"Where is she?"

"She's stuck beneath some large branches after pushing your neighbor out of the way. She saved his life. He might suffer minor bruising, but she couldn't move away in time."

I clutch my head, staring at the sky, trying to hold back the tears.

"But there's good news, Mr. Beckham. She landed away from the weightiest part of the tree. The medical team is doing everything they can to get her out."

I clutch the back of my neck and stare at the ground. This can't be happening. "Is she responsive?"

"You need to check with the paramedics assisting her. I'll escort you."

A crowd of medical personnel surrounds the fallen tree, and we push our way through. I must get to Isabelle. A glimpse of her green shirt appears through the leaves and debris. That's her. I grab my knees to fight the nausea rising in my belly. How can I get closer?

Chainsaws rip through the thick cedar, echoing throughout the hillside, deafening any chance she might hear my voice. I have to get closer, let her know I'm here. People scamper around like ants, removing branches and debris after each saw cut.

After a tap on the shoulder, I turn to see Pamela standing with a tall, brawny gentleman.

"Jacob, this is Lieutenant Steve Tyrell. He's in charge of Isabelle's rescue and will assist you from here."

I shake the lieutenant's hand. His grip is intense. "Hello, sir. How's she doing? How long until you get her out?"

His kind eyes meet mine. "I understand the urgency, and we're doing everything in our power to get your wife out safely. So far, she isn't responding and appears to be unconscious. The fallen branches create a house of cards. One miscalculation from the saw blade could shift the entire weight of the tree and crush her. We're avoiding that threat by cutting away each branch with precision. That takes time."

I blow air in and out, trying to think clearly. "I can't believe this is happening. She might respond better to my voice."

"Let's try."

Lieutenant Steve leads me to the worst scene of my life. Workers scurry around the tree among flurries of sawdust and the poignant scent of gasoline. I hold back the nausea again. If I can keep it together and speak to her, maybe she will respond.

Steve waves at the chainsaw crew to pause, giving me an opportunity to talk to my precious wife. Kneeling by a large branch, I squeeze through a gap to hear Isabelle or catch a glimpse of her face.

"Isabelle, it's Jacob. Can you hear me? Please say something."

Nothing but silence. I try two more times with the same result. "Hold on, honey."

With so much debris covering her body, I can't tell how badly she's hurt. What if she's gone? I clutch my mouth and my body shakes uncontrollably. Lieutenant Steve rescues me from the branches, away from the crew. I can't feel my legs. He holds me steady until I can walk on my own.

Minutes seem like hours, every second counts with saving my lovely wife. I can't help flashing back to our earlier conversations and her fragile emotions. I shake my head, refocusing on the nightmare in front of me.

Lieutenant Steve crawls into the debris. "Isabelle, can you hear me? Please say something or make a sound. Stay with us. We'll get you out of there." He repeats the same question a few more times, but silence lingers. He motions to the crew, and the buzz of chainsaws fills the air again, while firefighters clear the cut wood away from Isabelle. A petite medic makes her way beneath the tree and claws through a small tunnel in the dirt toward Isabelle's body. Please let the medic find a pulse. She struggles to reach Isabelle's small, still hand and wrist, pressing down to reveal the fateful outcome.

"I have a pulse, a weak pulse. Isabelle, my name is Alison, and I'm going to stay with you until you're out of here. Team, bring in the stretcher."

She's alive. My knees buckle to the ground as I whisper thanks to God. I have faith my sweet Isabelle is going to be okay.

The crew shouts, exchanging a quick high-five while Lieutenant Steve throws one fist in the air. "Excellent work, team. Isabelle, please make any sound."

Everyone is eager to pick up a murmur or groan, yet nothing materializes.

Alison turns to the Lieutenant. "Her pulse is very weak, sir. We need to move faster."

"Roger that, Alison." He claps his hands fiercely. "Team, time is critical. Let's move."

Distracted by a roaring vibration, I look up. A bright red helicopter appears in the sky, landing in our backyard, reminding me of the helicopter flying over the highway on my way here. With more debris cleared, I move closer to watch the medical team prepare Isabelle for the flight.

I clasp my mouth, holding back the nausea rising in my throat and the tears stream. Why is this happening? I stare at my wife lying in the rubble. Bruises and blood dominate her pale face. Covered in mashed leaves and sticks, her beautiful red hair is mangled, and her bottom left leg appears broken at the knee.

The medical team tries to pull her away but discovers her right foot trapped under a branch. A firefighter jumps in with large cutters to detach the tree limb, and she's free. On the second attempt, they place Isabelle's limp body onto the stretcher and check her pulse. It's barely detectable.

"She's out. Let's get her on the chopper," Lieutenant Steve says.

I run alongside the stretcher that carries my Isabelle, who is fighting for her life. Not a situation I could ever imagine. The paramedics continue checking her pulse, but there is no improvement.

The flight to the hospital seems like another eternity. I'm touching her hand, yet I can't grip the reality of my sweet Isabelle lying there on a stretcher, struggling to stay alive. What if she has internal bleeding? The weight of helplessness is unbearable. We need a miracle.

Two paramedics perform medical procedures on Isabelle. Their expertise ignites a spark of hope within me. *Please, God, help her.*

Moments later, we arrive at the emergency room. Medics hurry, and I feel a warmth for the first time since I saw Isabelle under the big cedar.

I rush in behind them, expecting to be with her in the examination room, but a short, stout nurse grabs my arm.

"Sir, you can't go in there. I doubt you want to interfere with the doctors' work. They need to prep her for emergency surgery. Step over here."

"I'm her husband, and I need to be with her." Then I gain my senses and realize I can't be in the doctors' way. The nurse steps back with her hands on her hips, giving me a warm smile.

"What's your name?"

"Jacob Beckham. That's my wife, Isabelle."

"Nice to meet you, Jacob. I'm Nurse Wanda, and I'll keep you updated about your wife throughout this process. Consider me your personal advocate."

I slap both hands against the cool concrete wall, sobbing. Why is this happening to Isabelle? The warmth of Wanda's hand on my back brings surprising comfort, and I pull myself together.

"Oh, my, Jacob. I see you've been through an awful experience. It's tough, but Isabelle needs you to stay strong for her. Do you understand me?" Her firm compassion pierces my heart.

"Yes, ma'am. You're right, and I appreciate your help."

"Okay then. Allow me to bring you a cup of coffee. How do you drink it?"

"Black."

We lock watery eyes. She gives me a thin smile and pats my arm. "I'll be right back."

Wanda shuffles away with a noticeable limp on her right side. My empathy must be on high alert. Others in the waiting area have weary faces and swollen red eyes. I'm a mess too. How will I tell the kids?

My mind replays the last few hours, but I shake my head to focus on the present. Wanda appears with coffee in hand. Good timing.

She hands me a Styrofoam cup. "I need to make my rounds. Will you be okay waiting here?"

"Yes, I'll be fine, and thank you for the coffee."

"You wait here while the doctors do their job, and we will update you as soon as possible. Any other needs before I leave?"

I clutch her arm. "Will you pray for her?"

"Child, I'm a prayer warrior. Better yet, let's pray together."

She sits next to me, extending her plump, leathery hands to mine. I face her, and we pray. For a millisecond, optimism enters my spirit from her kindness. I am grateful to God for blessing me with Wanda, my Nurse Angel.

"I need to visit my other patients, but I will check in with the nurses for a progress report soon. I'll notify you if I learn anything. Promise. The hospital chapel is down the hall. You'll see the sign. I'll be back later."

"Thank you, Wanda."

The kids. I'm dreading this moment. I'll call Travis first. The phone rings three times and he picks up.

"Hey, Dad. I'm glad you called, but I'm about to walk into my business class. Can I call you afterward?"

"Travis, listen to me. I have some news about your mother. Please sit down."

"Dad, you're scaring me. What's going on?"

"Your mother had a serious accident at the lake cottage. She's been air lifted to Atlanta and is undergoing emergency surgery. Her pulse is very weak. I can't tell how badly she's injured, but it's not good. I need you here with me."

"Oh, my gosh. I can't believe this. What happened?"

"A freak accident. The large cedar snapped and fell, pinning your mother beneath some heavy branches. She saved Mr. Merriweather from the fall. I'll share more details later. Please get on the next flight to Atlanta."

"Dad, I'll leave right now. Will Mom be okay?"

"I'm praying she will. We need to stay positive."

"You got it. Did you tell Katie?"

"I'm calling her next. I'll have her connect with you to coordinate flights from Austin and Denver into Atlanta. Please help keep her calm."

"Of course. I can't wrap my head around this yet, but you can count on me, Dad. I'll text you my flight information and keep you posted."

"Thank you, Travis. I love you."

"Love you too. Bye."

Even as a child, Travis owned an inner confidence. The type that handles pressure with steadiness and strength. Perhaps he falls apart behind closed doors, but no one sees. He will handle this like a soldier. My Katie-bug is another story. It's time to call her with the news. The phone rings, and thankfully, she picks up.

"Hi, Dad. What's up? You never call me on a Friday afternoon."

"Hi, Katie-bug. I have some bad news."

She gasps. "Is everything okay?"

"Are you in your dorm room?"

"Yes. I'm here with Alyssa."

"Good. Please sit down."

"Dad, I'm scared. What's this about?"

"It's your mother. She had a terrible accident at the lake cottage, and she's in the hospital having surgery."

Katie's shriek is no surprise. I clinch my teeth and cover my heart.

"What? Dad, no. Is she okay?"

"Please stay calm. We won't have the details until she's out of surgery, but you need to get to Atlanta immediately. I just called your brother, and he's headed to the airport." I grimace from the sobbing on the other end. Nothing prepares a father for these moments. She tries to get the words out between sniffles.

"Not . . . Mom. Will she be okay?"

"I'm praying she will, Katie-bug. Let's stay positive and hope for the best. Please catch the next flight from Denver." I'm not sure she hears me through her sobbing.

"Mr. Beckham, it's Alyssa. Katie put you on the speakerphone. I'm here to help."

"Oh good. Thank you, Alyssa. Katie, do you understand what I'm saying?"

"I need my mom. How did this happen?" The trembling in her voice breaks my heart.

"There's no time, I'll tell you everything when you arrive at the hospital. Now, pack a bag and call your brother to coordinate flights, if possible. Alyssa, can you drive her to the Denver airport?"

"Yes, sir. No problem."

"Thank you. And Katie, please stay calm. Everything will work out. I love you."

"I love you too. Bye."

The absence of being there to hug Katie is devastating. I've tried to be the tower of strength for my kids, but today, this tower is swaying. I pray my kids arrive safely.

The ticking of the wall clock in the surgery waiting room, although annoying, helps me focus. Hours pass, no sign of Nurse Wanda or doctors. I pestered the nurses' station too many times to face them again.

What is taking so long? With every sound, I stretch my neck to see if a doctor is coming. No such luck.

It's my fault. The last time at the cabin, Mr. Merriweather pointed out the rot within the enormous cedar tree to me. I put off cutting it down. If I had gone to the cabin with her, the outcome might be different. Isabelle begged for more time together, urging me to take Friday off. Once again, I chose work over her.

When will I learn? Now? When it might be too late? Oh, what have I done to us? I cover my face as tears stream down my cheeks.

With my third coffee in hand, I make another lap around the corridors. I spot Wanda heading my way. She forces a smile, but the gesture quickly fades. She tries picking up her pace and I rush to her.

"Wanda, how is she?"

"She just came out of surgery. The doctor will speak with you soon."

I hug my nurse angel. I'm desperate to see Isabelle and hear that she will recover. As I pull away from Wanda, the doctor approaches. His stoic facial expressions don't tell me a thing about Isabelle's condition.

"I'm Dr. Abbot. Are you Isabelle Beckham's husband?"

We shake hands. "Yes, I'm Jacob Beckham. How is she?" Wanda turns to walk away, but I ask her to stay.

"It's difficult to say this. Your wife's condition is critical. She's alive, but her pulse is extremely weak. We didn't find injuries to her neck, back, and spine beyond bruising, so that's the good news. The bad news is she's suffering from severe head trauma and multiple injuries. My primary concern is the brain hemorrhage causing internal bleeding. We stopped the bleeding, but we need to monitor her progress before we declare victory on the hemorrhage." He pauses, placing his hand on my shoulder. "There's more."

"What is it, doctor?"

"She's in a coma and unresponsive. Unsure if she'll survive the night."

Stabilizing my balance, I place one hand on Wanda's shoulder while staring back at the doctor in bewilderment. I rock sideways and she grips my other hand.

"I can't believe this. Anything else?"

"She has five broken ribs, a shattered bone in her left leg, and multiple fractures in her left arm and shoulder. If she's still with us in the morning, she will undergo multiple surgeries, and if she recovers from the coma, her brain could have permanent damage. I'm so sorry."

My knees weaken but falling apart doesn't help Isabelle, so I regain composure.

"Thank you, doctor. What's the next step?"

"We keep her in ICU for close monitoring, and I expect her to remain there for a while. I'll check on her throughout the night, and we'll know more in the morning."

"Is there anything I can do?" Wanda places her hand on my arm. The calluses tell me she's fought hard battles and survived.

"Stay strong. If you haven't notified your family, I recommend contacting them now. Be encouraged that we're doing everything possible to keep your wife alive."

My heart pounds as if it might burst from my chest, and I can't hold back the pain. I bend over and weep.

Dr. Abbot bends over with me, placing his hand firmly on my back. "I know it's hard, but please stay optimistic. We have our best on this."

Wanda steps in. "He needs a minute to process the news, doc. I'll stay here until he's feeling better."

"Thank you. I need to go check on his wife."

I hold up my finger. "Doc, wait. When can I see her?"

"A nurse will lead you to Isabelle's room once she's settled."

After a few steps, the doctor stops, and walks back to me. "Mr. Beckham, I heard how Isabelle risked her life to save your neighbor. I understand he's in his eighties, and it's likely he wouldn't have survived the same injuries. Your wife is young and healthy, with a much greater chance of recovery. She's a hero."

His words about Isabelle pierce me. She was already a hero to me. Wanda guides me to an empty seat, sits next to me, and pats my knee.

"This will work out, Jacob. Stay strong."

Speechless, I stare ahead. Powerless, I close my eyes and surrender to the darkest place. What if life as we know it, ends?

"Forgive me, Wanda. I'm usually much stronger than this. Helplessness is an unfamiliar enemy."

"Child, you have God on your side, and you must press into your faith. Seek His strength instead of your own. During times like these, we discover God's glorious power if we trust Him. You will get through this, and I'm praying for a complete recovery for your wife."

I nod and wipe my stinging eyes, throw my shoulders back and stiffen. For one split second, the mental shift seemed to wash away a nightmare, but the terror continues.

Wanda stands, pursing her lips. "Are you okay with being alone while I make my rounds again?"

"Yes. You've done enough." She smiles wide and turns to leave.

Watching her limp away reminds me of our blessed life. Until today, Isabelle and I were vibrant and healthy. Leaning back in my chair in the waiting area, visions of our interrupted weekend sink in.

This morning over coffee, Isabelle spoke about being nervous and excited. I sensed the same anxiousness. When she shared the level of her frustration with our marriage about a month ago, it stunned me. Yes, we have grown apart, but I never thought divorce was a possibility. Regardless of how much I try, I can't make her happy. Lord knows, sometimes I didn't care. Avoided her. Tuned her out. Will I get another chance?

Work consumed me after graduating from law school. That's my fault. Then having kids, we shifted our attention to them, snatching the romance from our marriage. My frequent work travels didn't help and poked at Isabelle's wounds from her past. Even though she assured me traveling was not a big deal, I should have been more aware of the potential impact.

She's an amazing mother, and we love our kids, but we took our relationship for granted. Not only is our marriage in shambles, but she's in there also fighting for her life.

Clutching my chest, I rock back and forth in my chair, trying to soothe the sharp throbbing in my heart. Nothing can stop this pain except seeing Isabelle's smile again. Our marriage problems seem absurd now. What if I lose her?

CHAPTER 3

The Counselor

ISABELLE

I open my eyes to a wide-open plantation of stunning colors, with gigantic green mountains, lush gardens, and crystal-blue lagoons. It's overwhelming. Imagine the largest box of crayons ever produced and multiply the shades of colors by millions. It's indescribable, like combining my favorite trip to Oregon and Hawaii into something even more breathtaking. I spin to absorb everything. Where am I?

Someone is whistling. I whirl around to a slender man with a peppy walk approaching me from a distance. I stiffen. He steps closer, sharing a friendly wave as if he recognizes me. Who is this mystery man?

As he approaches, the whistling stops, and he offers a warm, brilliant smile. His wavy salt-and-pepper hair glistens, and his face glows through flawless skin. I'm most struck by his piercing green eyes shining like diamonds and emeralds competing for dominance.

His attire is sporty, wearing lightweight khaki hiking pants and a lightweight beige pullover. No shoes? Despite being casual, his clothes are tailored with perfect stitching, and he exudes a joyful vibe, like no one I've ever encountered. My body eases.

I raise my hand to block the glare from the long chain around his

19

neck. As I lower my hand, I see it's a magnificent gold key hanging from the chain. Must be a rare form of gold.

"Greetings, Isabelle," he said.

Startled, I jump back. That voice. It sounds so familiar, and yet, I don't know Him. "Hello, sir. How do you know my name? Where am I?"

"It's okay, Izzy. You're safe here. Oh, may I call you Izzy?"

I take another step backwards and cover my gaping mouth. "The only person who ever called me Izzy is my late Grandpa Finny. No one else since."

He smiles, a perfect gesture that soothes me. "Why only Grandpa Finny?"

"That's a good question. I'm not sure. Grandpa's name was Finn, but as a little girl, I called him Grandpa Finny, so he nicknamed me Izzy."

I lean forward cautiously with my right hand over my heart. "I suppose you may call me Izzy. And you are?"

"Please forgive me for being so presumptuous. Call me, Counselor."

"Counselor? What is your name?"

"That's it, just Counselor. Soon, I will reveal where you are, and why. For now, let's take a stroll and admire our surroundings. Shall we? Allow me to show you around your new place."

"My place? But why am I here?"

He motions for me to follow, but my arms and legs won't move. He whistles an uplifting tune, which radiates like an angelic song, and instantly my entire body relaxes. This mysterious man is undeniably non-threatening and endearing.

I walk behind Him on a narrow path, covered with small and large round gemstones in a variety of sparkling colors.

"Mr. Counselor, these pebbles are remarkable. They . . . they glow like real gemstones."

He laughs. "Well, that's because they are. You're stepping in the purest sapphires, diamonds, jasper, emeralds, rubies, and others. Follow me. I've prepared a special place for our time together, and I'll explain everything there."

As we continue walking, my body seems weightless. No, it *is* weightless, and it's exhilarating. I giggle as the tiny gems slip between my toes. Majestic trees line the path with a myriad of colorful butterflies and large flower blossoms. Waterfalls rush into crystal lagoons and birds sing high above the trees. Imperfections do not exist. Blades of grass are the exact size in a deep shade of green. The combination of warm air and whispering breezes provides the optimal temperature.

I breathe the aroma with hints of lilac and fresh linens hung outside to dry. It's delightful. The world's best spa is no match for this invigorating fragrance. No wonder. Ahead, dazzling lavender fields stretch for miles wafting in the breeze.

I examine the obscure stranger, who goes by Counselor, and we share a familiar smile, as if we're old friends. His silver hair glistens with each step. I sense a safety beyond my understanding being near Him. I rub my eyes. Is this another one of my crazy dreams?

He stretches out his hand to help me through a small creek bed of smooth rocks and stones in various shapes and sizes. I love creeks. Reminds me of college and being with Jacob.

"This way, Izzy. Watch your step."

I take his hand stepping cautiously on the wet stones. After reaching the other side of the creek bed, I stop. A sense of clarity and peace from his touch soothes me, remembering my first memory as a child. It's so vivid but strangely, only the joyful memories appear, and the volume surprises me. I laugh and quickly cover my mouth. What about the tragic memories from my early years? What's going on?

"Almost there. Just over this hill," he says.

We climb to the top of a small hill and my mouth drops open when viewing the most exquisite fairytale garden I've ever seen. An English-style setting overflowing with whimsical wildflowers, soft shaded roses, and pink tulips. Precisely manicured topiaries line the outer edge of an outdoor sitting area. It's magical.

"Here we are." He gestures. "This is your sanctuary. A place designed for you and our private time together. You prefer the outdoors, don't you?"

"Yes. It's extraordinary."

We enter the sanctuary through a perfectly crafted white trellis covered in soft pink rose vines and lavender sprigs. At the top of the trellis hangs a wooden sign engraved with the words *Izzy's Sanctuary*. I pause and close my eyes, inhaling the intoxicating fragrance of a hundred rose bouquets.

He rushes to a cozy sitting area with two oversized chairs facing each other. The matching chairs appear super comfy and made of soft, white cotton fabric. Like a pair of old jeans. A sturdy wooden frame supporting a thick oval glass top serves as a small table between us.

"Come in. Make yourself comfortable while I pour us a hot cup of coffee."

"Okay. Thank you."

"Cream, no sugar, correct?"

"Yes." Is he a mind reader?

He gives me a wink while pouring the coffee into a delicate porcelain cup with a paisley design and pure gold handle. I sink into the down-filled chair made of the softest material. It's meticulously crafted, yet casual, reminding me of my favorite chair in college, minus the lumps, coffee stains, and duct tape.

In the garden, my teary eyes gaze at exquisite surroundings. All my favorites. Bougainvillea trees and lush hydrangea bushes stretch as far as I can see. An enormous weeping willow tree canopies the space, triggering memories of a similar tree my sisters and I climbed, where we sat and talked for hours.

The counselor stands before me, arms stretched wide. "What do you think, Izzy?"

I gulp. "The magnificent beauty overwhelms me, surrounded by many favorites. How did you know?"

He puts his hands on his hips and smirks. "I know all things, and I'm delighted the garden pleases you. How's the coffee?"

I take a sip and close my eyes to savor the flavor. It covers my tongue like a dark Belgian chocolate with a bold roast finish. Just the way I like it. "It's incredible. Starbucks should be nervous."

We laugh, and he sits with his coffee. I lower the cup on the glass table between us.

"Sir, why am I here? Where is my family?"

His bright green eyes stare at me with a sense of compassion I've never experienced.

"Fair enough, Izzy. I'll get right to the point. You've had a terrible accident, but your family is fine. I assure you. Distressed about your situation, but they are holding on. While trying to save Mr. Merriweather from a falling tree, you were struck by heavy branches. It was the old cedar tree between your properties. You saved your neighbor's life, but you couldn't move quickly enough to avoid the crushing blow to your body."

I freeze realizing the enormity of the separation from my family and lack of recollection of an accident. I peer down at my body to examine my arms and legs. Everything seems fine. Even my jeans and favorite green shirt are clean and my shoes intact.

"I must be dead. Am I dead?" The thought frightens me for my family, even in this breathtaking setting.

"No. You're not dead. Paramedics arrived quickly at the accident scene. However, it took some time to rescue you from beneath the tree and debris. Once out, they rushed you to the Atlanta hospital in a helicopter, where you now lay in a coma."

I stand and pace the area. "What? Are you serious?" I stare at the grass and press my stomach.

He stands, placing one hand on each of my shoulders, and I stabilize. "It's true."

"Why is this happening?"

"Let me explain. It's a lot to take in."

He lowers me into the oversized chair, and I breathe deeply.

"We brought you here to offer a brief pause from your current life."

"Who's we?"

"Consider it a brief gap in time."

"A gap in time? Can you tell me who you are and what this is about? Am I in Heaven?"

"I'm an old friend and you are safe here, I promise. But you're not in Heaven. Think of it as a gift. In fact, you requested this."

"What? I asked to be struck by a tree and separated from my family? They must be grief-stricken. Is this a joke?"

"Oh, it's no joke. It's profoundly serious. What I mean is, we are answering your prayer."

I want to run, but I'm captivated by this calm elusive man. "I pray many prayers." My voice shakes. "Please, tell me which one."

He rests his elbows on his armchair, tapping his fingers together. "You've spent years searching for answers to heal your deep sorrow and release the tormenting pain from your past. Plus, your marriage is falling apart with talk of divorce. In the lake cabin driveway, you called upon God urgently to save your marriage and heal your past. Did you not?"

I sit on the edge of my chair. "Yes. I was alone in my car. Who are you?"

"I am an old friend sent by God to be your guide and counselor."

"Do you mean Jesus sent you?"

"Well, of course. God is one."

My mouth drops open. Tears flow down my face. "Tell me this is a lucid dream."

"It's okay, Izzy. You are tenderhearted and to meet with me in person is extremely rare. No one will bring you harm or judge you. Your busy life moves too fast, making it impossible to connect otherwise."

"God wants me here?"

"Indeed. He loves you and wants to answer your urgent plea."

"Why this way?"

"A drastic interruption like this is the last resort. For some, it's necessary. The gap gives us uninterrupted space to work together so you can receive the spiritual guidance and healing you seek. Making sense now?"

I blink, trying to understand. "How does this work?"

"Your commitment and effort decide the outcome, just like in life. The task won't be easy."

"What am I expected to do?"

"Meet with me every day in this lovely garden to address your prayer. Are you willing?"

"Will I see my family again?"

"That's the plan. But first, you must decide to stay and take part in this rare gift."

I cross my arms. "Wow. I'm not sure how to respond. No offense, but I'm honored and horrified at the same time."

He grins. "I appreciate your candor."

I scratch my forehead. "Where will I stay? What will I eat and wear?"

"Not to worry. Your needs and desires are handled down to the last detail."

This place far exceeds any expectations, but it's not like being at home. "What if I don't agree and ask to return home right now?"

"Like at home, you have free will. At any moment, you may leave, but there are high stakes."

"High stakes?"

"If you leave now you risk going back too early, so we cannot promise you will wake up from the coma and recover. Each decision carries repercussions, even in this glorious setting. Also, if you return home now, you deny the unprecedented opportunity to heal the darkest places in your soul. You pleaded to God for help, telling Him you didn't want to live with the misery of the past any longer. Is that correct?"

What have I done? "Yes, that's true." I couldn't predict this type of response.

"He heard your cries, Izzy. God's responses are unpredictable. He's answering your prayer with this gap in time because He knows best."

"I'm thinking of my family."

"Then ask yourself this. If you continue doing life your way, what changes? Will you and Jacob restore your marriage, and will you heal your past wounds?"

I swallow a lump in my throat. The definition of insanity is doing the same thing repeatedly and expecting a different result. It hasn't worked yet. For over twenty years, I've read self-help books trying to move on from the shadows of my past and a stagnant marriage while neglecting the Bible.

"I'm exhausted by taking tiny steps forward and the void continues. That's why I cried out to God in the driveway. I'm sick of this hamster wheel."

"Yes. If there was a PhD for long suffering, you would qualify. You need God's help."

"That's me, Counselor."

"Indeed." We both grin.

"But wait, you mentioned healing the darkest parts of my soul. Will I have to talk about the family incident?"

"Eventually, you will, but we won't begin there."

Reality floods my mind. "I don't have a choice. If I go home, I risk staying in a coma, never seeing my family again."

"Choices always have some risk and consequences. Right now, your choice is fear or faith. Keep doing life your way or choose God's way. It's up to you. When you decide to return, it will happen at once. No questions asked with no judgement. Do you want to stay or go?"

"How long will this take? Days, weeks, months, or years?"

"As long as needed. That's all I can say. If you commit to this task and trust the process, the ultimate life awaits you."

I squirm. "Wait a minute. What am I doing? I want to believe you, but where's the proof? Maybe evil forces sent you to destroy me and my family."

"Izzy, I admire your gumption. You've always had a curious and fiery spirit."

With my arms folded, I glare back at Him.

"In fact, do you recall being nine years old on a sultry afternoon sneaking over to the neighbor's beehive to watch them make honey? Your mother forbade you to go there because it was dangerous. You wore your brother's Brave's cap and new tennis shoes. Do you remember?"

I nod slowly, the memory brings chill bumps to my arms.

"Good. You had a small window of time before your mother returned home from running errands, so you raced to the beehive. Once you spotted the hive, you downshifted to a slow walk to avoid attention from potential bystanders. Fascinated by the velocity of bees swarming around, the buzzing intensified as you tip-toed closer. Then it happened. The bees attacked you with multiple stings, and you dropped to the ground. Your throat swelled shut instantly. You clutched your neck, gasping for air. As you're passing out, you looked at the sky and prayed to God to save you and your throat opened. Your hands released, and you gulped in air until your breathing returned to normal. You sat tall in the grass and glanced upwards again. Only this time, you thanked God for saving your life. After brushing the dirt and grass from your knees, you stood, walked home, and told no one about the beehive attack."

He's right. I've told no one the beehive story.

With a sly grin, he pauses. "That's the day you discovered your deadly allergy to bee stings."

I shake my head slowly while tears cascade down my face. "It's impossible. I've told no one, not even Jacob. God must have sent you."

Our eyes meet. "What is your decision? Will you stay and work together?"

The idea of causing my family pain is unimaginable, but the thought of never seeing them again is unbearable. I want God's help, but not like this. They say the Lord works in mysterious ways, and He is always in control. It must be true.

"Counselor, when we finish our last session, will I be free from the torment of my past and my marriage restored?"

"That's our goal. It depends on your willingness to face your deepest wounds and darkest hour. I'll never mislead you. Significant effort is necessary and your two requests interconnect with tremendous complexity. If you fully surrender to God's strength, trust me and the process, all things are possible. God believes in you and has an incredible plan for your life. I encourage you to accept this precious offer."

I close my eyes, thinking I must be crazy. Am I dreaming? Regardless, I want answers to my prayer. "Based on the risks and potential rewards, I'll stay and work with you for a bit to test the waters."

He claps his hands. "Good decision. I understand your concerns, and I am thrilled to be appointed your official counselor."

I raise my hand to block the glare from the sun catching a gold key necklace around his neck. "That is a beautiful gold key. I've never seen gold shine so brightly, and the design is uniquely ornate."

"Oh, I almost forgot." He reaches behind his neck, lifting the necklace over his head, and holds it out for me. "This is for you."

"What? No. I couldn't."

"You don't understand. This is your key, designed for your journey forward. You must take it."

He lowers the gold chain around my head, and I hold the heavy key in my hand, feeling the weight.

Stepping back, he points at me. "We are going to unlock many mysteries together. This key will unlock your last mystery to release your ultimate reward."

"Wow. Can you tell me now?"

He chuckles. "And spoil the surprise? No way."

Interrupted by a deep loud barking, I turn to face a Harlequin Great Dane. His paws rest on my shoulders, and his tail wags uncontrollably, as if he's dancing. I fall in love instantly, and from the wet kisses, it must be mutual. I giggle.

"Who is this magnificent creature?"

"Izzy, meet Duke, your loyal companion. He will guide you to and from the garden and will never leave you during your stay. What do you think of him?"

Rubbing Duke's furry cheeks, I smile broadly. "I think you've provided another favorite thing. I am so grateful. Thank you, Mr. Counselor."

"Just Counselor. And it's my pleasure. We've prepared an exquisite bungalow for you a short walk from here. Duke and I will show you the way. I encourage you to rest this evening, and we'll begin the first session here in the garden tomorrow."

"What time should I meet you?"

"Whenever you arrive."

Duke nudges my hand. "I can't believe this is real. Or is it?"

CHAPTER 4

Misinterpretations

I t only takes a moment to realize the wet kisses are not from Jacob. Duke has lathered my face with his affection, serving as my wake-up call. I pat him on the head while wishing Jacob was here with me. I blink a few times and fall back on a mound of pillows. What must my family be going through? What if this turns out to be a hoax, and we live separately forever? The thought of their pain is excruciating. I press my heart. I don't understand why, but the counselor has an unfamiliar certainty I can't rationalize that persuades me to trust Him.

Refocusing on the moment, I look around my bedroom, taking in the opulent surroundings of my bungalow as the counselor described it. This is no bungalow—must be a room within a luxurious mansion. When I arrived here yesterday evening, I must have tumbled straight into bed and fell asleep since I'm wearing the same clothes.

Now I can take in the comfort and sweet serenity of my pristine environment decorated in my favorite French country décor with soft blue-grey tones and distressed-white furniture. The bedroom suite is the size of an average home equipped with an automatic fireplace and sitting area. The bed linens and comforter are cozy and thick, woven from the softest textiles. Gauzy, lightweight curtains hang from the soaring ceilings and border the tall windows equipped with pull-down shades. So much light. The walls are painted with a subtle, hazy sea-blue, reminding me of the ocean waters I love. The finest French country-style furniture fills the room. More of my favorites. This space makes the Ritz Carlton look shabby. I don't deserve such luxury.

Sliding my feet into the fluffy slippers by my bed, I step into the adjoining bathroom. It's massive and equally as luxurious as the bedroom. Pure gold faucets, towel warmers, and a deep, white porcelain tub to destress. I anticipate needing that. The huge shower is made of muted turquoise marble with skinny gold veins, unlike any I've seen. I turn on one of the shower heads and it flows like rain in my preferred temperature. Sensational.

Looks like Duke is back to sleep nestled in his thick, gigantic bed. What a doozy.

What will I wear today? A wooden hand-carved armoire with detailed cherubs down each side grabs my attention. I rush to see what's inside. After flinging open the two doors, I clap as I stare at a full wardrobe of the finest silk dresses. Garments hang in lovely florals and shades with matching shoes in my size. When I was little, I only wore dresses, and they were usually florals. My sisters teased me for being too girly, which I took as a compliment. Oh, I miss them.

Back to the armoire. On the casual front, I find soft faded jeans, cotton t-shirts in flattering colors along with hiking pants and boots. Hiking apparel seems odd. Good grief, this entire experience is beyond bizarre.

A deep purple dress covered in white orchids with matching flats looks good for today. I slip them on and twirl in front of the full-length mirror, admiring the feminine outfit. After years of wearing stuffy business suits, it's nice to feel girly again. The gold key hangs perfectly in place on my chest. What could this unlock?

Eager to meet the counselor for our first session, I realize my navigational skills will not get me back to our gathering place, so I call for Duke.

"Duke, come here, boy. Can you take me to the sanctuary where I'm supposed to meet the counselor?" He rises, twirls around a few times, barking, and bouncing. "Okay, show me the way." Could this dog understand English?

While walking to the sanctuary, the air is still constant. Warm, yet crisp, like fresh morning dew, only without the dew. Everything is better. Kinda like the Amalfi coast on steroids. I follow the same gemstone path aligned with flowering trees, waterfalls, and chirping birds. Duke is quickly becoming my personal navigator and loyal friend.

As we approach the garden entrance, I rub my hand over the engraved sign labeled *Izzy's Sanctuary*. My eyes tear up. Whoever designed this glorious place knows how to make a woman feel special. I sigh and take a seat. Guilt quickly takes over as my thoughts return to Jacob and the kids. The worry and suffering I'm putting them through is unnerving. I pray my time here is swift, transformative, and a bona fide answer to my prayers. It must be.

Thankfully, Duke chasing butterflies around the garden is a pleasant distraction. I hear familiar whistling and twist in my comfortable chair to see the counselor at the entrance. He waves, his lustrous silver hair and bright smile calm my nerves.

He approaches me, and I notice his piercing, emerald-green eyes again.

"Good morning, Izzy. Glad to see you up early."

"Good morning, sir."

"Did you have breakfast at the bungalow?"

"No. I was so excited to get here, I didn't realize . . ."

"No problem. How about a warm croissant, fresh fruit, and coffee?"

"Sounds yummy."

He gracefully pours each of us a warm brew with the precise amount of cream to my liking. "How is the bungalow? Does it suit you?"

"Bungalow? It's the most opulent mansion I've ever seen. I couldn't dream up such an extraordinary place. It's too much—but thank you."

"You're welcome. Consider it your home away from home."

He hands me a similar cup as yesterday but with paisleys in more vibrant colors. I blow on the cup and take a sip. "How did you learn so much about me, Counselor?"

Bending over the coffee table, he looks up. "You shouldn't fret about the information I possess. It's to your advantage. Instead, embrace it, so it doesn't become an obstacle with your progress."

"What do you mean?"

"It's crucial not to hold back sharing information, regardless of my knowledge." He takes a long sip, staring at me.

I fold my arms. "If you already know, why does it matter?"

"For our time to be effective, it's necessary we share two-way communications so I can hear your thoughts and stories in your words, not mine. That's a basic indicator of a healthy relationship, don't you think?"

"Sure, something I miss with Jacob."

"Yes. Never be afraid to ask me anything or worry about confidentiality. When you sense embarrassment or apprehension, say it anyway. I'm your friend, not here to condemn or harm you. Ever."

"Thank you." I fidget in my chair, wondering what's next.

"My pleasure. Now, let's get started, shall we?"

I hold my breath and then exhale. "I think so. Yes, I'm ready."

He runs his fingers through his hair. "Excellent. Let's begin with the most pressing matter."

I smirk. "That's easy. My failing marriage."

"Ah, yes. Except we're not diving into the marital problems yet. Let's start with the early days of Jacob and Isabelle. How did you meet?"

My arms relax. "Oh, I see. We met in college. As a non-conformist, ambitious student focused on studies, my first impression of Jacob was a cocky fraternity brat and football jock. A goofball. We had nothing in common except Blue Velvet Bakery, which we visited every morning before class. The smell of homemade cinnamon rolls two blocks away lured me to the bakery daily. I thought it was odd how we always coincided in line. It took me a while to realize Jacob's interest in the little redhead surpassed the donuts."

I point to my hair. "He asked me for a date multiple times, but I turned him down."

"You said yes, eventually." We laugh and sip our coffee.

"Yes. Jacob was relentless in his pursuit of a date, and eventually, we became friends during his flirting attempts in the bakery line. However,

I focused on graduating with honors and avoided romantic distractions, determined to succeed. On a Wednesday, the week of the fall homecoming game, we met in line at the bakery as usual and he gave me a proposition."

The counselor leans forward. "A proposition?"

"Yes. He understood my lack of interest in football, but if I agreed to watch him play the following Saturday, he would never ask me out again. He dug into his pocket and pulled out a crumpled ticket and handed it to me. Instead of watching the entire game, he said to come for the last quarter. The sigh of relief and a twinge of sadness hit an unexpected nerve. My conflicting reaction surprised me and made me sad that he would give up his pursuit. I accepted his offer, but I wrestled with the proposition over the days leading up to the big game. Saturday arrived, and walking to the stadium, I thought about Jacob never pursuing me again. I realized I had more than friendly feelings for him.

"I like where this story is going."

"The fourth quarter was starting when I arrived. The aroma of hotdogs and buttery popcorn caught my attention, and I stopped for snacks. I munched on the popcorn and stood behind the chain link fence, scanning the field for Jacob. He wore number eighty-seven. I spotted him on the sideline with the other players. Quickly, I climbed to the middle section and secured a clear view of the football field. Jacob put his hand over his eyes to block the sun and waved excitedly in my direction. I pulled my Atlanta Braves baseball cap down and gave a quick wave. He joined his team and ran onto the field into formation. It was interesting to watch the jokester I met at the bakery appear as a serious player. On the first snap, the quarterback lobbed the ball like a torpedo toward Jacob. He caught the ball and ran it down the field, scoring a touchdown. It was incredible. The crowd went wild, and I stood clapping and cheering him on."

"How exciting, Izzy."

"It was. He strutted off the field, took off his helmet, gave me a vigorous wave, and a big smile. He blew me away. All those times we met at the bakery, he never mentioned much about playing football. I found out he was the star wide receiver. That should tell you how much I kept my nose in the books."

"Then what happened?"

"After the game ended, I hurried down the bleachers, and we met at the sideline with the chain link fence between us. I congratulated him on the victory and touchdowns, and he thanked me for coming. We both froze for an awkward minute. His coach whistled loudly and motioned him into the locker room, and Jacob asked me to stick around, saying he had a surprise for me. As he was running away, I shouted, "Yes, I will.""

"I waited for him near the locker room and soon he walked out freshly showered, wearing a sneaky grin. We walked together down a bicycle path and talked about the game. He reiterated his surprise and kept me in suspense. We arrived at a wide stream of flowing rapids, and he asked me to sit next to him on a wooden bench and watch the trout run as we continued chatting. A live oak tree covered in Spanish moss hovered over the creek beside us. It was a cool fall day, and I never expected what happened next."

If the counselor scoots any closer to the edge of his seat, he might fall out of his chair.

I wiggle forward. "Oh, this is the best part. A few minutes passed when a guy arrived wearing Jacob's fraternity symbol on his sweatshirt. With a stoic face, he handed the guitar to Jacob and walked away. Before I could ask what was happening, I became hypnotized by Jacob singing a love song he wrote for me called 'Sweet Isabelle'."

The counselor's eyes widen. "What a romantic. I bet you were stunned."

"Dumbfounded."

The counselor and I break into laughter like two old high school friends. I tilt my head, peering at this mysterious man. His genuine care for me is undeniable.

"I love your story. Please continue."

I zero in on the day at the trout stream. "Stunned and captivated by his charm and hearing him sing for the first time, I fell for him, hard. I'd misjudged his personality. Until that day, I avoided relationships, even friendships. I learned he was more assertive than aggressive and confident vs. cocky. Traits I envy. From that day on, we were inseparable. We hugged and giggled in public like silly teenagers and spent late nights stargazing in the college park."

"Sounds like a true love story."

"We didn't always agree, but we were madly in love. As my biggest fan and protector, I felt adored and safe with Jacob."

I stare at my feet for a long silence. When I look up, the counselor scoots back with his fingers interlocked. "Try not to think about your current marriage problems. How does it feel sharing the beginning of Isabelle and Jacob's romance?"

I sit upright and remain silent a bit longer, allowing the early days to sink in further. My smile stretches wide, and I glance up with teary eyes. "It's reinvigorating. I haven't reminisced about my college days with Jacob for several years. A love so pure and powerful back then, but we're different people now who've grown apart. Disconnected. Our past was amazing, but today is reality."

"I understand how you feel, and I thank you for sharing such a beautiful story, which is also real. I encourage you to recall Jacob singing at the trout stream each day while you're here. It will help. Will you do that?"

"Okay. It might help offset the worry I have about the family as well."

"Good."

I pause picturing the romantic scene. "Jacob still has that guitar. It's been a while, but he would tinker with it and sing to me in the kitchen. I cherish those moments." I sigh heavily.

The counselor slowly nods his head with a warm smile. "That Jacob fella is one serious Romeo. The spark is still alive. Keep recalling those sentimental times during and after college."

"I guess I can do that."

The counselor's face shifts to serious. "Of course, you both are different people. Those two love birds in college grew up and took on major responsibilities as maturing adults." He squeezes his interlocked hands in front of me. "Don't you see? Your genuine love is the anchor that binds you together, tethering your fragile marriage. It's the same anchor to reconnect your souls today."

"What do you mean?"

"Isabelle, it's not over. You and Jacob built a solid foundation. Can't you see it?"

My face hardens, and I push back in my chair. "I'm sorry, I don't see it. An anchor to reconnect our souls? Really? With all due respect, sir, it sounds too fairytale to me. Not reality. The day at the trout stream created a phenomenal memory of our romance long ago. I'm grateful to relive it with you today. Truly. And I'll relive it each day because I promised you, but it's just a memory."

"Fairytale? Interesting choice of words as you sit here with me among fairytale-like surroundings."

Before I can utter a response, he raises one finger and clears his throat. "Please continue with your story. What happened after college?"

Should I apologize? He motions with one hand to keep the story moving.

"Two years later, after we graduated college, we were married. It was an intimate ceremony outdoors in late autumn. Our favorite season. Then Jacob went to law school, and I landed a lucrative job in pharmaceutical sales, which supported us through his continued law degrees. Our life was chaotic but felt perfect, rich with new and exhilarating challenges. We vowed to make it work, and I'm proud of our team effort."

"You still have vows to uphold."

"Touché, Counselor." We both smirk.

"When did the children enter the scene?"

I perk up to talk about my precious babies. "Just shy of two years after our wedding day, Travis was born. As a preemie, he gave us a scare for several days. Fourteen months later, we had baby Katie. Jacob's little Katie-bug. The opposite of Travis, she weighed almost nine pounds. A rough delivery. Somehow, I continued my career, and from then on, life was a blur. Today, the kids attend college full time in different states. I miss them." Duke whimpers, so I stroke the top of his head.

"That leaves you and Jacob alone. Empty nesters."

"Yes. We're like two strangers living in the same house. I wish we could reignite the spark we had in college. That's why the lake cottage weekend was so important. Now, I'm stuck here and uncertain about us."

I stand, holding my arms and pacing.

"What's really troubling you, Izzy? You can tell me."

"What am I doing here? This seems insane." My voice shakes as I pace faster with my fists clenched. He stands, stretching out his hand with an open palm. I look away.

"It's okay. You're not alone this time. Please sit down and take some deep breaths. Of course, your family is worried, but they are fine. I promise."

"How can I be confident you keep promises?" After a few huffs, I sit, and he captures my gaze. I stare back and my fists release. A calmness overtakes me like I just had the best massage of my life. How does He do it?

"I've explained why you are here. My promises are unbreakable, but you decide whether to trust me."

"Trust is difficult for me."

"Breathe."

"But I'm upset. What about my situation and my family?"

"It might sound harsh, but truthfully, you're choosing to be upset. Your current situation is sitting in a tranquil garden sipping coffee with someone who adores you and wants to help. The family is managing through your accident, and they have each other. Faith in this process is essential for success."

"Fine." I shut my eyes and inhale the deepest breath possible, exhaling slowly.

"Excellent. Are you feeling better now?"

"A little."

"Should I reiterate why you're here, or can we continue?"

"I'm good now. Let's keep going."

"Wonderful. Reflect on the years before the kids and ask yourself if Jacob was your top priority."

"Yes, of course. We were two inseparable love birds. We also made an oath not to let work or studies destroy our relationship."

"Did Jacob remain your highest priority once the children were born?" He scrutinizes me as though he doubts I'll be honest.

I pat Duke, trying to avoid the question. "Well, no. The kids became the highest priority for both of us. Besides, we're parents. That's how it's supposed to be, right? Kids first?"

"Before I answer that, tell me. With the kids at college now, are they still your highest priority?"

I bite my lower lip. Where is he going with this? "Of course they are. That's a mother's duty. I'm not perfect, but I didn't allow my career or anything else to take precedence over our kids, like Jacob." My right hand quickly covers my mouth. Did I really say that out loud?

"Don't hold back. Say anything."

My hand lowers. "I'm still getting used to it."

"It takes practice. I'm not questioning your abilities as a mother. Job well done. We will talk about your priorities further in a later session, but for now, let's shift to the resentment I hear in your tone toward Jacob. Is that what I hear?"

Great. First day with God's mystery man and I'm already showing my true colors. I ease back in my chair, formulating a proper response. He just said not to hold back. Aren't I the one seeking help? It's time to stop the charade of pretending everything is hunky dory at home while suffering on the inside. I prayed for a change, and now I'm fighting it. It's time to get over myself and embrace this opportunity.

"Yes, your interpretation of my tone is correct. I admit resenting Jacob's absence over the years, and when he was home, he spent his time playing basketball or getting ice cream with the kids while I did everything else. But for the record, Jacob is a terrific father, and the kids are crazy about him."

I roll my eyes. "Don't get me wrong, I'm thrilled that he has strong relationships with them, but I'm still jealous."

"Of what?"

I look at the sky. "It sounds petty, but I don't think the kids love me as much as they love Jacob. I'm not a fun parent, like him. They see me as serious, boring, and dependable. The kids and I are close too, but for laughs and fun, they call on Jacob. They turn to me for practical things."

"So, you believe having fun with the kids creates more love between them?"

My face heats. "I told you it sounds silly. I'm being ridiculous."

"It's not silly. You are saying how you feel. Please answer the question."

"No. Yes. I don't know."

"That's okay. Did you take part in fun activities with Jacob and the kids?"

"Frequently. But I felt like a fourth wheel. An outsider. I still do. When the feeling hits, I typically excuse myself and go to my office to be alone."

"I see. Do the kids avoid spending time with you or mistreat you?"

"Never."

"I'm confused. What evidence do you have they love Jacob more?"

I stare at my feet, creating an awkward silence. "It's obvious by how they light up around their dad, and it's not the same with me." I wipe a few tears from my cheek and fake a smile.

"Describe how Travis and Katie interact with you."

"Around me, they are more subdued. We have meaningful talks about college, current events, and relationships. Sometimes they ask me to book flights, do their laundry, or make their favorite chocolate chip cookies to take back to college."

"Do you find their requests offensive or burdensome?"

"Not at all. I love doing things for them, and I miss it while they're at college. I wish they lit up around me like they do with Jacob, that's all. It sounds childish hearing me say it aloud. As if I'm competing with my husband, which makes little sense, because I'm glad they have Jacob. It's ludicrous."

My face warms again, and I want to run to my room. Maybe I can change the subject. Where is he going with this line of questioning, anyway?

"Is it your belief that having fun with the kids creates more love than being dependable?"

The lump in my throat stops me from speaking, so I shake my head.

"Is Jacob dependable?"

I nod.

"Then what is it, Izzy? Let it out."

I squint at the sky and huff. "I'm not good enough, and I feel inadequate around my own family. Heck, almost everyone. But I've mastered the art of hiding my insecurities around others. When I see the kids extra excited and laughing with Jacob, it makes me feel detached and lonely. Kinda weird. So, there, I said it." I suck in a deep breath and hold it.

"Just exhale and take in a few more. The truth must surface for us to reach the core of your sorrow. Only then will you be free. Do you feel better now?"

"A smidge. I admit feeling lighter."

"You're doing great. Being vulnerable is unfamiliar territory."

"Definitely." After a few more deep breaths, my body melds back into my chair. "Would you like the truth about how your kids feel about you?"

"That depends on the truth." I touch my face to check the temperature.

"Your children love and adore you. They rely on you. You've always been there, even when Jacob wasn't. You guided their values, education, and wellbeing with extreme love and devotion, providing them with an incredible childhood well equipped for a bright future. You gave them stability and trained them to be responsible, respectful, and disciplined young adults. These are high-quality, solid life skills you fostered within Katie and Travis. Therefore, their reaction toward you is how you trained them, which is calm, loving, and communicative. They enjoy spending time with you. A classic example of conditioned behavior."

"That's fascinating. Never occurred to me but it sounds too simple. Otherwise, why would I feel so insecure with them?"

"Let's sort out the reason the kids respond to Jacob with more excitement, according to your perspective. Tell me about a typical week and how the kids interacted with their dad growing up."

I admit being envious of Jacob's business trips while I attended parent-teacher conferences and managed my busy career locally. He has a bond with the kids I envy.

"They had less time with Jacob because of his work and business travels. However, he called them almost every night from the hotel and intentionally talked about his day to make them part of it. Many times, we scolded Travis for rummaging through Jacob's briefcase, asking questions about his cases. Jacob lavished them with hugs and kisses before he left for his trips and was never stingy on saying 'I love you' to both."

"This Jacob fella sounds like a dedicated parent, just like you, Izzy."

I conjure up a slight grin. "He is. But that's not the slam-dunk, pun intended."

The counselor shimmies closer. "Tell me."

"Whenever Jacob returned from a business trip and the kids were home, he would stop the car and shout for them to come outside. He's a big kid at heart. Rolling up his white shirtsleeves and ripping off his tie, he'd scurry to the basketball hoop while leaving his luggage by the car."

"How did the kids respond?"

"Naturally, they came barreling down the stairs screaming 'Daddy's home' and made a beeline for the basketball hoop." I laugh. "It was quite a spectacle."

"And what were you doing during this slam-dunk event?"

"I stood at the kitchen sink and peered out the window as I prepared dinner. It's odd how my feelings collided."

"What do you mean, Izzy?"

"On the one hand, I was grateful and enjoyed watching my family play a simple game of basketball, but the outsider let loneliness seep in. It still does."

"Yes. Conflicting indeed. As we continue these sessions, the reason will become clear. But we have groundwork to do first. Trust the process."

"Trust is hard. How can I expect you to solve decades of sadness in a few sessions?"

"Are you annoyed, Izzy?"

I tap my chest. "I should apologize." Yikes. I heard the annoyance in my voice.

"No. I asked that you be honest, and building trust is a critical part of our time together."

A phrase I seldom use pops into my brain. "Yes. I am."

"It's healthy to express your feelings. Let's get back to your jealousy of Jacob's relationship with your children. Even though you've attached some emotional pain to the basketball game, isn't it obvious why the children respond to Jacob with excitement?"

I pause. "Not really."

"It's simple. Jacob figured out how to maximize limited time with the kids. He wasn't always available like you, and I suspect he regrets missing school events and other key moments you enjoyed. I bet the kids wish he had been there as well. Business trips throughout the years trained your kids to get excited when their dad came home, as he was always intentional in his actions. Based on your story, he wasn't motivated to make you appear boring. Through basketball, he found a way to reconnect after being away. Make sense?"

I cross my legs. "It sounds plausible, but I'm not convinced."

"Fair enough. Let's consider how the kids might interact with Jacob if he came home from business trips tired, stressed, and ignored them. Perhaps even hostile or abusive. Do you expect they would respond to Jacob the same way?"

"Of course not. I'm an expert receiver of consistent neglect, and it's not fun and games." I fight to keep my body language from giving away my inner turmoil. "And if I treated the kids negatively, they would react negatively, and we would not be close either. Right?"

"Exactly. We condition relationships through our interactions and inaction, both positive and negative. It's a blessing for Travis and Katie to have two equally loving parents with unique personalities and styles."

"But it doesn't explain why I felt empty watching my kids have fun with Jacob and then felt guilty for being jealous. It's awful. Am I just selfish and self-absorbed?"

"Selfishness would be an easier problem to solve, Izzy. The issue is misinterpretation and distorted views brought on by a deeply rooted trigger from your childhood. It's the first clue to unlocking the mystery of your long emotional sadness."

"Whoa. Are you taking me down the path to discuss the family incident now?"

"No. We must stay at the top level longer before we approach that specific topic, and besides, you will figure out the timing, remember? Trust me."

"Please don't use that phrase."

"Trust me?"

"Yes, please." My stomach sours. "A person I knew used to say it, but they were never honest."

"I understand."

Again, anger snaked through me. *Control, Isabelle.* With a deep breath, I release the grip on the chair arms and refocus.

"Seems odd that I can't recognize how much my children love me because of my misinterpretation, which I can't explain. Understanding why the kids respond to Jacob as the fun parent and me as the serious one helps. I get it. But I don't sense the resentment toward Jacob and feeling inadequate lessening much."

He scoots to the edge of his chair with a tender yet stern look. "Because prior experiences that are concealed and stored away trigger those emotions." He keeps eye contact.

I twitch and nod without a word.

"We will unlock the mystery, but not today. We're just skimming the surface."

"I need patience."

"Yes, healing takes time, Izzy. And I suspect you're misinterpreting other situations beyond your family, but we'll cover that later as well. Today, let's acknowledge your progress."

I shrug. "Doesn't seem like much."

"Nonsense, the first step toward unraveling the knots of your debilitating sorrow is understanding how the mind distorts simple interactions, like the love of your children, because of false beliefs."

"False beliefs?"

"Yes. Every time you perceive a situation based on negative triggers from your past, your mind creates lies. Unconsciously, of course. Which is why it's so tricky to unravel. But we will."

"I want to, but it seems complicated. Now what?"

He paces with his hands behind his back. "Before today, you believed the kids thought you were dependable but a serious bore and preferred their father. This false belief made you feel like an outsider and insecure. Did I capture that accurately?"

"Spot on."

He stops. "Now, you have two options. You can continue lying to yourself or accept the truth and start the healing process."

I sit on the edge of my chair. "How can I accept the truth?"

"You replace the lie with truth."

"I want that—"

"What, Izzy?"

I shake my head. "I'm scared."

"You're stronger than you think."

I study Him. He hasn't lied to me yet. Quite the opposite. "All right. I want to move forward."

He rubs his hands together vigorously and sits. "Let's try a visual exercise. Get comfortable, close your eyes, and take three deep breaths. On three, imagine the last time the kids returned from college. One, two, three."

After my third breath, the image is clear. Could this really work?

"Can you visualize the scene, Izzy?"

"I have it."

"Now, replace the lie that the kids love Jacob more because you are boring and inadequate with the truth about conditioned behavior. Recall as much detail as possible and embrace the memory in its true reality. When you're ready, tell me what you see."

"It's Labor Day weekend, and I'm in the kitchen baking the kids' favorite cookies before they arrive. Katie sends a text as Travis approaches the driveway in their rental car. I hear Jacob calling me to the back door, so I wipe my hands and rush over. He places his arm around my waist, tucking us in the doorway. We watch the kids park the car, but I pull away.

"When they step out of the car, they wave, smiling from ear to ear. Katie runs to the door, giving me a long hug, then shares a long hug and high-fives with Jacob. Travis follows closely behind, sharing a firm hug with each of us and high-fives with Jacob. The aroma of warm cookies grabs their attention, and they bolt inside. Jacob and I join them. He tries to put his arm around me, but I slither away."

I open my eyes. "I just blew him off. Why would I do that?"

"It's okay, Izzy. Keep going."

"With the oven alarm sounding, I take out the last batch of cookies and enjoy the kids' lively conversation about their travels from college. Katie places a plate of cookies on her glass of sweet tea and invites me to sit on the porch swing. Meanwhile, Travis and Jacob hurry outside for their first of many basketball competitions. Later that evening, we take in the latest *Mission Impossible* movie and relax the rest of the weekend at home. Oh, except for doing their laundry, which I enjoyed. A lovely visit." I stare at the cloudless sky. Tears flow, and I can't quit smiling.

"Well done, Izzy."

I cradle my face in my hands and sob. The counselor stands beside me with his hand on my shoulder. His love and empathy are indescribable. As I think about my wrong judgment, my face becomes flushed with heat.

"You'll be okay."

I take a tissue and wipe my cheeks. "I feel stupid and shallow. Why would I conjure up hurtful imaginary drama in my head?"

"Do you believe the truth as your reality?"

"I think so."

"Good. It's easier to dismiss your emotions as shallow than allowing your mind to confront the deeply rooted source of your distorted views. Your feelings are not silly because the false beliefs are real to you and cause genuine conflict with your family and beyond. Events of the past, firmly locked within your subconscious, signal those feelings to emerge."

I squirm. "The family incident again, I'm sure. Don't make me talk about it."

"Don't worry. We need to focus on today's lesson. Before we venture into the dark past, we must set up the foundation."

"Yes. I get it. But there's one thing troubling me."

"What is it?"

"My resentment towards Jacob. Not sure I fully understand."

"Ah. Glad you mentioned it. Your wrong ideas about Jacob caused insecurity and envy. But he's not the source of your suffering. Your natural response is to disengage from the situation to avoid further emotional pain. The outsider persona steps in. But this pain stems from wounds inflicted long before you met Jacob."

"You keep bringing up the past."

"I'm merely referencing the source. The truth must be faced at some point, but not today. Dare I say trust me?"

I scowl at Him. "I'm not there yet."

"I understand, but that's why you're here, isn't it? An answer to your prayer."

"But it's hard."

"Remember, I said this would be difficult. Easy street is not the pathway for healing pain like yours. Otherwise, through your many attempts, you would have solved it on your own."

"Good point, Counselor."

"Can we move on? It's vital to seal the truth about Jacob, too."

"Which truth?" I'm doing my best to stay on track.

"That Jacob is not the cause of your pain. It will not make sense until we reveal the genuine source."

I raise my hand. "But not today."

"That's right, Izzy. All in good timing."

"I need to process this further."

"Indeed, you must. It's a lot to absorb."

We smile and pause for a few moments. The counselor peeks at Duke, who appears to be sound asleep.

"If you recall, we started our session focused on your marriage as a necessary background. Although healing your sorrow and restoring your marriage might seem distinct, they interlock with great complexity. To answer your question about why you're creating imaginary drama, we need to shift our next session back to the beginning."

My eyes widen. "The beginning of what?"

"You. Your earliest childhood memories."

I shake my head.

"Izzy, we're going way back before the family incident."

His calming demeanor is convincing. "Okay, I believe you."

"Excellent. Allow me to stress the point. Despite the mangled complexities, the kids' reactions to Jacob are not about you. They are responding to each of you based on years of classic behavioral conditioning. They love you both dearly."

"I see that now."

"You're a sharp learner, and we're just beginning."

I sigh heavily. "Thank you. I could use a strong cup of coffee."

"Me too." The counselor pours our coffee as Duke stands at attention, wagging his tail. The intense dark roast blended with the sweet aroma of roses remind me of the cozy coffee shop back home. I welcome the silent breathing space to process the session.

He offers me the delicate cup. "I'm proud of you, Izzy. You're a courageous lady. Tomorrow, we unlock a significant clue about the mystery of your emotional pain. Now, it's time for an adventure."

My stomach flips. "Adventure? What is it?"

"Follow me."

The counselor walks away, motioning me forward, but my legs won't move. Duke twirls around me a few times, so I stand and take a step. Letting go, I follow.

CHAPTER 5

The Mountain

I jog to catch up with the counselor walking ahead of me. We're on the main path to the bungalow. My mind races. What kind of adventure? Could it be dangerous?

"Counselor, where are we going?"

He raises one finger and keeps walking. "We begin at the bungalow to switch clothes for the climb."

"Climb? What climb?"

"See that mountain over there?"

"Which one? There are many."

He stops and points up. "The tallest one, with the clouds surrounding the highest peak."

If it could, my mouth would hit the grass. "What? I can't climb a mountain."

"Don't worry, I will be your guide. I've conquered many mountains larger than this."

I run and catch up with Him as he keeps walking. "Perhaps you missed one detail about me. I'm petrified of heights, especially that high."

He grins impishly. "I'm aware of your crippling fears, including heights."

"This isn't funny. I'll never make it. Probably pass out and need a crew to carry me back. I'm begging you not to do this." I fold my arms, refusing to move.

He faces me with a stern yet caring look. "Izzy, I understand it's the first day, but we need to get to work. Serious work. Don't you want to see your family as soon as possible?"

"That's not fair."

"It's not about fairness. The truth is not always fair, but it's always righteous."

"What does that mean?"

"You're here because your mind is a mess. A master at keeping it together on the outside, but inside, your brain is like a bowl of spaghetti stuck together. Thankfully, you prayed for healing, but if you continue resisting God, you'll never be free."

"Being afraid to climb that enormous mountain is resisting God?"

"Yes."

I stomp. "That makes no sense."

"The mountain represents your greatest fear. Both figuratively, and in your case, literally. If you hike this mountain with me, you will receive incredible rewards. First, you must believe God is righteous in all His ways. Period."

An awkward silence lingers between us.

"Obviously, I want to see my family. I admit, doubting is my default mode. I hear you. Either I trust the process or go home, right?"

"Always your choice, Izzy."

I stare at the gigantic mountain with my hands trembling, but I have faith in God. I cannot make sense of being here or the upcoming adventure, but I long for freedom.

"Let's go, Counselor. I'll be back in a few minutes with the proper attire."

"Outstanding. I'll be right here waiting."

Duke trots ahead of me in what appears to be a victory prance. I roll my eyes and follow my spunky canine into the bungalow to swap outfits. In the armoire, a variety of earth-tone hiking pants and soft cotton t-shirts line the shelves. I change clothes and stand in front of the full-length mirror. As I tuck my shirt, I notice the gold key around my neck. Should I take it? I grab the key, contemplating and place it carefully in the top drawer.

"Come on, Duke. Let's get this over with." Outside the bungalow, we reunite with the counselor. Duke stands at attention beside me as if we are going into battle. I certainly hope not.

"Well, the hiking apparel makes sense now, and you look ready for a climb." I peer down. "Except, still no shoes?"

The counselor winks and hands me a unique walking stick made of gnarly blonde and mahogany wood. A brilliant blue sapphire sits atop the stick carved into an intricate butterfly glittering in the sunlight.

"You'll need this on our journey."

I hold the stick horizontally in both hands, feeling its heaviness. "Thank you. It's gorgeous. Too beautiful for a muddy forest, don't you think?"

"Nonsense. Remember, sometimes you must wade through the mud to receive God's greatest blessings."

I hold the stick in my right hand, placing it firmly on the ground. "Fair enough."

"Are you poking fun at our adventure?"

He turns to lead the way, holding a masculine walking stick made of an understated, thick natural wood I don't recognize. Over his left shoulder, he carries a worn leather backpack. He points to the left. "We'll take the smooth path around the lagoon toward the trailhead."

Duke sprints ahead of us and stops for a drink by the bank of the crystal lagoon. It's paradise, especially for a Great Dane. He splashes the water and runs back toward us with his tongue flapping. As we approach the water, a light mist engulfs us from the majestic waterfall pounding into the clear, aquamarine water. The crashing water is deafening. Colorful butterflies swarm around dense purple flower bushes and dainty wild orchids in every shade line the bank. Hints of sweet honeydew and orange blossoms ignite my senses. I close my eyes, taking in the atmosphere, avoiding my fear of heights. Duke stands along the bank barking.

"Okay, Duke. Have it your way. Let's follow him, Izzy."

"What's going on?"

"See those extra-large lily pads floating on the water?"

"How could I miss them? They're enormous."

"Duke loves riding on them underneath the waterfall. From his barking, it looks like he's wanting to share the experience. What do you say?"

I jolt. "Will it sink? We'll get wet."

"You won't sink, and we can maneuver around the waterfall to stay dry. Just use your walking stick as a paddle. It will be fun."

Duke leaps onto a nearby lily pad, wagging his tail and howling. The lily pad barely shifts.

"Well, if it can carry Duke's weight, I'm sure it can handle this pint-sized redhead. Let's do it, I say."

"Splendid. Pick your pad."

I walk along the edge, searching for a large and sturdy lily pad. The one I like glides over among loads of pink and purple water lilies.

"This one." I reach down and carefully step onto the lily pad with my walking stick in hand. I peer up to see the counselor standing on his lily pad, gliding gracefully. The best paddle board could never measure up to this experience. Duke bounces on his lily pad into the waterfall, drenching himself. He appears to be having a blast. Briefly, all concerns, fears, and doubts melt away. I watch the counselor paddle around the waterfall, but the mist still showers the area. Getting wet doesn't matter. I hear the counselor shouting among the crashing water.

"This way, Izzy."

I wave. We reach the other side and I dread hopping off my lily pad, anticipating the climb ahead. Duke sails to the bank, leaping onto the grass and shakes himself dry, keeping a respectable distance.

"That was a blast, sir."

"Yes. Duke loves having fun."

Two water bottles and large towels rest on a nearby wooden bench. My needful thoughts turn into tangible responses. We pat ourselves with towels and the counselor offers me a drink.

"I'm good."

He places the water bottles in his backpack and motions to a tunnel entering the mountain that's covered in densely twisted vines and velvety green ivy.

"Please stay close, Izzy. Once we get farther in, I will help you up the steep terrain."

"No pushback here. I welcome your help with anything steep."

Through the tunnel, we enter a lush tropical forest with squawking Macaw parrots, howling monkeys, and sounds of various wildlife amplifying within the massive jungle. I've never been to the Amazon rain forests, but I imagine it's similar. I stop and slowly turn around, absorbing the ripe essence of wet, mossy bark lined with ferns and undisturbed nature.

"Counselor, this is beyond anything I can imagine. A f fantastical place."

"And the adventure is just beginning. Stay close."

Back to the present. I follow Him with Duke a step behind me like a loyal protector. Where are we going? I love the majestic forest, it's the potential cliffs and climbs that concern me. I maintain a comfortable distance from the counselor. Without a watch, it seems like an hour of walking. He often looks over his shoulder.

"Izzy, just a few miles before we reach our first destination. This isn't so scary, is it?"

"Not yet, but I need a break." The counselor searches for a spot along the path.

"Over here. Let's sit on this smooth boulder and catch our breath."

"Thank you. The trail is easy, but my legs are shaky from the incline." He hands me the bottled water, and I guzzle it down. Duke and the counselor breathe normally as if the hike is effortless.

"Yes. The gradual incline is deceiving. We've climbed much higher than it appears."

"Oh, boy. I'm glad it's not obvious." I hold my stomach thinking about looking down from the mountain. We rest a bit and Duke paces with a few whimpers.

"That's our signal. Have you rested long enough?"

"I think so."

"Very well."

We hike a few miles, it seems, and the counselor stops to wait for me to catch up. When I reach his side, I look down and my heart seemingly stops. A long narrow bridge made of weathered wooden planks swings between two cliffs over river rapids. I try to calculate how high it is and begin hyperventilating.

"Izzy, breathe."

Stepping back from the edge, I hold my chest and sit on the ground, wheezing. The counselor rests one hand on my shoulder and my breathing normalizes.

He whispers. "We have to cross the bridge."

"Why?"

"There are rewards waiting for you on the other side."

"Any sane person would be afraid to cross that bridge. Did you see the rushing river below?"

"Did I say you shouldn't be afraid?"

"Didn't you?"

"No. Instead, I'm asking you to face your fear with me and do the scary thing, anyway."

"Huh?"

"Izzy, you're trying to eliminate your fear of the bridge, water, and height before taking a step. Your way is impossible. My way is to embrace the fear and walk across the bridge together, relying on my strength, not yours."

"So, it's okay to be terrified?"

"Potential danger should trigger fear. It's good to feel your emotions, yes. It's not okay to let emotions stop you from forging ahead."

I rest my arms on my knees and stare at the sky. "But how will I move if I'm emotionally paralyzed and hyperventilating?"

He reaches out his hand. "By holding my hand and taking one step at a time."

I look away. Duke rubs his large body against my legs, almost knocking me over.

"I'm sorry. I can't do it."

"That's right. You can't do it alone or eliminate fear, but you have courage to take the first step if we walk together."

He stretches his hand further. "Come on, Izzy." His face glows for a split second, and I take his hand, lifting me from the ground. I brush the dirt from my pants and shake my head, curious about the reward. Is it worth it?

"Whatever is waiting for me better be good."

He pats my shoulder, and we walk to the bridge. "That's my Izzy."

At the edge of the cliff, I can't move. What if I fall? What if I stop halfway and get stuck?

"Grip the railing with your left hand and my hand with your right. I will lead you. Fix your eyes on me and avoid looking down. Can you do those three things?"

I nod. Grasping the frayed rope railing, I breathe in hard and exhale. I squeeze the counselor's hand like a lemon into sweet tea.

"Wait. What about Duke?"

"He waits here. Now, take your right foot and step on the bridge."

My leg trembles. After one attempt, I step onto the first skinny plank, and the bridge bounces. I close my eyes as my knees buckle.

"Look at me, Izzy. I won't let you fall."

Opening my eyes, his emerald-diamond eyes pierce me, and my body decompresses. He takes one step, guiding me forward. My left leg moves easier, and I've taken my first step into the abyss of a debilitating phobia. What have I done? The counselor's stance and strength are unwavering, as if fear doesn't exist with Him. Can I take a hundred more steps?

"You're doing great, Izzy. One step at a time. It's working."

I must be having an out-of-body experience to explain me walking on a swinging bridge over crashing rapids at least a hundred feet below. I admit, each step is a little less threatening, and the bouncing is becoming tolerable.

The best part is witnessing the counselor's genuine concern for my safety. I saw a glimpse earlier in our session, but this is another level. My feet seem weightless, and my pace increases. I catch a glimpse of the last plank.

He points to his eyes with two fingers. "Almost there."

We reach the end, and the counselor stops. He smiles widely. "Close your eyes and plant this moment permanently in your mind and let it penetrate deep into your soul."

I squeeze my eyes closed and embrace the thrill of sweet victory.

"Take your last step, Izzy."

I leap over the plank onto the grass and fall to the ground. Jumping back to my feet, I dance around the grassy area like Rocky Balboa. We share a high-five. He clutches both of my arms with an affectionate look.

"I'm so proud of you."

"Thank you. I'm blown away." He releases my arms and I stare at the long skinny bridge swaying from our journey. It's still scary.

"I couldn't do it without you."

His mouth softens into a warm grin. "Are you ready for the reward?"

My eyes light up. "What? Isn't crossing the bridge reward enough?"

"There's a special treat waiting for you here. Never forget, fear conceals the ultimate future from you."

"Tell me. What is it?"

"Follow me."

We climb a small hill using tree roots and rocks for support. Once we reach the top, I pull myself up to see over the ridge. In the distance, a burly man stands with his back to me. I squint. Being curious, I scoot on top of the hill, dusting debris from my clothes. I glance at the counselor leaning against a large tree and grinning like a Cheshire Cat.

I point to the man. "Counselor, there is a big man standing there. Who is it?"

"Go find out. It's okay, I'll wait here."

"We're deep in a jungle. Who could it be?"

"Patience, Izzy."

I inch closer. He's wearing a green plaid flannel shirt, faded jeans, and an Indiana Jones hat, revealing wiry red hair underneath. Kinda reminds me of . . . he turns around, and I cover my mouth.

"Grandpa Finny?" I blink.

He turns facing me. "Izzy, my sweet girl. Come here." With his arms outstretched, I race to him, and we embrace. His strong arms envelope my entire body, just as I remember.

I step backward. "You haven't aged. Same red hair and bushy beard."

"Look at you, darlin'—all grown up."

"I'm delighted, but shocked to see you. How did you get here?"

"Slow down, Izzy. We're on borrowed time. He extends his hand and I take it. He guides me to a mammoth tree with a heavy rope swing attached to a sturdy limb. The swing is a carbon copy of the one at Grandpa Finny's farm. Climb aboard and give it a whirl, like the good old days."

"Are you serious?"

"Are you too grown up, darlin'?" His peculiar laughter rumbles.

"It's been years, but oh, well." I hop on the large swing, and he pushes me carefully back and forth, rekindling a comfort long forgotten. I close my eyes, savoring the sweet moment.

"Do you remember? It's just like our swing at the farm. Oh, how I treasure those times with your Grandma Millie."

"Yes, it's fantastic." After several more pushes, he holds the rope steady on the last return to stabilize the swing. He walks behind the large tree and appears holding a three-legged wooden stool and sits facing me with a caring smile within his red mustache and beard. His green eyes twinkle.

"Izzy, seeing your precious face again is a glorious gift."

"Am I in Heaven now?"

"No, darlin'. We're in your special place, as the counselor explained. Heaven is even more grand than this. Can you imagine?"

"I can't."

"You're safe here. I promise."

"You never broke a promise—like someone else in the family."

He drops his head. "If I could fix the past, I would. The counselor will help sort it out if you trust Him. He's a good lad." He takes hold of my hand.

"Is that why you're here? To convince me?" He shares a sly grin.

"No, darlin'. The Lord thought you could use a familiar face, so He sent me. You must miss your family dearly."

"So much. I want to accept this time gap, but it's too outlandish to comprehend."

"Most of the time, we don't understand God's ways. That's why we have faith."

A long silence hangs between us.

"Funny, I've been praying since I was ten for one more chance to see you because I missed saying goodbye in the hospital. In my youthful innocence, I couldn't accept losing you, so I held out my goodbyes believing you wouldn't die. It sounds ridiculous."

He roars again. "My sweet Izzy. Your heart is as big as a whale." He caresses my hand.

"On your dying day, I hurried to your room, but I was too late. Now, here you are, and I'm astonished."

"Well, that's what happens when you delight in God's ways like you're doing here. He gives you your heart's desires."

"Really?"

"God knows what He's doing. If you believe, there's a bigger reward beyond this brief pause in time and reunion. But you must face your deepest fears to get it."

"Not you too."

"Were you afraid to walk across the swinging bridge?"

"Terrified."

"In your humbleness, he guided you the entire way and look at the reward. A chance to see this ugly mug again." He pats his jiggling belly.

I shake my head. "I'm relieved your humor hasn't changed either."

"Just imagine if you chose not to cross the bridge and missed this lovely moment."

I nod.

"Keep trusting God's plan and lean on your counselor."

"But . . ."

He wags his finger. "No more excuses, Izzy. Get on with it. Be brave and get back to your family where you belong."

He stands with his arms wide open. We cling to each other, reluctant to separate. Then he kisses my forehead. "That's my girl. Now, go on. No need for goodbyes, we'll meet again someday."

I step backward and look up at his woolly red beard while squeezing his hands tightly. His features blur through my watery eyes. I flinch, hearing the counselor calling for me in the distance.

"It's time to go, Izzy."

Grandpa Finny nods. "Go on. You are in the best of hands."

Choked up, I slowly release my palms and turn to the counselor's voice. Walking slowly, I stop to peer over my shoulder, and Grandpa Finny is nowhere in sight. I continue walking with a taller stance, reflecting on the day's events. The gift to overcome my deep sorrow sinks in. It's time for me to trust God's ways. After all, this could be my last chance. My pace speeds up. I reach the counselor standing in front of the swinging bridge.

"Surprised to see Grandpa Finny?"

"Shocked. The best reward. Thank you so much."

"My pleasure. Ready to conquer the bridge again?"

"We're going back?"

"Yes. You're not ready?"

I point toward the peak. "Aren't we hiking to the top?"

"I said we needed to climb this mountain, but I didn't say how high."

"I assumed the worst."

"Ah yes. Making the problem bigger than reality is a common occurrence. Let's work on that."

He's right. I assume the worst in most situations. So much enlightenment in one day. What will tomorrow tell?

"Izzy, are you ready?"

"It's still scary, but with you, I can do it again."

Duke's barking on the other side echoes throughout the canyon, as if he's cheering me on. Same strategy. I grip the rope and the counselor's hand and take one step at a time. Midway, a fierce wind shakes the feeble bridge and I freeze with panic.

"Steady, Izzy. Don't look down."

I refocus on his serious face until the wind gusts settle into a comfortable breeze.

He points to his nose. "Eyes on me. You're doing splendidly."

Still frozen, he coaches me on farther, and I take another step. We reach the last plank and I leap to dry ground. Lying face down, I hug the grass while Duke licks my ears. The counselor extends his hand and I take it, rising to my feet.

"Izzy, after this, there's nothing we can't accomplish together. The ultimate reward is coming."

I stand erect. "I believe you."

On the trek down, the counselor whistles a smooth melody, making the time seem quicker than the climb. I see bright sunshine ahead as we exit the dark tunnel. Duke stops at the lagoon for a drink of water, bypassing the lily pad ride, and we approach the bungalow. The counselor wraps one arm around me with a casual squeeze. I face Him and we hug, Grandpa Finny style. The purest love is unmistakable from our embrace.

"Thank you, Counselor. I don't understand God's plan, but I trust you to lead me forward."

"I'm elated to hear it. Rest well and I'll see you at the sanctuary tomorrow."

"Yes, sir. See you then."

In my room, Jacob comes to mind. I want to tell him about my adventure and meeting Grandpa Finny. Being apart in different worlds makes our emotional separation back home seem trivial. Will I make it back to his arms?

There's no denying what's required to reunite with him. Shadows of the family incident roll in like dark stormy thunder. Victory over the crippling misery held captive in my mind is the ultimate reward. A full life awaits—but is it truly possible? I must find out.

CHAPTER 6

Suitcase Ride

After the usual morning routine, I retrieve the key necklace from the drawer and place it around my neck before walking out the door. I stop and rub the key. God must really love me to bring my beloved grandfather into this fantasy world for a brief encounter. I can't imagine a better way to offer assurance about my special time with the counselor.

Back to the present, I stroll towards the garden sanctuary with Duke by my side. We crisscross through the majestic labyrinth of dense shrubs and flowering bushes. Disney World landscapes seem amateurish compared to this. I slow down, close my eyes, and breathe in the stimulating aroma of cut grass blended with fragrant flowers. Grandpa Finny claims Heaven surpasses this place. I can't fathom.

A heavy sigh overpowers my imagination. Even a paradise like this doesn't compare to being home with Jacob, Travis, and Katie. God went to extraordinary lengths to pamper me, and I'm grateful, but it can't replace life with them. I imagine Jacob singing to me by the creek with his guitar, and I flick a tear from my eye.

We arrive at the sanctuary, and Duke races ahead of me through the rose-covered trellis, but as usual, I stop below the engraved signage bearing my name. I kiss my fingers and tap the wooden sign. The scent of fresh roses and hydrangeas tickles my nose. I plop down, sinking into my white, cushy chair, while Duke circles the area beside me, preparing his resting spot.

My hands twist together, thinking of my family. How are they coping? Distracted by the counselor approaching the trellis, I release my hands. He walks closer and waves.

"Good morning, Izzy. Glad you're still here, and I didn't scare you off with the climb."

"Good morning, sir." He stands before me with hands on his hips in nylon hiking pants with a matching pullover and no shoes. Another day of hiking? I hope not.

A shiny, silver coffee carafe with pure gold inlays and two matching cups sit on the table between our chairs. Must be a rare antique set. He bends over to pour our coffee. I relax my eyes and sniff the bold coffee aroma in the air.

"Jacob and the kids are the only reason I'd ever leave this place. Are they okay?"

"They're doing their best and praying for your recovery. Jacob is clinging to his faith and staying strong for the kids. He's a good man." He hands me the shiny coffee cup with an empathetic look.

He sits across from me, quietly respecting the somberness because of the separation from my family. I place the coffee cup back on the table.

"Counselor, I'm eager to start our session, even though I'm nervous about what's coming."

"Happy to hear that. Confronting your fear yesterday is the first step, but I warn you again, it's going to get tougher as we continue, so it's imperative we move at your pace. Are you ready?"

"I have to be."

"Good. Today we go way back to your earliest childhood memories. Get comfortable, close your eyes, and take three deep breaths. On the last exhale, share the memory that instantly pops into your mind without any hesitation.

I follow His instructions as flashbacks form in my mind, yet one specific memory dominates.

"I'm about six years old. It was a cool Sunday evening, and Mother ushered my three siblings and me outside to play like she did every week for the past year. I rode my Big Wheel around the driveway while my brother, Roger, eavesdropped outside our parents' bedroom window. Occasionally, he allowed my eldest sister Abbey to listen, but he didn't allow Shannon and me to join. When the argument escalated, even Roger couldn't keep us from overhearing. That's the year everything changed." My fingers press into the arms of the chair.

"Did the argument become violent?"

"No, never. Just verbal. Sometimes the feud was brief, other times longer. Once the yelling stopped, Mother appeared at the front door, forcing a smile, and ordered us into the house to say goodbye to our father. Every week, I went through the same routine of jumping off my Big Wheel and bolting to my parents' bedroom where the begging began."

"Begging?"

"Yes. As Father packed his clothes, I begged him to stay, but he ignored me. I didn't let up. Once he finished packing his silver, hard-shelled suitcase, I jumped on top of the roller bag for my weekly ride to the back door."

"You mean you sat on top of his suitcase while he rolled it through the house?"

"That's right. From bedroom to garage, I rode, suitcase between my legs, begging him to stay. Once we arrived at the back door, I had a melt-down—feet kicking, arms flying. Like a robot, he gripped underneath my arms, lifted me up and over the large bag. He placed my feet firmly on the floor, away from his suitcase. I sobbed hysterically, but he left without a hug or a goodbye."

I press my fist over my mouth to hold back the tears. With staccato-like words and tears rolling down my face, I continue.

"I relived that scene at least a hundred times, trying to erase the emotional scars and convince myself it doesn't hurt anymore. I'm in my forties and should be over it, but in sharing the same pathetic story, wounds are still raw. How is that possible?"

"It's complicated, but you'll get there. Please keep going with your memory."

"Okay. Father walked casually to his red Cadillac convertible, mumbling he'd be back in a week. I stomped my feet screaming, 'No, Daddy.' He threw his suitcase into the trunk, climbed into the Cadillac, and once again, I couldn't make him stay. He was gone."

"Did you believe you could convince him otherwise?"

I tilt my head back. "When I grew older, yes. Every week I hoped for a different outcome and believed he would stay if I tried hard enough."

"That's concerning. Let's come back to that. Where was your mother during this suitcase episode?"

"On my ride, I remember passing her in the kitchen washing dishes. She never looked my way or intervened."

"Where was your father going?"

"Good question. He worked as a sales executive for a large steel manufacturer. That same year, he told my mother he accepted a promotion that required weekly out-of-town travels to meet with clients. He took the new position without consulting her. She was furious. They had several heated discussions about her needs at home to ensure a stable family. Mother didn't care about the extra money because we already lived an abundant lifestyle. To make matters worse, he told her his traveling was temporary. She trusted his word."

"As you would expect a wife to trust her husband."

"I agree. She did her best to keep us together and didn't waver in her position. As an orphan from birth, Mother grew up in different foster homes, graduated high school, and went to college on a ballet scholarship. She never spoke about the details of her childhood except for her dream of a happy family, which came true until that fateful year."

I wring my hands, questioning my sanity to rehash my childhood.

"Your mother endured extreme suffering. We will talk about that later."

I flinch and stare straight ahead. "Sorry for getting off track."

"It's okay, Izzy. You're doing great. But let's finish the suitcase ride memory first."

"Sure."

"How many times did you ride your father's suitcase when he left home?"

"Countless. The Sunday night ritual lasted for years until I outgrew the luggage, or I gave up. Not sure which. With time, the childish fits faded, and the suitcase ride became a disturbing game. After a few years of this, my gut instinct told me he had a choice to stay, and when he left, I slowly grew to mistrust him. He never waffled from his decision to leave, and every time he stepped over the threshold into the garage, my anguish deepened. I clung to the hope that I could persuade him the following week and saw the eerie suitcase ride as a chance to draw his attention to me before he left because time with him was scarce."

"You mean this is the only time you spent with your father?"

"He spent weekends at home, mostly disrupted by mysterious phone calls."

"Why mysterious?"

"He took his calls outside sometimes at the edge of our driveway. If it was raining, he murmured in the garage. It seemed secretive."

"I see."

"Yeah. The tension between my parents was thick and silent, so we learned to keep our distance by playing outside until dusk or arranging sleepovers at the neighbor's house."

The counselor presses his lips together before speaking. "I am so sorry this happened to you, Izzy. You deserved better."

"Thank you." I search for courage to continue the session.

"Are you okay? Do you need a break?"

"No, let's keep going."

"How many years did your father's traveling continue?"

"About eleven years."

He raises an eyebrow. "That's a significant amount of time. How did your mother handle it?"

"Approximately five years in, she gave up and stopped fighting with him on Sunday evening. She spent many nights crying in her bedroom with the door locked, but around us kids, she pretended everything was fine and dandy. Father convinced her he couldn't replace his income with a local job, and he preferred to stay with his current company for the perks and benefits. End of debate. She loved my father passionately and held on to her dream of a united family, but separation was her reality. Sunday evening cast a gloomy darkness, but we pretended it was normal. No longer ushered in for weekly goodbyes. As a teen, I remember waving half-heartedly to my father from my pink banana seat bicycle as he drove away. I hated it. Although acceptance became ordinary, Mother assured us he would stop traveling. He never did."

The counselor rubs his chin. "The pain was obvious to each of you. You were incredibly young, but what about life prior to your father's promotion? Do you remember anything?"

"Barely. We laughed together, even Father. I vaguely recall my parents dancing in the living room to romantic music, and they giggled a lot. Once, we went on a trip to the southern California coast and visited a beautiful beach. Mother caked me with sunscreen. My first experience in ocean waters, and I fell in love with palm trees. As the youngest, my siblings recalled more stories about life before Father's big promotion." I gesture with air quotes and roll my eyes.

"What else can you tell me about the years leading up to him traveling?"

I rub my forehead and look down. "I was so little, but I craved being Daddy's little girl. Before his so-called job promotion, I never let him out of my sight at home. He tried to read *The Wall Street Journal* with me on his lap, pestering him for attention. He let me ride along when the Cadillac needed an oil change. I loved being around him because he was fun and gentle during those years."

"Things certainly changed, Izzy."

I nod.

"Anything else you want to share?"

"Oh yeah. Father was nuts about aviation. Model airplanes hung from the ceiling in his home office. In the summertime, he would take us kids for donuts in his convertible and then to the airport to watch the planes. It touched me, watching his face light up when the jet engines roared—the only images I recall of him being excited, like a big kid. A simple, yet unforgettable tradition."

With my hands interlocked, I whisper, "Can you imagine my devastation when he went absent, both physically and emotionally?"

"Yes. You've suffered severely. Something drastic happened the year of his career advancement. Please recall the memory once more, despite the pain. This time, we're going to probe deeper. Are you up for it?"

"Not sure. I fear getting too far into the past."

"Remember the mountain and the swinging bridge? It's okay to be afraid."

I raise one finger. "Do the scary thing, anyway."

"Exactly. Now, sit back and close your eyes, taking three deep breaths. After the third exhale, imagine you are that six-year-old child riding your father's suitcase. Once you have the visual clearly in your mind, describe the scene again."

I wiggle in my chair and close my eyes. Will this really work? After my third exhale, I envision myself back in our childhood home, walking to the master bedroom. I'm wearing blue polka dot leggings with a white kitten stitched on my long-sleeved shirt. I loved those leggings.

"I got it. I'm in my parents' bedroom, bouncing lightly on the king-sized bed next to the open suitcase, watching my father pack his suits and ties. We've had no interaction until I ask him if he would stay home this time. He huffs and shakes his head without making eye contact and keeps packing. I stop bouncing, sit, and stare at the floor, swinging my feet to hit the side of the bed, seeking his attention. Once he zips the suitcase shut and places it upright on the floor, I jump on top of the bag. He shakes his head and mumbles my name under his breath. Once we're in the hallway, I kick the sides of the bag and beg him to stay."

"Stop there," the counselor says. "What's going through your mind?"

"If I beg hard enough, he will stay this time."

"How does it feel?"

"My stomach aches. Questions flood my mind like, what can I do differently to make him stay? What if I am better? Why doesn't he like me? What is wrong with me?" I pause. "I'm surprised by these thoughts."

"That's okay. You're doing great. Describe the emotions popping up?"

"Frustrated, desperate, disappointed, crushed, hurt, and devastated when he leaves. He let me down again and I don't understand why I can't convince him to stay. After he picks me up to remove me from his roller bag, the heat within my body intensifies."

"What is the ultimate feeling?"

"Rejection."

I hold my stomach as tears stream down my face. But this time, I'm not crying like a hurt child anymore. I'm grieving the loss of the father I lost.

The counselor hands me a tissue, and I wipe my eyes to regain composure.

"Izzy, when you were a child, did you share these feelings with your mother or siblings?"

"No way. I didn't want them to blame me too or feel worse about his absence."

"Blame you?"

"Yes. Because I couldn't convince him to choose us over his job."

"It's surprising to hear you take responsibility for the situation, being so young."

"Remember, his traveling lasted for years. But it surprises me too. I wasn't aware of feeling responsible until today. I've focused on being hurt and angry."

"Do you still believe you could have prevented your father from leaving?"

"No. Based on later events, the truth came out. Regardless, the scars are raw from being rejected."

"Have you considered that the suitcase ride was not about your father rejecting you?"

I shrug my shoulders. "He rejected me every time he walked through the garage door."

"Is it possible his decisions, although neglectful and painful, had nothing to do with you?"

"I don't understand. It had everything to do with me."

"Yes. His decisions made an impact on you. But he didn't choose to leave *because* of you nor anything you did. Nor could you have persuaded him to stay. Do you see the difference?"

"I do, but the pain I carry is the same."

"I understand. But it doesn't have to be."

"How so? I feel the pain of those recurring rejections."

"Hear me out. The pain your father caused is legitimate, but your interpretation of rejection is not."

I stand, pacing in front of my chair. "My sorrow is my fault?"

"No. It's not about blame. Your father neglected and deceived you and your family. There's no excuse for his choices and behavior."

"I'm glad we agree on something."

He gestures me to sit. "Open your mind, Izzy. To heal the emotional scars from this specific memory, we must separate the false belief from the truth. It doesn't excuse or erase the mistreatment by him."

I huff and sit down. "I'm listening."

"As a little girl, you believed you could change your father's decision. When he left, you concluded his choice was because of your inadequacy and ultimately felt rejected. The recurrence created an emotional groove, forming a mind trap."

"Mind trap?"

"Yes, it's a negative thought pattern made of up false beliefs trapped in your mind. Let's save mind traps for later."

"Why would those beliefs continue once the truth was out about Father?"

"You mentioned not being aware of those thoughts on the suitcase until today because they were buried deep within your subconscious."

"Why does it matter?"

"As an adult, situations arise pricking at subconscious emotions of rejection."

My eyes widen. "Like the misunderstanding about Jacob and the kids?"

"Bingo. Your father made mistakes at catastrophic levels, but your father's actions had nothing to do with rejecting you. It doesn't mean his actions didn't cause genuine disappointment and a lack of love. It did. What you must see is that your belief about inadequacy is not valid, but it's the source causing your current emotions of inferiority."

"I was just a little girl wanting to be with her dad."

He gives me a tender look. "Exactly. You couldn't possibly understand what was going on, and he wasn't thinking of you or the harm he would cause. Truly. He thought only of himself. The weekly event and his callous behavior presented an opportunity for you to interpret the situation as your fault by convincing yourself you could change his decision to leave."

I wipe a tear from my eye. "I looked up to him."

"As a child should."

"I believe you're saying that although his leaving was illogical, I denied any potential wrongdoing on his part and blamed myself instead."

He forms a fist. "That's when the false beliefs took hold, Izzy. Can you see it now?"

"I think so, but it's hard to wrap my head around."

"It's tricky. Plus, based on your input, roughly 52 weeks times 11 years equals 572 recurring beliefs of rejection."

I raise both hands. "My point exactly. So how can you say it's not true?"

"Your recurring interpretation is wrong. You know the reason he left every week."

"Hold it, Counselor."

"Don't worry. We're not going down that road today."

I shake my head, blowing off stream. "If I'm wrong, why do I still feel rejected and unloved by him?"

"We're dissecting a tiny fraction of the overall pain you endured. Narrow your focus to the beliefs you had riding the suitcase and no further."

I slap my thigh. "He rejected us."

"You believe that, but it wasn't his intention. The year he started traveling, showing love toward his family faded, leaving a void he once filled. The change created the loss and genuine pain you felt as a child and still today. But believing you were the reason he left is not true or real. Are we getting anywhere?"

"Maybe. I admit a sense of peace by revealing my subconscious thoughts as a little girl. It helps. The sudden loss of his presence explains why I'm grief stricken for the first time. Still doesn't change how I feel about him."

"Baby steps, Izzy. We're not attempting to erase every emotional scar in one hour. I'm asking you to accept the truth about the suitcase ride. That's it. He didn't leave because you were a terrible child or not persuasive enough. It wasn't your fault."

I swallow the lump in my throat. "I see the truth. But I still despise the man."

"It's okay. We're making progress."

"Are we? How can I remove the pain forever?"

"Patience."

I perk up. "Can I truly move forward and live without this heavy burden?"

"Yes."

I shrug. "What could get me there?"

"At your discretion, confront your entire past and release the anguish holding you hostage."

I squirm in my chair. "I can't."

"No, but *we* can. I warned the process is challenging and complex with each twisted noodle in your brain interconnected." He grins slightly, lifting the atmosphere.

"Great. I'm a messy head case."

"You're human. Think of each session as olive oil pouring over a bowl of overcooked spaghetti, lubricating the sticky strongholds until untangled."

"I guess. Let's keep going before I change my mind."

"We've covered enough ground today."

"Really? That was quick."

"Information overload will hinder our progress. Allow your mind to marinate on our last two sessions. We tackled boulders." Besides, I have another surprise for you after lunch."

I stiffen. "Mountain climbing?"

He laughs, "No, an afternoon of movie watching in the theater room next to your bungalow."

I pause momentarily.

"What is it? Don't you like movies?"

"Yes, and I appreciate your kindness, but my family must be worried sick. Shouldn't we keep going with our session?"

"Few things are more important than enjoying the life God grants His children. You'll understand once you watch the first movie. They are favorites, I assure you."

I stand, stretching my arms over my head. The heaviness of our session lessens. "Okay. I'll take your advice."

"Izzy, before we close, I want to share one more truth."

"What is it?"

"Your mother didn't look at you or intervene during the suitcase ride because she was crying quietly at the kitchen sink and didn't want you to see her upset. It's the only way she could cope."

His words pierce my heart. It never occurred to me to consider her pain during my ride of perceived rejection. Thoughts of my mother are daunting. I'm aware of what's nearing, unsure if I can confront it. Duke nuzzles my hand and brings me back to the moment.

The counselor touches my shoulder. "Izzy, are you okay?"

"Yes. Thank you, sir."

"Go enjoy a hearty lunch."

Duke takes my hand gingerly in his mouth and pulls me forward. I pat his head and we mosey to the bungalow. Butterflies of every color flutter around us until we reach our lunch destination.

After a cup of clam chowder and Caesar salad, Duke leads me to a cinema that reminds me of the iconic Fox Theater in downtown Atlanta. I stop and press my heart. On the digital marquee reads *Izzy's Matinee*. I peer at the spiral stone columns on each side leading to hand-carved ornate towers. When we enter the lobby, the sound and smell of popcorn popping overtakes me. Duke prances through the red velvet roped walkway to the concession stand and barks. I assume he wants popcorn too. With no one in sight, I pour a soda for me and water for Duke and fill a large bucket with warm buttery popcorn. Duke's nose twitches as he sniffs the air. Large double doors line the entrance to the theater room. I open the middle section and enter a timeless auditorium. The art deco style, rich gold colors, and architectural elements create a nostalgic atmosphere. A nice reminder of watching movies with my high school girlfriend, Misty.

Duke runs to the front row, faces me and wags his tail. I take a seat and sink into the blue velvet cushion. Duke stretches out beside me. I place his water and a few kernels of popcorn on the floor and he devours them.

Tall, heavy red curtains open to an enormous movie screen displaying a countdown from 10. What appears when the screen reads zero is unimaginable. I stand, dumping my popcorn and stare at a video of our family beach vacation in California. I hear my mother's laughter and watch my siblings swim in the ocean through my water-filled eyes. Mother waves to the camera. I wipe the tears and lower to my seat as I gaze at the screen. Duke gobbles up the popcorn on the floor. I've never seen this video before.

Roger moves out of the water and runs forward until his face covers the entire movie screen. He makes a funny face, and the camera jostles sideways. After the picture stabilizes, my father enters the scene and runs to my mother lying on a beach towel. He extends his hand, and she stands. They embrace. After a long hug, he kisses her cheek, and they dance slowly in the sand. He twirls her around like a ballerina and they laugh. I close my eyes for a moment. What happened to them?

The camera zooms in on me. I'm digging in the sand and building a sandcastle. Roger yells for my sisters to join me and they run over with plastic shovels to help. I marvel at the sounds of our innocent giggles. The scene transitions back to my parents, with a close-up on their faces. Their eyes meet and they continue to sway gently. After several minutes, the video abruptly changes to a scene in our living room with Mother performing ballet. I can see the top of Father's head. Soon he joins her, and they waltz through the house. I sniffle. Duke rises and rests his paw on my knee with droopy, sad eyes. I stroke his forehead.

Hours pass and I experience the erratic emotions of jubilation and despair. My heart aches. Questions about their marriage scramble in my mind. They appear deeply in love on the movie screen. Like them, Jacob and I shared a deep love in our early years. Maybe they prioritized us kids over romance and drifted apart. Even though I blame my father, I've never felt empathetic about their marriage situation. On the screen, I see flawed humans, like me. Could my marriage end in disaster too?

CHAPTER 7

The Blame Game

JACOB

Isabelle is still unconscious. I can't bear watching her lie in the hospital bed, lifeless. Her face bulges with blue and purple bruises, and apparatus is attached to her from all directions. I rub my face briskly, listening to the repetitive pumping of oxygen and beeping sounds keeping her alive.

Nurse Wanda enters the room holding a steaming cup of coffee wafting a welcome aroma. She must have read my mind.

"You really need this. Your eyes are so bloodshot that I can't tell what color they are anymore." She hands me an oversized coffee mug with the hospital logo and whispers, "Don't tell. I'm borrowing this from the cafeteria."

"Mums the word, and perfect timing. Thank you, Wanda."

She steps back with her finger pressed to her lips.

"You've been here two days straight wearing the same clothes. Go home and take a nice, hot shower. You'll feel better."

I blow on the coffee. "Is that a polite way of saying I stink?" We laugh, lightening the heavy mood.

"Not at all. You just need a break. Travis and Katie said they will stop by later. Go on."

"I can't leave her, Wanda."

She pats my shoulder. "I understand. Take a walk, stretch those long legs. You can't be all cooped up in that small recliner forever. Plus, you're in my way to work with Isabelle. Now shoo."

"Fine."

I stand beside Isabelle, scan her body, and walk out with my coffee mug in hand. The ICU corridors are full of people crying over their loved ones. There is no escape from this crisis. I keep walking and spot the chapel sign ahead. As I approach the sanctuary door, an unfamiliar wave of rage sweeps through my body. I fling open the door and march down the red carpeted aisle and stand in front of a large cross surrounded by brilliant stained-glass windows. I kneel, placing my coffee mug next to me, and I pound the wooden floor with my fists shouting, "Why, God?"

The blows on the hardwood floor increase with intensity. I can't stop. Startled by a warm touch on my shoulder and a whisper saying my name, I turn to see Mr. Merriweather standing over me with big watery eyes.

I stand clutching him in my arms, wailing. When I stormed in, I didn't check the chapel for anyone. After a long embrace, I release him. He hands me a handkerchief, and I wipe my nose.

"Jacob, are you okay, son?"

"Obviously not."

"I'm sorry to interrupt what looks like a private moment between you and God, but it broke my heart seeing you in such pain. I had to come over."

"I'm glad you did, but I'm embarrassed. Thankfully, you are the only one here. I've never felt rage like this before, and it scares me."

He grips my arm. "I understand, son. You can't imagine the hostile conversations I had with God when my beloved Rosemary transitioned to Heaven. Too long, I blamed Him for taking her and leaving me behind in this crazy world. Releasing emotion is healthy."

I drop my head. "Why did God allow this to happen?"

"Oh, how I wish it was me instead of Isabelle. If I hadn't taken my walk that day, this would not be happening. Besides, I'm ready to see Rosemary again."

"No way. It's not your fault. I'm relieved your injuries are minor. If anyone is to blame, it's me."

"How so?"

"Remember, you showed me the rot in that old tree a few summers back, and we talked about cutting it down, but I put it off. Too busy with work."

"Jacob, listen to me. When accidents happen, it's human nature to look for someone or something to blame, believing it eases the pain. Don't fall for the lie. It was an accident, and unfortunately, your sweet Isabelle is the victim. She's also a hero. I feel terrible that she's suffering the consequences of saving my life. I'll live my remaining days haunted by that, but I'll be here praying until God brings her back to you and the kids."

I stare at the hardwood floor, allowing his wisdom to sink in. "That's why you're in the chapel?"

"Yes. While only the immediate family can visit Isabelle, I can still pray near her room. Prayer is powerful."

"You *are* family, but you don't want to see her yet." I pause. "She's unrecognizable."

He closes his eyes and nods slowly.

"Mr. Merriweather, your kindness is overwhelming, and you're a sincere man of God. I can't say that about myself."

"Son, give yourself a little grace. Besides, Isabelle is fighting for her life and needs your courage, not your anger at God. Believe me, I've been there. For you and your family, I urge you to keep God in the forefront of this battle, and don't turn away from Him now because you can't reconcile the reasons for this trial."

I share a slight grin. "That's what lawyers do."

"And you're a darn good one." We smile. "Trust in God's strength, and I am confident she will come back to you."

"How are you so sure?"

He holds his stomach. "Eighty-seven years with faith as my compass. Something deep in my gut tells me she will wake up, and it's not false hope. I can't explain the feeling."

"I hope you're right."

"Trials in life are opportunities to grow closer to God. When we do that, miracles happen. Don't let the alternative block those miracles."

"I hear you. Thank you for being here and keeping me straight. Before it ends, I might need this discussion again."

"You can count on it."

We shake hands, and he turns to leave. "I'll see you here tomorrow, Jacob."

"I'm going to stay here a little longer."

He waves and slowly shuffles down the aisle with his wooden cane. Mr. Merriweather's presence here is ironic. He's right. Even though it's tough, I can't fall into the trap of blaming God and separate myself from the mightiest strength of all. Most importantly, I must stay grounded in the roots of my faith and be strong for Isabelle and our two kids.

I take a seat in the front pew, mesmerized by the stately wooden cross before me. Where would I be if Mr. Merriweather hadn't appeared today? As if God arranged our chance meeting. A calming sensation overtakes me, and I thank God in prayer for His strength.

"Dad, there you are. We thought you might be here." I twist around to see my two beautiful children entering the chapel.

"Travis, Katie, you are a welcome sight. Come here."

They rush down the aisle and we embrace. Katie sobs in my chest, and Travis steps back so I can hold her closer. We nod at each other. My son appears strong as a soldier, but I'm concerned about him. His eyes express a heartbreak like I've never seen. He treasures his mother. Together, we will get through this with the Lord's help.

I notice Nurse Wanda poking her head in the chapel entrance with a frantic look. "Jacob, please hurry. The doctor needs to see you about Isabelle."

CHAPTER 8

The Mind Trap Method

ISABELLE

The sun beams through the window, warming my face. I overslept. After a quick shower and teeth brushing, I pull on a pair of faded jeans and a cotton t-shirt with white sneakers. Calling for Duke, we sprint through the bungalow to the sanctuary. How can I be so rude? I skid into our meeting spot like I'm rounding home plate. And there's the counselor, sitting patiently drinking coffee. He appears calm. I stop beside his chair, panting.

"Counselor, forgive me. I'm late. I never sleep in like this."

"Good morning, Izzy. There is nothing to forgive. Take a seat and catch your breath."

"But I'm late."

"Says who? Your concept of time differs from mine. Rest is what you needed, so you rested well. Let's start the morning with some hot coffee, fresh fruit, and an English muffin, since you didn't have time for breakfast at the bungalow."

"Oh, thank you. I'm so embarrassed."

"Why? Do I seem disturbed?"

77

He pours the coffee and shoos Duke away from the table.

"Not at all."

"Let's use this moment to disrupt your old thoughts and respond to reality. Shall we?"

He smiles widely, and I snicker.

"Yes, sir. I think that's a terrific idea."

He hands me a delicate cup with a red paisley design and takes his seat.

"Perfect. In our earlier sessions, we revealed the mind trap of rejection, and we worked through the stages of revealing the lie and owning the truth. Our focus today is on renewing the mind by replacing old lies with truth. Make sense?"

"It does. Sounds like a mind trap method."

"You can label it if it helps."

I inch forward. "I don't want to forget anything."

"You won't. As noted, the hurtful emotions continue even though you confronted the lies and own the truth intellectually. You also said you wouldn't continue believing a lie once it's exposed."

"That's right. It's illogical."

"Good."

Out of nowhere, he whips out a piece of paper on a clipboard. He hands me the clipboard and a gold pen. It's heavy. Could it be pure gold? I take both.

"Remember, prayer is always the first step in seeking guidance."

I chuckle. "My last prayer landed me here. But I'm not afraid to pray."

"And we are delighted to host you, Izzy."

The counselor leads, and we pray together aloud, seeking God's direction and Holy Spirit discernment. Then, I call on Jesus to help ease the discomfort through my time with the counselor. Once we conclude, he continues.

"Please title the paper 'Mind Trap of Rejection' and draw a straight line down the middle. A few lines down on the left side write 'Current Thought Pattern' and underline it. Below that line, write the list of lies we revealed within the negative pattern."

"Okay. Why am I doing this?"

"So, you don't forget." We smile. "Also, when you write on paper, the brain activates a heightened focus and retention while serving as a reference document."

"Makes complete sense."

I tap my chin contemplating each lie. A lengthy list. Tears fill my eyes as I read the deceit in print. I've been living through a lens of lies since childhood. My hand shakes.

"It will be okay, Izzy. We cannot rewind time, yet through God's strength and guidance, you can restore your mind to find peace and joy. Plus, you have support and new teachings to support you."

"I understand." I cover my face with both hands.

"What is it?"

The long silence becomes awkward, and I blurt it out.

"I'm too old."

He laughs hysterically. I cross my arms and stare back at Him with pressed lips.

"You find this humorous, but I'm serious. I'm too old to change."

"Are you doubting the one God sent as your advocate?"

"You? No. I'm doubting my abilities to change my thick-headed skull."

"I'm not laughing at you, but at the belief that age prevents change. If you're mentally sound and breathing, you can make choices that bring change. And with God—"

"Let me guess. All things are possible."

"That's right."

"Pardon me, but I'm sitting here with a messenger from God, surrounded by what looks like Heaven, but it's not. Can this get any more surreal?"

"Why are you stalling? What is it, Izzy?"

I stare at my feet and see Duke looking at me with huge brown eyes. "I'm frustrated and scared."

"What are you most afraid of?"

Breathing deeply, I exhale. "I'm afraid of failing again. I'm tired of digging up the past and getting nowhere. Even with God's help, I'm not convinced."

"You don't need convincing. You only need a little faith."

His gentle smile gives me hope. I bite my lower lip to fight back the tears.

"If you commit to the process, I guarantee you will see this is possible by the end of our session. Can we continue?"

When I nod, he speaks again.

"Put your age aside and let's focus on the next step. Shall we?"

"All right."

"Where were we? Ah, yes. After jotting down the lies, please add a heading titled 'New Thought Pattern' at the top of the page on the right and underline it.

I peer at the ground, searching for the right statements to counteract each lie.

"I was a good kid, often having fun with lots of friends."

"Do you have any evidence?"

"Yes. Positive relationships and experiences."

"Excellent. Write that down."

"The next three are more difficult to write."

"You can do it."

"I couldn't control my father's actions. I'm not responsible for his decisions, and his choices were not about me."

"Impressive, Izzy."

"Plus, excluding parental dramas, our life was good until the family incident."

"Outstanding. Everything you stated is one hundred percent reality. You're an exceptional student."

He applauds. Duke howls, which I interpret as his way of celebrating my progress.

"Thank you. It feels good. Without your guidance, I would have remained unaware of the lies and truth within me."

"My pleasure."

A new peace lives in the garden. I can't describe it with words. "What's next, Counselor?"

He tops off our coffee and takes a sip. "Understand, the daily work renews your mind. Don't expect the mind trap to disappear instantaneously. It's a process."

"I'm listening."

"Always look forward, Izzy. Never backward."

"I will do my best. Where do I go from here?"

"Start each day with prayer, seeking the Lord's wisdom and guidance. Become a partner with God through continuous awareness and participation. With time, the mind trap fades away, replaced by a new thought pattern. Attempts to recall the old thought pattern become futile."

I write feverishly to capture every word, then glance up. "Wow. This is a game changer. Going backward is not an option."

"That's right. It's vital to leave the past behind."

"Thank you, sir." I stare at my life-changing notes, tapping the pen on the clipboard.

"Izzy, do you realize your thoughts of rejection affect other relationships?"

"How so?" I stop tapping the pen.

"Well, even the smallest encounter can trigger a related emotion. For example, a friend makes dinner plans with you, then cancels at the last minute, and it's not an emergency. How do you react?"

My lips pucker. "Oh, my gosh."

"Strike a nerve?"

"Yes, I feel rejected."

"Why?"

"Because I was not important enough to keep their commitment. Negative chatter floods my mind, like why am I not a priority? Maybe they dislike me. Did I do something wrong?" I put my hands on my head and grit my teeth. "It's the suitcase ride."

"That's correct. The same negative thoughts and emotions established during the suitcase ride trigger the deeply rooted mind trap."

"Unbelievable."

"And now you will continue recognizing the triggers and respond based on reality instead of past hurts. You might learn to trust people at face value."

"You hit a crucial point, Counselor. I don't trust people, and I don't believe their excuses. Why should I when I couldn't trust the man who gave me birth?"

"It's hard, but it's time to stop assuming everyone is treating you the same as your father. It's unjust, Izzy. It applies to both the other person and you. Do you see?"

"I guess. The pain from disappointment or betrayal is too severe. Why risk it? I refuse to be a fool riding a suitcase again." I fold my arms across my chest.

"What about Jacob?"

"Huh? What do you mean?"

"Do you trust him?"

I glance at Duke while forming my thoughts. "He's never given me a reason to distrust him. I can count on Jacob for anything, especially with our kids, but you're putting me on the spot so I can't honestly say I trust him 100 percent."

"Why not?"

"Because he can leave me anytime he wants."

He tilts his head. "Has Jacob ever threatened to leave you?"

"Never."

"Has he broken his commitments?"

"Not Jacob. He warns me when he's running late. His integrity is impeccable."

"I guess it's true that Jacob could leave you anytime he wants, but I don't hear any evidence to justify the belief that he would. Jacob hasn't left, but who did?"

I slump in my chair and sigh. "I'm comparing Jacob to my father."

Great, my life runs on fear and disappointment because of a man I haven't spoken to in over twenty years. This is maddening.

"Stay with me, Izzy. We need to push through, and you're so close."

"If you say so. Let's keep going."

"When you are elusive or defensive towards people, what occurs?"

His insights are rattling. "Isolation."

"Right. It's your coping mechanism. Isolating yourself symbolizes a barrier of protection from pain. However, it doesn't fix the problem."

My shoulders ease. "I disagree. It's my safety zone where I'm in control."

"Not exactly. Your *perceived* safety zone is also rooted in lies."

"What are you talking about? It protects me from being hurt again."

"How so, Izzy?"

"Well, let's use the example of the friend canceling dinner at the last minute for non-emergency reasons. If they ask again, I'll think twice before committing. Distrust begins because they didn't keep a promise. If they cancel more than once without a good reason, we're probably finished. Why invite rejection again? I'm back in control."

"Do you recognize what's happening?"

"No. What?"

"It's *dinner*. Not a rejection of *you* as a person. They chose to dine with you at some point. If they disliked you, why would they even schedule time with you?"

I drop my head. "Ugh. It's the suitcase ride again?"

He nods. "It's the lies created from the suitcase ride triggering the mind trap of rejection repeatedly in simple daily interactions."

I clutch the armchair and look at the sky. "I'm doomed."

"On the contrary. We're uprooting the source that plagues your soul to establish a new way of thinking. A new life."

I nibble on my fingernail. "True."

"Let's keep pouring oil on the sticky spaghetti. What else do you believe about the person who cancels dinner plans at the last minute?"

"That's easy. They don't value my time. I'm not a priority, and they're untrustworthy. I can't depend on them to keep commitments."

"Who are you really describing?"

I throw my head back and close my eyes. "Oh, my gosh. It all points to my father."

Everything is spinning. One minute I gain a moment of clarity and the next, I'm frazzled. Should I keep doing this? The counselor stands and presses one hand on my shoulder. A soothing sensation like a warm blanket covers my body, and I relax. I stare into his compassionate eyes.

"Izzy, I said it will become more painful as we move along, didn't I?"

"Yes sir. And we haven't touched on the family incident yet. How will I get through it?" I shudder.

"Together, one step at a time. You're doing so well."

"Am I? I'm disheartened to realize I've been living through the lens of a hurt six-year-old child my entire life. Comparing people and situations based on grave decisions by my father is a disturbing viewpoint. Makes me wonder how I accomplished anything with this mangled mindset."

"Great point, Izzy. You've established a remarkable life despite the past. Hold on to that. Otherwise, you'll get mired farther into the pit with more guilt and shame."

"I can't imagine adding more. Is it normal to feel stupid and sad about my past actions and wasted time?"

"Yes, it's normal to feel this way, but it's not okay to dwell there. You can't change what happened twenty years ago or an hour ago. Embrace your emotions, feel them completely, and then move on."

"Your encouragement helps. I worry more about how I shouldn't feel, which blocks my ability to accept and move on."

"Our work together is one big breakthrough after another. I've pulled you far beyond your comfort zone. Get used to it. Brilliantly wired, your mind offers so much more than traps to overcome. Your life is beautiful. You just can't experience the full richness because the mind traps create limits. Instinctively, you realize you're not fully alive because you prayed for marriage restoration, and soul healing."

"Yes. Please keep reminding me. Otherwise, I'll lose sight of the end goals."

"I will. Remember to stay on high alert because once the trap springs open, the negative thought pattern races through your mind. Your guard goes up and you react simultaneously. Subconsciously and automatically, which makes it tough to recognize and disrupt."

I nod slowly. "Often, I overreact when people fall short on keeping their word with minor situations, and I never understood my irrational behavior. During the situation, I convince myself they are taking advantage of me, which is an exaggerated perspective. I also believe they want me to look foolish and are out to get me. After the contentious exchange, I suffer horrible feelings of remorse admitting my reaction wasn't proportionate to the situation. Now, I can visualize the mind trap releasing and the flow of thoughts taking over my ability to think clearly. I lose control like the hurt child having the tantrum beside the suitcase at the back door with my father. Wow."

"You nailed it. The positive view is that you recognized your reaction was off balance, which led you to seek the Lord's help. That's the true path forward for transforming your mind."

"It's clear, but I'm struggling to believe I can change permanently. My responses are instantaneous. In the heat of the moment, I can't stop myself from overreacting."

"It takes practice. Not if, but when you overreact again, give yourself grace and seek forgiveness for any transgressions that may occur."

"You said earlier, I only need a little faith. So, there's no turning back."

He reaches forward to offer me a fist bump. I fist bump back, and we sit quietly for a few moments sipping coffee. Duke lets out a loud snore, and we laugh hysterically. Leave it to Duke to lighten a somber moment. The counselor peers over his coffee cup, and we lock eyes. He places the cup down.

"We've covered a lot of territory today. Tomorrow, we venture into deeper waters."

"Oh, boy. If today wasn't deep water, I'll need a snorkel and life vest."

"You'll be fine."

We chit chat, then he stands like a soldier, one hand extended and the other behind his back. I take his palm and he lifts me out of my cozy white chair.

"May I escort you to the bungalow?"

"Certainly."

"I've arranged a selection of your favorite movies in the theatre room. Mostly comedies. Please relax and allow the mind trap teaching to take hold."

"Popcorn too?"

"Of course."

I smile. "Thank you, sir. You are so kind." We link arms and slowly wander to the bungalow. Watching Duke chase butterflies is a new favorite pastime. His playful, carefree charm is childlike, yet I feel safe with him like a fierce protector. The perfect companion.

We approach the bungalow entrance, and I turn to say goodbye to the counselor. He wraps his arms around me, again like Grandpa Finny's hug, except the purest love rushes through me.

My body goes limp as I sense a release of the wounded child who stood at the back door begging her father to stay. Tears roll down my cheeks, and he tightens the embrace, delivering an overwhelming peace into my spirit.

I remind myself to savor this moment instead of dreading the day I must face the family incident.

CHAPTER 9

The Purpose of Trials

As I contemplate starting the day, I stare at the ceiling thinking about my family. I miss them. What if my soul is beyond repair and this never ends? Duke rests his gigantic head on the bed. He's extra quiet, as if he realizes how much I miss my family.

I stroke his head and crawl out of bed. What's the rush if the counselor measures time differently? I hear a knock at the door, but nobody is there, just a tray of mouthwatering breakfast foods on a waiter's stand. I bring it inside. I didn't feel up to dining outside the room this morning. A welcome coincidence.

After indulging in delicious fresh fruit and an omelet, I take a long hot shower, dress in casual jeans, and a soft green t-shirt. I curiously stare at the gold key necklace in the mirror. It's time to make our way to the garden sanctuary. Duke and I stroll leisurely, dazzled by the scenery, and I try to cultivate optimism for the next discussion. I miss Jacob's smile.

We arrive before the counselor, and I tap the sign bearing my name over the trellis and touch the gold key hanging around my neck again. It's still there. Two precious gifts from a mysterious man while Jacob and the kids deal with my tragic accident back home. I don't deserve any special treatment. What must the kids be thinking? I've abandoned them to be here in luxury while they suffer. And Jacob. He's always been my protector. He must be crazy with worry. Perhaps I should go back today. After all, I've unearthed the mind trap of rejection, and I think I can change.

Instantly, the counselor appears at the trellis, jogging to our sitting area. Instead of his usual dull pullover, he's sporting a bright and colorful paisley-patterned silk shirt. He raises his arms out to his side and turns around.

"Well, what do you think?"

"About the shirt?"

"Yes. Do you like it?"

"It's snazzy." I pause. "Seems a bit out of character, though, don't you think?"

He chuckles. "Your candor is always welcome here, Izzy."

I hold up a brightly painted paisley coffee cup. "Obviously, you know I love paisley prints. What gives?" I put the cup down, and he pours the coffee.

"In due time you will discover the significance of paisley prints, and why you admire this creative design. The shirt? I thought we could use some cheerful color in our conversation today. That's all."

I rub the key necklace with squinty eyes, looking around at the brilliant flowers surrounding our space. "I have something more pressing than paisleys to discuss with you."

"Sure, what is it?"

"This is hard. I'm so grateful for this time with you, and I've gained so much already about mind traps and coping mechanisms." I hesitate. "I think I should go back to my family today."

"Oh, what brought this on? We made tremendous progress yesterday."

"That's why it's so difficult. Although I admit there's more to learn, it doesn't seem fair. In my extravagant bungalow, I'm surrounded by lavish décor, having counseling sessions, while my family worries if they will see me again. It's cruel and selfish of me."

"I understand you don't feel worthy of these things as your family faces a tragedy, but what if I told you, it's more unfair to take this experience away from them?"

I stand, sloshing coffee on my jeans. "Are you kidding me? They are suffering because of me, and the burden is too harsh. How can you say such things? I need more details about their well-being."

"Absolutely. You can ask me about them as often as you wish."

I ease down onto my chair and dab at the spilled coffee on my jeans. "Understood. I'm growing more anxious about them each day."

"I understand. Naturally, they love you and are seriously distressed about your condition, but they stay hopeful. Considering your situation, they're handling it well."

"Oh, thank goodness." Tears roll down my cheeks.

"They pray together daily, especially Jacob and Mr. Merriweather, who is still a little sore from falling. Through this experience, they are learning valuable lessons, and it would be more unfair to cut the growth potential for them."

"What valuable lessons?"

"For starters, their busy lives are being disrupted like yours, forcing them to pause and reflect on how much they love and value their family. They're gaining a deeper appreciation for life, but it's also challenging their faith. They will need your help."

I flinch. "How can I help them from here?"

"Many people find their way during the darkest hours. Times of revival and renewal are challenging for a reason. Life without fluctuation inhibits growth of heart and mind. Your instinct is to protect your family, which is honorable. However, by cutting your time short, you rob them of critical lessons in their spiritual growth process along with yours."

I scoot forward. "But these are my kids and husband. I hate that my accident is causing them pain."

"It's messy, and I mean this in the most loving way." He looks for a moment. "But it's selfish of you to return early."

I rush to my feet to dash out of the sanctuary. Instead, I pace the sitting area. The counselor sits back in his chair, crosses his legs, and watches me pace with the calmest demeanor.

I sense the heat rising from my neck to my face. "Selfish? Are you serious? I risked my life by pushing Mr. Merriweather out of the way of that old cedar tree to save his life. Now, I'm here and my family is suffering because of my actions." I keep pacing.

"Calm down, Izzy, and hear me out. Please sit."

I scowl at Him and plop back into the chair.

"You're correct. Saving a life is the ultimate act of selflessness and honor. The Lord recognizes your distinguished heroism. But let's not entangle the selfless act of saving Mr. Merriweather with your current family situation."

I relax my arms. "Saying I'm being selfish just hit the wrong nerve. Help me understand."

"It's okay. Remember, I asked you to hold nothing back."

"You're not the one with the family in misery."

"Let me explain another way. People wish and strive for utopia, a life free from accidents, illness, pain, and mistakes. Have you met someone with such a life?"

"Of course not."

"It's unattainable. The trials in life shape and mold a person's character and spiritual maturity. Because free will exists, people choose how they respond to tough times and crises. Some will grow closer to God while others turn away from Him, and others claim indifference. Every trial is an opportunity to develop a deeper relationship with God."

I hold up my palm. "Wait, I want that statement to sink in."

He pauses as I repeat the phrase, and I drop my hand.

"Okay, by selfish, I mean you rob the opportunity of growth for yourself, Jacob, and your two children if you leave too soon. It's a decision based on fear, not faith. Plus, putting your physical recovery at risk."

"Oh, yeah. If I go early, I might not recover." I touch my churning stomach. "You're saying trials are good?"

"Trials are necessary. There's a difference."

I press my lower lip. "So, we should seek trials to create more opportunities to get closer to God?"

He waves a finger in front of me. "I wouldn't advise that, Izzy. Each day already has plenty of troubles. A distressful situation provides a time to lean on God for strength and trust Him while riding the storm.

Regardless of the outcome, important lessons surface. Your family is riding a storm for a valuable purpose."

"This is a mind bender, but it's making sense."

"Good. If you're diligent in seeking the truth and gaining answers to your prayers, you will be free. Life transformed. Will you stay?"

I look at the sky, then down at Duke, who's sleeping soundly beside my chair. "I will stay."

He claps his hands. "Excellent decision."

He rises and pours us another cup of delicious coffee. A needed break. I push back on the armchairs. I'm questioning my sanity, but believing this is my only choice to heal, both emotionally and physically.

"Can we continue from yesterday's session?"

"Yes, I'm ready."

He grins at me with twinkling, diamond-emerald eyes, and our connection strengthens. Viewing trials in life as opportunities for spiritual growth is a new concept. I always muscle through adversity on my own, blocking the peace and comfort only God can deliver.

"Izzy, you're going through a lot, but you appear extra agitated today. Is there something beyond the worry about your family that's troubling you?"

"Yes. Last night lying in bed, I reflected on our conversation about not fully trusting Jacob and how irrational that is. Despite our emotional distance, I have no reason to distrust him. I admit, my father's wrongdoings influence my relationship with Jacob, and I'm at a loss on how to fix it."

"You've made a brilliant observation."

"Bottom line, how can I believe any man would truly love me if my father didn't?"

"First, Jacob is not your father and even though you won't believe me, your father loved you from birth and still does."

I stand, pacing the area. "You're right, I don't believe you, and I don't want to hear it."

"Please sit, Izzy. You will not find clarity or peace with this until we unravel the entanglement between your father, Jacob, and God. We will eventually, but not today."

"God? What connection does he have to Jacob or my father?"

"Your distrust starts with Him, doesn't it?"

A long pause as I ponder his question.

"While I believe in God, I've given little thought to placing my trust in Him. How could I trust a God who allows such painful tragedies?"

"Are you mad at God, blaming Him for your father's actions?"

"Not mad. Disappointed."

"Can we revisit the trials we discussed?"

"If it helps."

"Did you learn anything from the negative experiences with your father?"

"It never occurred to me, but a few lessons come to mind."

"Tell me."

"I learned not to marry a deceitful, cold-hearted man like my father. I learned self-reliance, independence, and . . . " I pause mid-sentence.

"What is it, Izzy?"

"The home movies."

"You haven't mentioned the movies until now. What about them?"

"After watching my parents together in those early years, they became more human. I realize they have flaws like me, and my marriage is vulnerable as well."

"How does this relate to you being independent?"

"Maybe my independence strengthened from subconscious fear."

"Of what?"

"A failed marriage." I press into my temples. "But, Jacob is nothing like my father. That's why I struggle with the exposed feelings of distrust."

"And how does this translate to your relationship with God?"

"God let me down. Unknowingly, I seized independence from everyone, including God. I want control. Also, since God created man in His image, I assumed the Lord didn't love me either. After all, He created my father, who deserted us. Therefore, God must reject me, too." I hold my stomach. These confessions make me woozy.

"Is it fair to say you've kept God at arm's length, but in your desperate hour, you called on Him to intervene?"

"Yes."

"Are you going through a trial now?"

"Let's see. Coma, mysterious gap in time. I believe so."

"And here you sit with me, building a deeper relationship with God."

I lean back like a lightbulb just lit. "Oh, my gosh. I am."

"Not only with your current trial, but the trauma from your past. Fasten your seatbelt because it's going to get bumpier."

"I'm motivated to be reunited with my family." My eyes well up.

"Of course. There's one more thing we need to cover."

"I'm listening."

"As you grow closer to God, your true identity unfolds."

I hesitate. "My identity?"

"Yes. Your identity in Christ."

"What do you mean?"

"Once you're willing to fully accept God's love and trust, over time you will blossom with more developed Christlike qualities. No more oscillating in your independence and sorrow, like the wind. You become rooted in God's love. You will never walk alone again."

"Even though you're aware, I want to confess it aloud."

He nods. "Go ahead."

"I'm a luke-warm Christian. Still a newbie in biblical knowledge. I surrendered my life to Christ and water baptized back in college, but I haven't been a committed believer. I'm ashamed."

He scoots forward. "It will be okay, Izzy. Repentance is necessary. God hears you, and He meets you right where you are. Indeed, He constructed a special place to foster a deeper acquaintance."

"Yeah. His generosity is overwhelming."

"I sense you need some time alone. Am I correct?"

"That would be appreciated. Mind if I sit here for a bit?"

"No problem. I'll check on you later."

He walks toward the lavender field, and Duke stays beside my chair. I'm a long way from understanding God's ways. How strange to learn there's value within the tragedy of my accident. Lessons I missed decades ago.

How sad that it took a separation from my family for God to gain my full attention. Where have I been? I neglected my faith while wrapped up in the hustle and bustle of life.

I find solace in knowing my family is safe and view this tragic experience as a chance to connect with God, but will they do the same?

I squirm. As their mother, I should know the status of my children's relationship with God, but I don't. Outside of going to church based on convenience, we haven't talked about God much as a family, and now I understand my critical role in guiding them on their spiritual journey. Jacob's bond with the Lord is unwavering, and although he doesn't discuss God often with the kids either, he leads by example. We both do, I guess, but it's not the same as genuine discipleship. This must change.

To reach my family faster, I must focus on this endeavor. The mystery of God's ways offers a gateway for me to enter and learn His character. Each day unlocks another key to the mystery of my past and its effects on my marriage . . . on my entire life. We are literally worlds apart, and yet I feel closer to Jacob than the day I left for our special weekend at the lake cottage. I can't wait to see his face again. I hope it's not too late for us.

Duke rises and sniffs the air while stretching his legs, and I stroke his back. The counselor returns and stands beside his chair. We chit-chat and I stand to say goodbye.

Duke barks and twirls, signaling it's time for our walk back to the bungalow. He races ahead of me and stops to look back with his tongue hanging out. I wave my hand, motioning him forward.

"I'm coming, Duke."

He trots ahead. How long until I confront the unthinkable? I've buried it for so long. Tomorrow could be the day.

CHAPTER 10

More Unwelcome Surprises

JACOB

I run to Wanda standing in the back of the chapel.

"Wanda, what is it?"

"Come with me now. Dr. Abbot wants to see you. He said something about an anomaly on Isabelle's brain scan."

The kids and I race to Isabelle's room with Wanda limping closely behind. When I enter, Dr. Abbot stands with his back to me examining an x-ray on the wall.

"Doc, what's going on?

"Ah, Mr. Beckham. I'm glad you're here. We have a new finding that offers a concern."

By his serious expression, it can't be good news. Travis wraps his arm around his sister, and they stand patiently.

"New finding?"

"Yes. The latest scan reveals slight swelling on the left side of her brain known as cerebral edema. I don't want to alarm you, but we cannot be too cautious."

I press on my forehead. "Too late. I'm alarmed. What does this mean?"

"We need to bring the swelling down. First, with medications. If that doesn't work and swelling increases, decompressive surgery might be necessary."

I hold my stomach. "Another surgery?"

"Only as a last resort if medication doesn't work. Because of Isabelle's weak pulse, recent surgeries, and her condition, her odds of surviving this type of surgery are not high."

I blast out a deep exhale. "What's next?"

"Let's give the medication a few days and go from there. Hopefully, she will not require surgery. I thought you should be aware."

"Thank you, Doc. I want to be informed."

"Certainly. Any questions?"

My brain cells are shot, and I press hard on my temples. "I can't think right now."

Dr. Abbot slides next to me and helps me into the green recliner. "Please rest. If you think of anything, Nurse Wanda will find me. Okay?"

Travis and Katie step in for Dr. Abbot, place their hands on my shoulders, and thank him. The doctor walks briskly from the room while Wanda hangs back like a watchman. I close my eyes.

The chatter from the nurses' station, loud beeps, and oxygen pumps awaken me to the real-life nightmare again. Foggy, I squint at the wall clock and realize it's the next morning. I don't recall saying goodbye to the kids or anyone else. I've hit a brick wall. What if the medication doesn't work and she needs brain surgery? I can't go there.

Another night sleeping on a recliner in Isabelle's hospital room is taking a toll on my body. I stand next to her hospital bed, stretching my arms and twisting my head from side to side. There's no sign of improvement since the day of her fateful accident. And now, brain swelling. It's unnerving. I take her limp right hand in mine and hover over her wounded body.

"Isabelle, it's me, Jacob. I miss you. Please wake up, my love."

Tears fall on her hospital gown, and I pull away. Katie and Travis enter the room with a tray of coffee and donuts. They are pale, and lines are etched in their faces showing what this crisis has done to them.

Looks like Travis grew two inches since his last trip home. People say he's my mini-me with his sandy brown hair, although a much hipper haircut. Same blue eyes. I admire his conservative nature and attire to match. It's rare to find Travis not in preppy business casual, wearing pressed shirts or sweater vests with stylish shoes. Is preppy still a word? He takes life seriously, and I constantly encourage him to lighten up and have fun.

Katie-bug is the complete opposite. She loves flashy urban living and fits the part with her sleek, long brown hair and bold make-up. She loves tennis and stays fit. I remember sleepless nights over Katie's boyfriends in high school. She's beautiful. Although I'm not a fan of her wild nail polish designs and obsession with black urban wear, it suits her personality, and I want both kids to be themselves. I'm proud of them.

Travis hands me a Starbucks coffee cup. "Dad, how are you feeling? You crashed after the doctor left."

"Despite the leg cramps and back aches, I feel better. Didn't wake up one time through the night. That's a first."

I stretch to the floor touching my toes.

"How do you manage sleeping in that awful vinyl chair? It's not healthy, Dad."

"It's fine, Katie-bug. Small sacrifice." We hug and I kiss her forehead.

Travis steps forward. "Still, you need a break from this room. Give us a moment alone with Mom. We need that too."

"Okay, Travis. I'll take a walk."

Travis grips my shoulder, giving me a stern look. "Not a walk. I'm begging you to go home and get some meaningful rest. There's nothing you can do. Katie and I will look after Mom and call you if anything changes."

I clear a large lump in my throat and fight back the tears. "I can't. Leaving her is not an option."

Travis grabs me in a bear hug and the painful emotions break out like a tidal wave. Katie joins the hug sniffling, and the added stress becomes clear. I squeeze them tightly and let go.

"Okay. To make you both feel better, I'll go home for a few hours. You're right about needing time alone with your mom. I'm being stingy."

"It's okay, Dad," Katie says. "We understand, and we love you for not leaving Mom's side."

"Thank you. I'll be back soon. Call me the second anything changes."

Travis pats my shoulder as we force smiles. "You got it."

I walk out briskly before my mind changes. While passing through the corridor, I quickly check the chapel for Mr. Merriweather. Praying with him keeps me going. It's empty. I approach the elevator and the phone rings. The number on the screen is from Katie's college. I bet they are checking on Isabelle's condition. I'll call back later.

As I walk to the car, I cover my eyes from the brilliant sun. Daylight. I haven't been outside for days. I check my phone and see a new voicemail. Before taking off, I dock the phone to listen to the message.

Mr. Beckham, this is Sarah Chambers, Katie's academic advisor. First off, I am so sorry to hear about Mrs. Beckham's unfortunate accident. My thoughts are with you and the family. If this wasn't an urgent matter, I wouldn't be calling during this difficult time. Please call me back at your earliest convenience regarding Katie's academic status.

My heart sinks into the pit of my stomach. What's going on? I hit the call button on the screen.

"Sarah Chambers."

"Hi Sarah, Jacob Beckham here. I listened to your voicemail."

"Mr. Beckham, thank you for calling me back so quickly."

"Call me Jacob."

"Certainly. I hope your wife is doing okay."

"She's holding on."

"I see. I'm so sorry to burden you with this news, considering all that you're going through."

"What's going on?"

"I'll get right to the point. Katie does not attend most classes and failing her exams in every course except one. I'm concerned about a failing GPA for her first semester."

I sigh heavily. "What? I had no idea."

"I understand. There's one more thing."

"There's more?"

"She appears to be in denial. Every week, we meet to discuss her poor grades, and she expresses little concern."

I scratch my head. "What does she say?"

"She agrees to working harder, but nothing changes the following week. I've taken a personal interest in Katie because I see potential, but I'm not getting through."

"I'm speechless."

"I realize this must be a shock, but if Katie doesn't improve her grades, they will place her on academic probation."

"I can hire tutors to help."

"That's a good next step." She pauses. "Because of her cavalier attitude and skipping classes, I'm not convinced she's committed to a college career. If you want my advice . . ."

"Please."

"I suggest having a serious discussion about her decision to attend college. So far, she tells me what I want to hear but doesn't follow through with the agreed-upon corrective action."

"Thank you for bringing this to my attention. I'll get to the bottom of it. Let me speak with Katie and get back to you tomorrow. Please don't give up on her."

"I won't. Have a good day."

"You too, goodbye."

I end the call and rest my head on the steering wheel when I want to pound my head on the windshield. This doesn't sound like Katie. Why wouldn't she tell us about her struggles? I raise my head and pat my cheeks. We'll solve this and help her get back on track. Katie, a college dropout. That's not in the plan.

I need a hot shower to get refreshed. Now this, on top of Isabelle's situation. What's next?

Please God, give me extra strength.

Now I question Travis. He's been an open book with his challenges and progress, whereas Katie is not. Thinking back, I recall her avoiding my questions about college. I should have seen the warning sign.

I start the car to drive home. As I cruise down the highway approaching our neighborhood entrance, a car passes me, honking their horn. I glance at the scowling driver who's shouting words I'm thankful

I can't hear and speeds ahead. If he only knew. I check my speedometer, and it reads thirty miles per hour. No wonder.

I press the gas pedal, reach our home, pull into the driveway, and shut off the car. The dread of entering an empty house quickens, but I force myself inside. After showering and napping, I drive back to the hospital.

Katie is already fragile, worrying about her mother. How do I approach this conversation about her failing grades? *Be open-minded, Jacob.*

After a text exchange with Travis about lunch plans, I pick up sandwiches at a Chick-fil-A drive-thru around the corner. The thought of eating a meal with Travis and Katie brings a welcome smile. We will overcome these obstacles.

I arrive at the hospital, park the car, and walk inside. With a tray of drinks and a Chick-fil-A bag on top, I walk past the nurses' station where Wanda gives me a firm nod. I wink back at her.

Before I reach Isabelle's hospital room, Travis steps outside her door.

I speed up to him. "Is everything okay? Did something change?"

"No, Dad. I'm just stretching my legs and giving Katie a private moment with Mom."

"I see. Ready for lunch?"

"Yes, I'm starved. I'll tell Katie to meet us at the cafeteria when she's finished."

"Thanks, Travis." He steps back into the room briefly and returns. We walk together to the cafeteria.

"Travis, I'm impressed with how you're handling this crisis with your mother. I'm not sure where you get your strength, but it's helpful to everyone around you."

Travis stops and turns to me. "From you, Dad. I get it from you. We're like ducks."

"Ducks?"

"Yeah. The duck glides calmly on the water while its feet are flapping like crazy below the surface where no one can see. Am I right?"

I laugh. "I hadn't thought of it, but yes, we're like ducks. Honestly, I'm not feeling so tough on the inside or outside these last few days.

Without God's strength, it's doubtful I could handle your mom's condition."

"Dad, your faith is obvious."

"That's a relief. I don't share my faith enough with you kids."

"I see it through your actions."

"Maybe."

"You're doing great, Dad. Don't be so hard on yourself."

"Thank you, Travis. There's no rush, but after you finish lunch, I need some time alone with Katie. Is that okay?"

"No problem. I'll sit with Mom."

We find a table, and Travis sits first. I place the bag and sodas on the surface. He mentions college, so I probe hard with targeted questions to confirm he is doing well.

"Everything okay at college?"

"Dad, it's tougher this year."

"I remember."

"I'm worried about making the Dean's List this semester."

"That, I don't remember, but your mother would." We chuckle, lightening the mood.

"I'm doing my best and studying hard, but physics is killing me."

"Do your best. That's all I ask."

"Thanks, Dad."

"Any other challenges? Girlfriends?"

"Who has time for girlfriends?"

"Now I'm worried. Don't miss having some fun at school, Travis. It flies by fast."

"Don't worry. I'm having a blast with the entrepreneur incubator programs in my spare time. Girls and the party scene are overrated."

"Ladies and gentlemen, I'm sitting with the next Jeff Bezos."

"I wish."

"You can be greater than him if you set your mind to it. I believe in you, Travis. God believes in you, too."

"Thanks, Dad."

"Anytime."

Our conversation is a welcome distraction from the pain of Isabelle's accident and the news about Katie. About thirty minutes pass and Katie arrives. She takes a seat beside her brother with a grimaced face.

"What's wrong, Katie-bug?"

She gathers her hair into a ponytail, fidgeting. "It's just hard. Mom is a force, and I hate seeing her so wounded. Parents are supposed to be invincible."

"We're human too, honey."

"It sounds dumb, but this is the first tragedy we've experienced together. I'm still a kid."

"It's not dumb, it's natural. I put your grandparents on a pedestal my entire childhood until the day they proved to be humans, too."

"Really? We've had it so good. I never imagined this could happen to us."

I place my hand on top of Katie's. "Me either."

She forces a grin and eats her waffle fries. After several minutes of casual chit-chat, Travis stands, placing his meal containers in the bag.

"Dad, thank you for lunch. I'm going back to Mom's room to spend time alone with her if it's okay with you and Katie."

Katie nods while sipping her soda.

"Please take your time. Katie and I will join you later."

Travis pats me on the back and leaves the table. His maturity amazes me, and I can't take all the credit. Through this trial, my admiration and respect for Isabelle's motherhood deepens.

My attention shifts to Katie. I gather my thoughts to speak with her delicately.

"Katie, I recognize you're dealing with a heavy load right now. Life throws us curveballs when we least expect it. I'm proud of the way you're managing through this crisis with your mom."

"Seriously, Dad? Without you and Travis, I would be bonkers."

"I understand. Which is why this next conversation is extra painful."

"Now what?"

I pat her hand. "Your academic advisor called me today. She said you're skipping classes and failing most of your exams."

Katie covers her face. "Ugh. No way. She called you?"

"Yes. What's going on? You can tell me."

"Promise not to get mad?"

"I'm not mad. I'm concerned and want to help. But no more hiding. You have nothing to be afraid of telling the truth. Now, spill it."

She huffs. "I can't believe Miss Chambers betrayed my confidence."

"Katie Beckham, there's no room for self-righteousness. She's on your side. You're facing academic probation and potential suspension if your grades don't improve. Now, tell me what's going on?"

She bites her lower lip as tears well up. "I'm not smart enough. I can't do it."

"Are the classes too hard? Did you pick the wrong major?"

"It's worse."

"How?"

Katie looks away and then stares at the table. "I never wanted to attend college, and I don't want to stay."

My mouth drops open, and I can't speak. Katie continues.

"I went to college to make you and Mom happy, hoping I would change my mind. But it's not my thing."

"It sounds like you're not even trying."

"See, you're mad."

"I'm not mad but help me understand. You never mentioned you didn't want to get a college degree. Never."

"I didn't have a choice."

"How so?"

"You and Mom spoke about us attending college since kindergarten, sharing your dreams about the perfect schools for us, but never asked if I *wanted* to go."

I rub my forehead. Is she right?

"Dad, let's be real. I'm an average student, rarely making the honor roll in high school, while Travis achieved valedictorian with multiple academic scholarships for college. He's so sure of himself and I'm not. Travis loves college and has his entire future figured out. I'm happy for him, but I don't have a clue about mine."

I stammer, seeking my words carefully. "Katie-bug, I wish you'd spoken up before now."

"I was afraid."

"Of us?"

"Afraid of disappointing the two people I love and admire most. Plus, you both are ultra successful with amazing careers. Now, Travis. I will never measure up. I'm just piling more on top of Mom's situation. It's too much. Dad. I'm so sorry."

I swivel around the table and take a seat next to Katie as she sobs into my arms. I look up, seeking God's comfort. My little girl is hurting, and I can't fix it.

"Katie, it's going to be alright. I'm glad you shared the truth. Your Mom and I love you and want what's best for you, which is why we stressed the importance of a college education. I stand firm on my belief. Perhaps it's not the best path for you, and we should examine other options. There's no rush to decide on college or the future."

"Really, Dad? You're not disappointed?"

"I'm hurt that you didn't confide in us, but I'm more concerned about you feeling inferior. I'm not sure why because you are extremely bright with lots of untapped potential."

"You really think so?"

"I do. Not today, but soon, let's evaluate your passions and develop a plan. It may or may not include college. But your mother requires our attention now, and I need you to be here with me."

I share a warm smile, trying to calm her nerves. She forces a grin.

"What about Miss Chambers and my classes?"

My smile fades. "Let's be clear. You're not off the hook with your irresponsible behavior. We'll talk more about how to reconcile your actions later."

"Okay, Dad."

"Tomorrow, I will call Miss Chambers and request a leave of absence for you to focus on your mom."

Katie's shoulders slump. "Thank you. I'm truly sorry."

"I forgive you. We all face setbacks. What's most important is how we respond. You and I will work on a proper response to this challenge. No more hiding."

Katie swivels around beside me and hugs my neck. I sense her relief, and I'm saddened by the negative views of herself and the future. Somehow, we failed her through our assumptions and expectations. Another reason Isabelle must return to us. She is a master at resolving problems with the kids. I need a miracle.

"Let's check on your mom." I stand and extend my hand to Katie, and she takes it. We walk arm in arm.

As we enter her room, Wanda greets us.

"Hi Katie girl. Jacob, I see you put on some clean clothes and combed your hair. Aside from those bloodshot eyes, we're making headway."

"Cut me some slack, Wanda."

She presses her mouth and giggles. "You got it. Just keeping you on your toes."

"I appreciate it."

"Oh, you just missed Mr. Merriweather. He came by the nurses' station looking for you. He mentioned being in the chapel if you'd like to visit today."

"Good. I need to see him." I glance at Isabelle lying in her bed lifeless and close my eyes. No change.

"Dad, go visit with Mr. Merriweather. We won't leave until you return."

"Thanks, Travis. I'll be back."

I exit and rush to the chapel, believing Mr. Merriweather's timing is a gift from God. His wisdom is the medicine I need. The large, heavy wooden doors are closed, and I open them cautiously. In the first pew sits Mr. Merriweather, facing the large cross and intricate stained-glass windows. My steps cause the wooden floor to creak, and he turns around. Mr. Merriweather stands with his wobbly cane, extending his other hand and I shake it.

"Good to see you, Jacob. Any improvement?"

I inhale and exhale a long breath. "Not yet. I'm so glad you're here. It's been quite a day."

"Sit and tell me all about it."

"A few days ago, I thought my life was in complete control. Turns out, I'm oblivious to many things. Especially related to the women in my life."

"You mean, Isabelle?"

"She and Katie. I'm embarrassed to share this, but Isabelle and I hit a rough patch in our marriage. Years of drifting apart led us to plan a weekend cabin getaway, hoping to rekindle our connection. What a turn of events."

He flinches with surprise. "Oh dear. I never suspected."

"We've mastered the charade of being the envied couple by others while we continue widening the gap between us."

"Every marriage goes through rough patches. Rosemary and I certainly did."

"You two lovebirds? I'm shocked."

"Yes, indeed. Our love was constant, though we briefly fell out of it. Do you follow?"

"I sure do."

"Our spark dimmed, requiring significant effort to reignite. Boy, once we did, the marriage was better than the honeymoon days." He nudges me with his elbow.

"Wow. How did you light the flame again?"

"Lots of prayer. You see, we were butting heads over petty things competing for control, I guess. We were confused and frustrated."

"That sounds familiar."

"After a terrible argument, I prayed desperately. I didn't want to lose Rosemary. Then God showed me our marriage was not about either of us. Instead, it was about putting Him first and us united beneath His command. Soon, I started seeing Rosemary differently through God's eyes instead of mine and loved her with more humbleness and grace. Unconditionally. More than ever, I wanted to bring her joy through acts of kindness. Simple things like filling her car with gas or making the bed first. And . . . the red rose."

I snap my fingers. "That's why you take a red rose to her grave every day?"

"Yes, sir. Oh, how she loved her roses. During that difficult period, I decided to give her a single red rose every day, and I never stopped. Not long after this shift, she reciprocated, and the arguments became rare, instead of frequent."

"Sounds amazing. Could it be that simple?"

"People rarely consider work to be easy. For me, the effort was more fun than us fighting over nothing." He presses his fingertips together, forming a pyramid. "It worked because we put God in top position, and we aligned equally below Him. The kids next. We learned to love each other according to His ways instead of our convoluted perspectives."

I gaze at the enormous cross in front of me. "We never had a conversation about putting God first in our marriage. The kids have always been our number one priority, and our careers a close second."

"A common mistake among parents. We did the same. Once we experienced a deeper connection with our children by placing God first and watching our marriage improve, it was a breeze to keep it going."

I lower my head. "Question is, will I get another chance to re-prioritize and save our marriage?"

"Time will tell, son. Time will tell. You also mentioned Katie."

I roll my eyes. "Yes, I learned today that she is failing her college courses and facing academic probation."

"Your Katie? She's such a smart girl."

"She is. Apparently, she doesn't think so. She might drop out of college, but we will not decide today. We need to focus our energy on Isabelle."

"My goodness. How are you holding up?"

"Like Tom Cruise in *Mission Impossible*, hanging from the ledge of a skyscraper by my fingertips."

He shakes his head. "Oh, Lord, have mercy."

"I'm okay. I hide it well, but inside, I'm torn up. My family means everything to me."

"That's obvious. You're a good man, Jacob."

"Thank you, sir. I'm not sure I would make it without these chats."

"I'm glad to be here. You are family to me."

I cover my heart. "We feel the same way. Still heartbroken over the loss of Rosemary."

"Oh, me too, son. Me too."

We sit quietly, gazing at the large wooden cross. The light shines brightly through the stained-glass window, warming the sanctuary like a heavy down-filled comforter.

"Jacob, there's one thing I've learned from every trial in my life."

"Please tell me."

"Good awaits beyond the storm. We can't see it with the dark, dense clouds whirling around, but it's there waiting patiently for the dust to settle."

I snicker and fold my arms. "You're right. I can't see it."

He raises one finger. "You can't see it *yet*. Every trial in life is an opportunity to grow closer to God. Surrender fully and draw upon His power."

"I call on Him for strength, but I hadn't thought to ask about strengthening our relationship. Your wisdom is golden, sir."

He lets out a belly laugh. "It's not wisdom, it's age and hard knocks experience."

"You age well, my friend."

"You're too kind, son. Let's pray for sweet Isabelle."

We pray for a miracle. After saying goodbye, I walk out with new optimism about our marriage potential, but seize the reality that our future together could be ending.

CHAPTER 11

Unconditional Love

Isabelle

After a restless night, I wake up to no daylight. More rest is what I need, but my mind races with concern for my family and the information I'm learning about my past. I glance with envy at Duke, sound asleep.

Pulling the covers back, I climb out of the cozy bed. I kneel beside Duke and caress his silky head. He opens his eyes, then closes them slowly.

There's a prompting in my mind, specifically directing me to read the book of Malachi. I reach for the NASB Bible on my nightstand and open to the book of Malachi. I blink. At the top of the first chapter, it reads 'God's love for Jacob.' I blink and the same words appear. Even though the Bible is referring to Jacob, the son of Isaac, it sparks thoughts of my Jacob.

I feel the Lord's presence and His overwhelming love for my husband. I sit upright with teary eyes. A visual of the Lord accepting Jacob exactly how he is enters my mind, and He calls me to love Jacob unconditionally as well. In a millisecond, the image fades, and a veil lifts, revealing my love toward others with conditions, especially Jacob. I just experienced loving Jacob through God's eyes, not mine. It's obvious now.

Hours later, I awake with my head resting on the Bible. I'm refreshed, and I can't wait to share my divine encounter with the counselor. As I get ready, Duke stands wagging his tail, eager to be the tour guide to the gorgeous garden. Once out the door and walking our usual route, he races ahead of me and turns back to make sure I'm coming. I giggle watching this canine and pick up my pace. Arriving at the sanctuary, the counselor meets me at the rose-covered trellis.

"Well, this is a first, Izzy. We arrive at the same time. How are you this morning?"

"I'm wonderful. My sleep was restless, but the early morning hours made up for it. I had a divine encounter."

We approach the sitting area, and the usual aroma of freshly brewed coffee consumes me.

"Really? I can't wait to hear about it over coffee."

He hands me a porcelain cup with a vibrant paisley pattern. I notice his shirt. No paisley pattern today or shoes but a similar pullover and nylon hiking pants. I rub my gold key necklace. What's behind the paisley prints and mysterious gold key?

"Tell me about your encounter this morning." I lower my cup and rub my hands together.

"I couldn't sleep, and a thought prompted me to read in the book of Malachi." I shared with the counselor all God had shown me. "The entire experience lasted only seconds, but it was life changing."

"Sounds like a revelation from the Holy Spirit."

"Yes. A revelation."

"I'm thrilled for you, Izzy. Did you learn anything else?"

"I think I've been pushing Jacob away, perhaps for a long time. Our marriage isn't in crisis because of an affair or a single event. It's been slowly dying for years, and my constant need for validation and repeated disappointment are major factors in our disconnect. The realization this morning made me aware of the conditions I put on my relationships—especially with Jacob."

"Excellent insight. Can you go even deeper?"

"Yes. I've been creating expectations in my head and placing them on Jacob. When he doesn't deliver, I label it another disappointment. Like a notch on a scorecard." My stomach sours, but I press on it. "Unaware, I set him up for failure by withholding my thoughts as if he's a mind reader." I pause, hearing my voice admitting this aloud.

"You're fine, Izzy. Keep going."

"The outcome justifies the sadness in my heart, which is rooted in past disappointments. I interpret Jacob's lack of awareness about my needs as lacking love and interest in me, triggering the mind trap of rejection all over again."

"You nailed it."

"I feel sick. This mind trap runs deep."

"Yes, the boulder. Don't stop now."

I press my stomach to ease the nausea. "I appreciate your encouragement. Jacob and I have weak communications. I admit, we're both at fault. He's kind, but he loses patience with me, and empathy is short-lived if he senses the slightest drama. His body language tells all. So, I shy away from creating controversy, fearing rejection again, and the wall gets thicker."

"What else?"

"Regardless of how he tries to please me, I find something wrong with his attempt. It's like I want him to fail." I hesitate, embarrassed. "That sounded insane. Why would I do that?"

"Can you give me an example?"

I rub my forehead, thinking. "About a year ago, we confronted the need to spend more time together and agreed to schedule date nights. It was painful to require a dedicated time because our early years together were spontaneous and fun. Due to our financial constraints, we rarely left our apartment, making every night feel like a special occasion. Anyway, we agreed to alternate the duty of planning date night each week. This time, it was Jacob's turn, and at 5:00 p.m. he came to me with a few options, expecting me to decide the ultimate plan. It crushed me. I interpreted his indecision as uncaring and thoughtless. In the extreme sense, he didn't love me enough to plan a romantic date night on his own."

The counselor glances down, trying to hide his smile. "I see. You're right about the mind trap of rejection, Izzy. What else do you think is happening?"

"I wish I had the answer. Hearing myself describe this sounds like an oxymoron, with me being the moron. Lord knows my poor husband tries to make me happy, but I won't let him. It's like we're playing an invisible game with secret rules. It's nonsense."

I rock back and forward, holding my stomach.

"Don't hold back, regardless of how silly it sounds. You're doing great."

Am I? I've never felt so vulnerable, but I must keep going.

"When he asks what will make me happy, it hurts. He should know. It's not rational, but that's how I think. After our discussion yesterday, I realize there's nothing he can do because the source of my sorrow lies within me, not with him. His question presses on the bruise of my childhood sadness. I hate it. In response, I retreat inwardly for comfort, widening the distance between us."

"What is that comfort?"

I glance beyond the counselor. "Control."

"Precisely. You've trained your mind to believe comfort equal's control. Once the mind trap triggers, the invisible fence goes up. Through isolation and independence, you believe you're back in control."

My eyebrows rise. "Wow. Is that what I'm doing? Seriously?"

"Yes. But there's good news. You and Jacob can overcome this."

"I want to believe, but the mind plays tricks. Even though the process is painful, it's also familiar. It seems the mind defaults to the dominate and familiar patterns more than my genuine desires."

"That's right. Until we confront and heal the deeper wounds of the soul, the painful past is the ultimate controller. If you delight yourself in the Lord, He will give you the desires of your heart."

"How do I delight myself in the Lord in a practical sense?"

"Good question. Surrender control to the Lord, learn to embrace and enjoy His ways. After all, He knows what is best for you. By doing so, you empower God to lead your life and He delivers your true heart's desires. Sorrow stagnates your aspirations."

"This sounds wonderful, but the past seems to have a choke hold on me."

"That's why I'm here. You may not realize it, but through your prayer at the cabin and agreement to stay and resolve your issues, you've surrendered to God's control. He's attempting to deliver your heart's desires right here, right now. You're receiving the supersonic version of the sanctification process."

"Sancti what?"

"Sanctification. It's God's process for restoring the souls that give their life to Christ. Like yours."

"I didn't realize there is a literal process."

"Oh yes. It started the day you surrendered to Christ back in college. Problem is, you are stuck."

"That's an understatement."

"Now we have dedicated focus to decouple your past sorrow towards freedom. Discard the old, embrace the new. Your desire to heal and willingness to bring to light the sources of your pain are part of the process. Enlightenment brings healing. We haven't touched on the later trauma in your life, but when you're ready, we must expose the darkest place in your soul for you to achieve the life you crave."

I sink in my chair and lower my head. "Oh no. We can't go there today."

"I said, when you are ready. Besides, I'm getting off track from your revelation about Jacob in Malachi. Please continue."

"The scripture made me ponder the entangled views of my father, Jacob, and God, forcing me to remember how much I appreciate Jacob. In those few seconds, realizing I will never fully love Jacob as the man God created until I see him through God's eyes. My distorted human perspective evaporates, and I see God's creation, regardless of flaws."

"God is never the author of confusion."

"I must remember that. Especially since I overcomplicate everything by creating invisible fences and limit interactions with Jacob to avoid potential disappointment. He doesn't have a chance. After so many failed attempts trying to meet my unstated expectations, he stopped trying. That's where we are."

"I'm so proud of your courage and determination. Excellent job."

"You're too good to me, but I need the encouragement."

"Good. You've defined a critical step toward restoring your marriage. It might seem awkward, but defining where you and Jacob are today helps us figure out where you go from here."

Another rock lifted. "It's certainly awkward, but I didn't realize how much progress we've made until hearing my own words."

"Well done." He smiles widely.

I stare at the ground. "The divine encounter reading Malachi opened my eyes. Heck, it opened my heart and for the first time in my life, I'm not alone. Even though I believed, I felt separated from God."

"Wonderful, Izzy. More progress indicators."

I lean in. "Yes. Finally, faith makes sense to me. Whenever I hear the Holy Spirit or Holy Ghost mentioned in church, it didn't seem real until today. No one teaches like you."

"I understand and regard that as the highest compliment."

After a deep breath, I exhale, and we sip more coffee. My head is spinning from the fire hose of information, and I pray I can remember everything he says. I place my cup down gingerly.

Reality punches me in the stomach, and I gasp.

"What's troubling you, Izzy?"

I fiddle with my hands. "What if I'm too late? What if I pushed Jacob away one too many times?"

"This is a great opportunity to give God control."

I sit upright. "You're right. Automatically, I focused on the worst-case scenario and controlling the outcome."

"Remember, it's a process that requires patience and practice. If you trust God and do your part, the outcome is in His hands. You will get through it."

I clutch my hands together. "I want to trust God."

"You trust Him more than you realize."

"I suppose."

"Believe it. Now, before we close today, let's do another visualization. Sit back, close your eyes, and picture you and Jacob together at home. It's the same date night scene you described earlier, so it's his turn to make plans. He approaches you at 5:00 p.m. with the same options, requesting you to choose. Describe how the scene plays out based on today's session."

With eyes closed, I concentrate on recalling the same memory from God's perspective.

"Okay. First, I'm impressed that he remembered date night and grateful he took the time to research some options for our date. We collaborate to ensure I'm satisfied with his selections, which I find respectful and thoughtful. We agree on our favorite eatery, followed by an action movie. The interaction is fun, considerate, and loving. It just hit me. It doesn't matter what we do if we are together." I smile as tears roll down my face.

"There's one more thing," I say.

"What is it?"

I wipe the tears. "I believe Jacob truly loves me."

He claps his hands. "Magnificent. Love without limits."

"Oh, yes. The joy and freedom are undeniable."

I wave my hands over my face and blow. He scoots to the edge of his chair and leans forward, his eyes beaming with serious intensity and we lock eyes.

"That's the same type of love God wants you to experience toward your earthly father."

The fight is over. I place my limp hand in his palm as we walk somberly to the bungalow in silence. Tomorrow is the day I face the family incident.

CHAPTER 12

The Incident

I open my eyes and clench my teeth together. I hide under the covers, hoping the day is not real. Even the sweet melody of unfamiliar birds cannot soften the dread of facing the worst experience of my life. The one that's secretly tormented my soul for over two decades.

After a few more moments wrapped tightly within the covers, I fling the thick blankets off and hop out of bed.

I process every teaching moment from the counselor and practice applying the lessons in my head. Will I remember? One minute I'm clear about misinterpretations, mind traps, and relationships, then it's murky. How will I recall these teachings and apply them in real life? The doubt reminds me to release control and trust in the Lord.

Standing in front of the armoire, I select a soft cotton, baggy dress with subdued florals. It looks nice against my pale skin and auburn hair. Duke rises and shakes from head to tail along with a few deep stretches. He appears extra cautious this morning, as if he detects my anxiety about what's coming in today's session. We walk outside and instead of running ahead like usual, Duke matches his steps with mine. The distance to the garden sanctuary seems longer. The uncomfortable anticipation throttles my usual peppy stride. Once we reach the trellis adorned in pink roses, Duke trots to his favorite spot by my chair and twirls a few times before plopping down. He peers up at me with his large brown eyes. The kind that melts hearts.

The counselor arrives a few minutes later, meticulously dressed in a white linen shirt and matching trousers. His perfectly styled silver hair is extra wavy. He strolls toward our sitting area and towers over the usual ensemble of paisley cups and coffee. He offers me a full cup.

"Good morning, Izzy. How did you sleep?"

"Good morning. It took a while, but it was restful, considering. Typically, dreams are part of my nightly routine, so it's odd that I haven't dreamed at all. Does it matter?"

"Dreams can cause distractions when you wake up. It's best to achieve a full rest to focus on our time together."

"Seems logical." My stomach is icky, matching my emotions. "Shall we dive right in? I can dance around the inevitable topic all day if you let me."

We both grin at my honesty while sipping on the delicious coffee. Each day, the coffee is more satisfying.

"Izzy, what do you think will happen if we talk about the family incident?"

My eyebrows squeeze together. "What do you mean?"

"Physically or mentally. What is your fear of confronting the memory you've avoided for over twenty years?"

"Hmm. I never thought about the outcome. I was too busy avoiding the topic altogether."

"What would be the worst-case scenario?"

"I might freeze like a zombie and not recover. I've seen cases in documentaries and movies where the trauma was so severe it caused mental disorders. Physically, I can't imagine feeling the suffering in my heart. I've mastered the art of avoiding pain, and it's safe."

"Do you ever think about the incident?"

I clench my eyes closed. "With the slightest recollection of those two days, my heart races, tears flow, and my mind goes into a frenzy until I push the images out of my mind."

"I understand. You experienced a serious trauma. Under God's protection, if I guarantee you will not become a zombie, can you trust me to help you confront the past?"

"Counselor, I trust you. But the pain is unimaginable." I squirm.

"That's because the fear of pain is stronger than your desire to confront the situation and heal. Remember, you prayed for God to heal your sorrow, and it won't happen unless you allow me to help you work through the incident. Because you cried out to God, your desire is stronger than you realize. With me, you can gain the courage to face frightening events. Alone, you can't."

"I want to heal, but is it possible?"

"With God, it's always possible."

My fingers grip the fabric on the chairs. "Counselor, you weren't there. It was horrific."

"I understand. Recall when you prayed for healing in the past. Why did you pray if you believe it's too painful?"

Hesitating, my mind scrambles. And then I blurt it out. "Because I hate myself."

The counselor closes his eyes and presses his heart. A long silence hangs between us. The pure love he has for me is clear.

"There it is, Izzy."

"What?"

"The truth."

I look away. "It's humiliating."

"No, it's being humble. The key to victory."

He hands me a handkerchief.

"My stomach quit churning, but I don't feel victorious."

"Yet. Keyword is *yet*. Now, tell me what you hate about yourself."

"I sound like a broken record. Despite the blessings in my life, I'm tired of feeling miserable and guilty for feeling this way. I'm exhausted with being offended by petty situations and believing no one likes me. When I misinterpret people's motives and shut them out, I despise my reactions and isolate myself. Showing kindness and being considerate are easy and safe emotions, but I have more love to offer that's held back. I don't understand it, but darkness is my captor."

"You've suffered tragically during your childhood, and the trauma you endured in your late teens compounded the torment. Facing the incident could last hours, but you've spent over twenty years in misery."

"Good point."

"Naturally, the healing process continues long after today, but it can begin right now. Isn't it worth experiencing some intense short-term emotional pain to free yourself of the long-term choke hold?"

My grip releases. "I suppose. With you here, I'm willing to try. It's foolish to keep fighting against an answer to prayer."

"Excellent. Before we begin, think about your marriage and overall life once you're set free."

I scratch my nose. "Maybe I can stop being an unconscious emotional pin cushion waiting for someone, anyone, to trigger my invisible wounds."

He beams. "There you go. And what will you gain?"

"Joy, free of guilt and shame, experiencing relationships without conditions and worry of acceptance."

"And what is that worth?"

"It's everything. I crave the steady joy I experience from Jacob. His mind is solid, and he loves life without limitations."

"What would joy look like for you? Describe your new life."

I close my eyes. "My mind is empty of turmoil, carefree, and content. Of course, I still have difficulties, but my joy is constant regardless of my interactions. No more time wasted on others' thoughts, imaginary drama, or creating sadness. Guilt and shame about the past vanish. I embrace my life as a blessing and open myself to deeper connections instead of pushing people away." I glance at Duke. "I'm ready, let's go."

"Good decision. Take three deep breaths and get comfortable. Start with events leading to the tragic day, considering your limited perspective. Way back, how did your mother and father meet?"

I wiggle back in my chair. "That's easy. Mother shared this story a hundred times when we were kids. She was an accomplished dancer with a prominent ballet company in Chicago where she lived. Dancing was her passion. My father lived in Atlanta, and one year he traveled to Chicago over Christmas break to attend a client's holiday party. The client offered my father front row tickets to the Nutcracker ballet as a gift, so he went. Mother was the lead dancer, front and center for much of the show. According to mother's story, the moment she approached the stage, he never took his eyes off her. After the show, he made his way backstage to meet her. He pushed through, stood face to face, and she peered up at him, hand outstretched. She reached out and touched his palm, and he bent over and kissed the top of her hand. Their eyes connected until her manager whisked her away. She said he was the most handsome man she'd ever met, with thick, light-brown hair and mysterious hazel eyes. Father sent six dozen red roses to Mother's dance studio the following day."

"Such a romantic story. Then what happened?"

"She boasted about Father pursuing her with phone calls, flowers, and chocolates, relentlessly trying to win a first date. She resisted because of the distance between the two cities and dancing was her top priority. But persistence paid off, and she agreed to have lunch if my father came to Chicago. They had lunch at her favorite café and spent the rest of the day together walking the city. They dated long distance for a few years, and she continued dancing before they married and moved to an Atlanta suburb where I grew up."

"Did she give up her dance career for your father?"

"Yes, even though dancing was her passion, her ultimate dream was a happy family. So, when they married, she hung up the ballet shoes and devoted her life to us. As a kid, I loved watching old footage of her ballet performances."

"Did they have much in common?"

"Beyond dancing in the living room in my toddler years, not much. She didn't join us at the airports to watch takeoffs and landings. Knowing my selfless mother, she probably wanted that time to be special between us kids and my father. She said he promised to buy a plane someday so he could fly her to ballets all over the country. Her face lit up when she told the story. What a fantasy."

"I heard sarcasm, Izzy."

I grimace while reaching for my coffee cup.

"I wish their outcome had been better."

"Oh, me too, Counselor."

"It sounds like they loved each other early on and had four children together. But when you were six years old, you said everything changed."

I clutch the gold key necklace. "Yes. From the time Father started traveling every week, he withdrew from us physically and emotionally, leaving Mother in a fragile state. She suffered for years. I hated watching my mother hurting, especially after her parents abandoned her as a baby. My brother Roger asked her about her childhood only once. Mother grabbed Roger by the shoulders and scolded him for asking. That was the only time she showed any anger toward us, and we avoided the subject afterwards. Mother was timid and kind, never raising her voice. I believe the grace within her dancing flowed from her gentle nature."

"Izzy, your mother endured a turbulent childhood. She didn't want her children to feel any of her pain, so she protected you all by not sharing her story. Through her bold courage and grit, she harnessed her talent to its fullest potential for an improved life. Remarkable lady, your mother."

"Thank you for sharing that, sir."

"Over the next eleven years, your father continued traveling, even though he promised your mother he would find a local job. Correct?"

"That's right. He always offered excuses for why he couldn't leave the company and stop traveling. It became normal, even though none of us liked it."

"Did you take family vacations after the California beach trip?"

"No. Every summer, we went to the family lake cottage, which belonged to my Grandpa Finny on my father's side. We always arrived without our father, and on Friday, he showed up at the lake cottage for the weekend. Like at home, the distractions of phone calls continued, and he claimed they were work-related calls. Despite Father's lack of attention, we loved our time at the cottage. Some of my fondest memories."

Bolting out of my chair, I pace our sitting area. I begin hyperventilating. "I can't do this."

"Izzy, it's okay. Slow down, take your seat, and breathe in and out slowly. You are not alone anymore."

Back in my chair, I focus on his eyes. "It's over and I can't change the outcome. Why am I so afraid?"

He stretches his hands to me. I grasp both hands and receive an unspoken message of acceptance. I regain composure and continue the story.

"I'm seventeen. A senior in high school. Since Roger, Abbey, and

Shannon went to college, I'm the only one at home. It was on a Wednesday, and my best friend, Misty, was playing in a regional volleyball tournament a few hours hour away. I begged Mom to take her car and drive to the game by myself. Reluctantly, she agreed. I gave her a kiss, grabbed the car keys, and darted to the wood-panel station wagon. On the way to the tournament, with the radio blaring an 'Eagles' tune, I sang at the top of my lungs. I arrived a little early and entered a quiet gymnasium. I waved at Misty practicing her serve and found a mid-level seat in the bleachers. The match ended in overtime, but our school won, and Misty received the most valuable player award. I hustled down the bleachers, waved my hands in the air, and gave hugs and high-fives to Misty and the other players. The assistant coach invited me to meet the team for pie and ice cream at a nearby diner before heading back home, so I accepted. After a short drive to the restaurant, I pulled into the parking lot and spotted a red Cadillac like my father's. He refused to drive anything else. Curious, I pulled up behind the vehicle and noticed the familiar right rear dent and vanity tag. My heart pounded. It's pounding like that right now." I press my chest with both hands.

"Take a deep breath. You're doing so well."

After three deep breaths, I exhale, clawing the fabric on my chair.

"Something didn't add up. Although my father was supposed to be at a hotel in another state, I'd spotted his car parked at a diner a few hours from our house. I drove to the back and parked discreetly. Leaving my car, I tip-toed to the building's side. From there, I could peer through a large corner window. My heart was racing so fast that I felt like it could jump out of my chest. I knelt beneath the window with both hands on the brick ledge and scanned the restaurant, searching for my father, then blinked several times because I couldn't believe my eyes. In a corner booth, he sat beside a slender woman with long, curly blonde hair. Across from them, a petite little girl wore a pink ruffly dress. My heart sped up faster as I watched them laughing over dinner. The little girl laughed while sipping on a tall milkshake, as her feet swung back and forth under the table. I wondered who they were and why he was here on a Wednesday evening. Then it happened."

I pause and close my eyes. I'm reliving this nightmare, and it's only the beginning. Tears roll down my face, and my hands grip tightly in my lap.

"Keep going, Izzy. It's okay."

"He put his arm around the woman and kissed her cheek. She turned to him, and they kissed on the lips. The little girl sucked on her milkshake straw, as her legs swung back and forth faster under the table. They looked so happy. I slid onto the sidewalk, nauseous and nearly fainting, but I gathered my courage. I peered over the window ledge again. Shortly after, they stood up and left the booth. Father helped them with their coats, and they headed to the cashier. I ran to my car to drive home. How I arrived safely is a mystery because I was in shock."

"What happened when you returned home?"

"I pulled in the driveway, shut off the car, and stared at our garage door, hoping to escape the nightmare. But it wasn't a dream. The shock wore off, and I wailed, hitting the steering wheel with both fists. The reality of betrayal and deception came into focus, and hatred for my father took root. How could he do this to us? For at least an hour, I sat in the dark car, then realized Mother would look for me soon and worry. I had to face her."

With streaming tears, I tremble, replaying the shocking moment in my mind.

"Izzy, are you alright?" the counselor says.

"I'm terrified."

"I'm right here with you, and nothing can harm you. Focus on the progress you've made. It's remarkable how well you're doing, and you will move beyond this. I think it's best to pause and continue tomorrow. What do you think?"

"I agree."

Duke jumps to his feet and places his head in my lap. The trembling weakens by rubbing his heavy jaws.

"Very well. It's never wise to rush God's timing. I think it's a good idea that we both walk you back to the bungalow. Tomorrow, we continue."

CHAPTER 13

Consequences

The next morning, I stare at the ceiling, I cannot force myself to get out of bed. The dread settles in thinking about Jacob, the kids, and what I'm putting them through. Why did I pray for healing? What have I done to my family? It's torture, making them wonder if I will recover.

Wait, is this about my family, or me avoiding the next conversation with the counselor? For nearly twenty-six years, I have kept silent about the worst day of my life. Now I'm facing the darkest hour again. How will I get through this?

There it is again, disbelief and doubting God. I have two choices, continue living with familiar darkness or face the truth with God's help and be free of the guilt and sadness. Despite fearing the unknown, staying the same is unthinkable. I must lean on God's strength, not mine.

Duke grabs my attention with a whimper. I turn to see his big chin resting on the bed. His huge body wiggles. Concerned about his tail knocking over the lamp on the side table, I roll out of bed. He's such a blessing.

I browse through the dresses and choose a solid pale green. I admit, any shade of green looks good on us gingers. Duke and I stroll to the sanctuary, where a fresh sweetness fills the air. Butterflies and birds flutter around like they're escorting us to the garden. Could they sense my anxiety about today's session? I sense God's presence speaking bravery over each stride. My stance straightens. I'm ready for battle. We arrive at the trellis, and I tap the engraved sign over my head. Yeah, this is my sacred sanctuary, but today, it's my battleground. I roll my shoulders back while Duke runs to greet the counselor.

"Good morning, Izzy. How are you feeling this morning?"

"Good morning, Counselor. I woke up restless but gained some confidence walking over here."

"I'm delighted you are confronting fear. Each time you recognize disbelief and correct yourself, faith increases. Something to celebrate."

"Yeah. I think you're right."

"Let's have coffee and blueberry muffins, then continue from where we stopped yesterday. If you're up for it."

He gives me a stunning paisley cup. I sip, searching his kind eyes for courage. I lower the cup slowly and rub the gold key necklace.

"I'm not sure if I can get through the entire story, but I'll try."

"That's all we can ask. Let's begin with your arriving home after discovering your father at the diner with another lady and the little girl. What happens next?"

I take two gulps of coffee. "Before going inside, I pondered whether to share the news with Mother. I walked into the kitchen greeted by the scent of oatmeal cookies and Mother in her embroidered apron. We chatted about the volleyball game, but I quickly excused myself to finish homework. I couldn't tell her. In my room, I paced the floor, wringing my hands until they ached. I couldn't sleep. Believing my decision to share what I saw would decide our family's future, I kept asking myself what to do. I wanted to call my father but couldn't. It's not like today, with mobile phones at our fingertips. Regardless, what would I say? The thought of my father having a second family made me dizzy and nauseous. I recall falling to the floor, holding my stomach."

The counselor reaches across the table and gently squeezes my hands. "I'm sorry you experienced this. No one should bear such a burden."

His validation offers slight relief and yet exposes the naked truth of the disturbing reality. With lips trembling, tears flow down my cheeks. I can't speak.

"Let it out, Izzy. You must let loose of the gripping pain you've held back for so long. We have all the time you need. Just let it go."

Sobbing for what felt like an hour, I release the agony. There's nothing left. The counselor offers a perfectly starched handkerchief. Mopping up the tears, I gather my composure and continue.

"At around 5:00 a.m., I considered calling Roger or one of my sisters to share my observation but decided not to involve them. A decision I regret. However, to keep a tragic secret and pretend nothing happened wasn't an option. Confronting my father seemed horrific, so telling my mother privately appeared to be the only way forward. Another decision I regret. Standing at my bedroom door for several minutes, I build up the courage to turn the knob, walk to Mother's bedroom, and wake her."

He takes my hands again. "Izzy, your decision made sense based on the circumstances. You're not responsible for the outcome. Please continue."

"With a gentle touch of my hand on her shoulder, Mother opened her eyes and asked what was wrong. I stared at her, not able to speak or breathe, giving her time to get up. From the troubled look on her face, I realized I must appear frightened. I stuttered and tried to speak, but the words would not form. Concerned, she grabbed my shoulders and demanded I continue. Finally, I blurted it out like a cannonball from a cannon. I explained what I'd witnessed at the diner and that I didn't understand what father was doing there. Her hands dropped from my shoulders. She stared at the floor, appearing utterly defeated. The moment the words ejected from my mouth, I wanted them obliterated, but it was too late. I tried to convince her of a logical explanation, but she just stood there staring, motionless."

"Your mother deserved the truth, and this was not your fault. Please accept that."

"How can I? My choice to tell her cost us everything."

"That's a lie."

"How so?"

"Your decision to tell your mother didn't cause your family's destruction. It was the choices made by your father and your mother. Please continue with the story."

I sigh. "I stood with her for a long time asking if she was okay and encouraged her to call my father at his office so he could clear this up. It must be a misunderstanding on my part. She didn't respond but lowered to the edge of the bed staring at the floor. With hollow eyes, she peered at me, revealing her soul. In a soft, monotone voice, she reassured me not to worry and to prepare for school. Her instant transition from despair to apathy alarmed me. As usual, she pretended to be fine, but there was a noticeable difference. She was emotionless."

"Then what happened?"

"She kept insisting I go to school, but I didn't want to leave her alone. After several minutes, I left her room to get ready, and before leaving for school, I returned to check on her and say goodbye."

I tremble. The counselor steps forward and hugs my shoulder tightly. His love envelopes me. After a long squeeze, he releases me and takes his seat.

"When I entered Mother's room again, she was sitting in the same spot on the edge of her bed. With a chilling smile, she peered up and wished me a good day. I kneeled in front of her and offered to stay home, but she insisted I be on time. We hugged, and I kissed her cheek and said I loved her. Again, I assured her father would sort this out. Before leaving her bedroom, I apologized for sharing what I saw. She thanked me for telling her, waved her hand, and said she would be okay. The final decision I regret."

"She wanted the illusion to end, Izzy."

I can't speak, knowing the worst is yet to come. Petrified, I whisper, "I shouldn't have left her alone. How could I leave her after dropping that bombshell? What was wrong with me?"

"Izzy, you were only seventeen, reacting to a terrible situation, and you obeyed your mother's request. Any adult could have made this assessment. Please accept you are not to blame for anything that happened."

"I remember backing out of her bedroom, reluctant to leave. The ten-minute drive to school seemed like forever. I considered turning around to go back home, but I didn't. As I reached the school parking lot, I noticed Misty leaving her car, prompting me to approach her and share the news. Before I could speak, she told me she was running late for first period and rushed toward the entrance. I wandered into the building, and each class seemed twice as long. I couldn't focus. Then, around 2:00 p.m., my name was announced over the loudspeaker calling me to the office. My heart leaped into my throat as I shuffled my papers and grabbed my backpack, then sprinted to the principal's office. When I entered, I noticed Mrs. Wilson sitting in the waiting area, Mother's best friend. She dabs her eyes with a tissue and stands. My knees buckle, and I grab a nearby armchair to break the fall."

I pause, breathless, and reach out to the counselor. He kneels before me, our hands tightly intertwined.

"I need your strength."

"I'm here."

I close my eyes and continue.

"Before Mrs. Wilson spoke, Mr. Copeland, our school principal, interrupted telling me Mother was in an accident, and we needed to get to the hospital right away. He gave Mrs. Wilson an awkward stare. She hugged me closely, and we walked to her car. Mrs. Wilson's eyes were red and swollen. As we traveled in the car, I asked her multiple times about Mother's situation, but she only assured me that we would receive more information at the hospital. My instincts told me Mother was not all right. Mrs. Wilson said she spoke to my father at his office, and he was on his way to the hospital. I sat there, numb. My mind raced, recalling the conversation with Mother and the scene at the diner. Considering a probable connection between Mother's accident and our morning discussion, I felt sickened by the remorse."

I open my eyes and look at the counselor.

"You lived through unthinkable consequences, and you're still punishing yourself through guilt and shame, but it serves no one. Please keep going."

"After a short drive with Mrs. Wilson, we pulled into the emergency area parking lot. Looking out the window, I spotted my father's red Cadillac a few rows over. I shuddered, thinking about facing him and what I might say. Mrs. Wilson got out of the car, and we walked to the hospital entrance together with her arm wrapped snuggly around my shoulder. I felt secure with her, but I hesitated to go inside. As we approached the glass doors, I could see Father and Shannon hugging each other inside the foyer. Her college was nearby, but Roger and Abbey were farther away. I hesitated. Mrs. Wilson faced me with puffy, red eyes and placed both hands on my shoulders. She asked if I was okay. I said I didn't want to face my father. She raised one eyebrow, grabbed my hand, and we scurried through the automatic doors. Once inside, Father glanced up from Shannon and motioned me to form a group hug. I was queasy, but the concern for Mother overshadowed the negative emotions towards him. After a lengthy embrace, he released us and directed us to a waiting area sofa. Shannon and I sat beside each other, holding hands as our father bent on one knee. He stared Shannon in the eyes but looked down when he glanced at me. Tears streamed down his face, and his head dropped. He uttered the words that froze time. He said, "Your mother took her life and passed away this morning. She is gone."

I hunch over, holding my stomach, sobbing. The counselor kneels beside me with one hand on my shoulder. His fatherly love envelopes me as I release years of pent-up anguish over my mother's death. I hold nothing back.

Visions of my mother travel through my mind. I recall fond memories of her performing the Nutcracker in our living room, reliving the dance as she twirled me around, gaining a whiff of her exotic perfume with every turn.

She was amazing in the kitchen, transforming the ordinary oatmeal cookie into a gourmet sensation. Walking into our home was like stepping into a bakery, filled with a permanent aroma of apples and cinnamon. In the background, scores of Tchaikovsky or Mozart echoed, and Mother glided around pretending to be on stage. My body tingles, admiring her graceful spirit and gentleness towards life. She taught us to approach each day with passion and chase our dreams with confidence. From her, we learned proper citizenship, discipline, and respect for others. She loved us and we loved her. I couldn't dream up a more devoted and generous mother.

How is this possible? For the first time since my teens, I'm reliving positive memories instead of painful scenes. My sobbing turns to sniffles, and I sit upright. I reach for the saturated handkerchief, and the counselor hands me a clean one. He strokes the top of my hand patiently as each touch sends a sensational wave of pure love. Words cannot describe ethereal comfort.

He whispers in a calm voice, "You did it, Izzy. The scariest part of your healing process is over, and you survived, even though more of the story remains untold."

I catch my breath. "I can't believe it. Wonderful memories flooded my mind just now, overpowering the tragic accident. Things I had forgotten or repressed because of my focus on her death. Before today, when I thought of Mother, I only recalled the events surrounding her death. I was stuck. Now, my mind is open, remembering the glorious seventeen years I had with her instead of obsessing about time lost. I am grateful beyond words."

"Incredible breakthrough. Like your mother, you are extraordinary."

"Thank you. That's a lovely compliment."

"Let's rest a while longer and call it a day. I realize there's more to share about the days following your mother's passing, but it's too much for one day."

"What's coming concerns me." I play with the gold key necklace.

"You survived today, not a zombie, nothing to worry about, right?"

We chuckle, and I welcome the needed laughter. Felt like medicine.

"Seriously, the next phase of healing is crucial, even more so than coping with your mother's tragic suicide."

I stiffen and my smile fades. "How can that be?"

"We tackle the deep wounds caused by your father's choices before and after your mother's death."

Staring at the counselor in silence, I close my eyes.

"Can't think about more healing, just memories resurrected today. I need to rest."

"Indeed. Come, let's return to the bungalow."

We rise and embrace like Grandpa Finny. I sense his presence, too. Duke stands, eager to lead the way. We release and I pet Duke's back, feeling the comfort of our companionship. I thank the counselor. He's made this possible. I buried the burden so deep, never believing I could face the loss of my mother. I now understand the damage caused by harboring emotional pain. I should have called on God sooner and faced this battle with Him. A lesson I'll never forget.

Boulders lift, but more rocks remain.

CHAPTER 14

Betrayal

After rising, Duke and I take an early morning stroll through the forest beside the bungalow. At a slow pace, I walk along a wide dirt path and enjoy a granola bar. Thoughts of my mother are like reuniting with my long-lost friend. For the first time in over twenty years, I celebrate memories of her life instead of mourning her death. I'm healing.

The truth is the guilt from telling her about seeing Father at the diner and leaving her alone that fateful day still grips my throat. But with fond memories taking root in my heart, over time I expect to move beyond my fatal mistake. I can't change it, only my attitude.

It's different from my father. Whatever the counselor has in store for today, I must keep believing and trusting God to carry me through the pain. I'm ready.

Duke bounds ahead and I linger behind. My mind continues with thoughts about my life with Mother. The good stuff. There's a pleasant punch in the air, like a crisp, green apple. I hold tight to this moment before the familiar bitterness chokes out the welcomed joy.

I catch up to Duke who's stopped at the bank of a wide creek. The shallow water flows gently over large rocks. Reminds me of the trout stream in college where Jacob sang to me. Duke jumps in the water and splashes around. I peer down at my wet pants and shoes.

"Hey. Take it easy." He moves closer and flips water with his back legs toward me.

I tighten my face to avoid water in my eyes and mouth. "Duke, I'm soaked." Wet from head to toe, he continues splashing.

I cover my face. "Come. Get out of the water."

He ignores my command and prances in a circle as if he's taunting me to join him.

"I mean it, come here, boy." No change.

Playfulness seeps in and overtakes me. I jump in the water with Duke to engage in the water fight of the century. I haven't laughed this much in a long while and Duke has never howled so boldly.

After several minutes splashing each other, I climb out of the creek onto dry ground and sit.

"Duke, the counselor will be waiting. Let's head back to the bungalow for dry clothes. Duke leaps onto the bank away from me and shakes his body until there's no water left on his fur. I notice his demeanor transitions from playful to protective, as if he's my guardian.

Before I complete my worrisome thought of being late to meet the counselor, a gust of wind rushes over me and I cover my head. When the breeze stops, I stand with my mouth gaping open and touch my dry, clean clothes. And my hair—bone dry. I giggle. God takes care of every detail.

"Duke, let's go. A change of clothes won't be necessary."

He barks loudly and leads me out of the woods toward the sanctuary. Duke's escapades remind me to enjoy the present moment. Something I've forgotten.

At the sanctuary, the counselor sits and sips his coffee. He's wearing a loud paisley print shirt today with teal and yellow designs. The pattern is lovely, but what's with the paisleys?

I touch his shoulder lightly. "Good morning, sir. How are you today?"

He looks up, blinding me with his radiant eyes. Whoa, too close. I shield my eyes.

"It's a fine morning. I'm delighted to see your warm smile and dry clothes." He winks.

I jerk sideways. "You know about the water fight with Duke?"

He chuckles. "Absolutely. Please sit and have some coffee."

"Hot coffee is what I need." My eyes widen as he hands me a steaming cup. We chit chat about the morning walk and water fight for a while. I prolong the conversation to avoid the inevitable. He leans forward as if he's catching on.

"Izzy, I'm amazed by your courage and openness to this process. How a person interprets and responds to life's trials affects everything. It's understandable to zero in on one traumatic event over the volume of wonderful memories. Trauma is a shock to the entire system. Not intended as permanent. Is this making sense?"

"Yes. I understand how my trauma kept me stuck in the time of her death, never recalling our good life together. And despite our marriage problems, Jacob and I built a good life with two amazing kids. Even so, a gloomy darkness hovers over that too. Life will improve, but the feeling of dread is inexplicable. With each session, another boulder lifts and the gloominess fades. I am hopeful. Finally, I am confident in becoming the person God intended. It's exciting."

He steeples his fingers together in a prayer position. "I'm overjoyed about your lovely memories of your mother. Remember to recall more details of your life with her to avoid relapsing into the tragic memory of her death. Let the seventeen joyful years spent with her build and outweigh the memories of losing her."

"I will. I don't want to fall back into the darkness again."

"Excellent. Let's continue uncovering the story. What happens next at the hospital?"

I wiggle back in my chair.

"Right after Father shared the news about Mother's suicide, I ran to Mrs. Wilson, leaving Shannon with my father. I couldn't look at him. I'd lost my mother, and Mrs. Wilson lost her best friend. They were like sisters. We hugged each other and sobbed. Father said he needed to call Roger and Abbey at college and shuffled Shannon to us. The room spun, time stood still, yet nothing stopped. People scurried around us in the waiting area, some annoyed by our obstruction. I'll never forget how strange it was to observe the outer world move ahead without skipping a beat while my inner world collapsed around me. The insensitivity from my surroundings pricked at my heart like thistles."

"The initial shock and heartbreak increased your awareness and need for comfort, which no one could fulfill. Only God's love is sufficient during these times."

"I get it now."

"Keep going."

"I sat close to Mrs. Wilson in the waiting area, and Shannon kept asking why Mother would do this. Mrs. Wilson stroked her hair and tried to comfort her without an explanation. I couldn't tell if Mrs. Wilson knew anything about Father's affair at this point. Sitting there numb, thoughts of my conversation with Mother replayed repeatedly. I tried to discern if I should share what I saw the night before at the diner and my discussion with Mother this morning, but I remained silent. After all, the last time I opened my big mouth, the most unimaginable tragedy struck. Even though Mother appeared distraught, committing suicide never entered my mind."

I pause and put my thoughts in order.

"After several minutes, Father returned to tell us he'd reached Roger and Abbey and expected them to arrive within a few hours. Again, he locked eyes with Shannon, but avoided looking at me. I couldn't look at him either. Shannon clung to him, asking why Mother killed herself. She asked if he'd spoken to her before she died. He didn't respond to Shannon and stared at the ground. He patted the top of her head and excused himself to make more phone calls. We sat there, shocked, holding one another."

"When did the others arrive?"

"A few hours later. Father walked back into the waiting room at the same time Roger and Abbey entered the hospital. They rushed to us with panicked looks on their faces. They asked about Mother. Shannon and I fell into Roger's arms, crying. Roger stared at my father. Obviously, he needed a response. Father asked us to sit so he could explain. He knelt in front of Roger and Abbey and told them Mother committed suicide. The shock struck me once more, like a slap to my face. Abbey fell into Father's arms, but Roger didn't move. The pain of watching my family suffer was unbearable, so I ran to the bathroom. I had to process the situation and decide how to handle the information about Father and my conversation with Mother."

"What did you decide?"

"I didn't. After a few minutes, Mrs. Wilson called my name outside the bathroom door. She came in to check on me. The family was leaving the hospital and going to her house. As we walked through the parking lot, Mrs. Wilson led me to Father's red Cadillac. The same one at the diner. I stopped and grabbed my mouth, holding back the vomit as my three siblings climbed into his vehicle. I asked Mrs. Wilson if I could ride with her so she wouldn't be alone. She clutched my shoulder and shouted to Father that I was riding with her. He waved his agreement, and we left for Mrs. Wilson's home. My mind raced as we rode along in silence."

"What were your thoughts?"

"Would Father share anything with my siblings before arriving at Mrs. Wilson's? Then it hit me. I asked her who found Mother and where. She covered her mouth as tears rushed down her face. Shaking and sobbing, she pulled the car over. I put my hand on her arm and tried to comfort her. After several minutes, she looked at me with the deepest regret and told me she found Mother at home in her bedroom. She said there was a large empty pill bottle lying on the floor next to her bed, and she believed Mother died peacefully. Stunned, we sat silently until Mrs. Wilson put the car in drive and started back on the road."

The counselor sighs. "Mrs. Wilson loved your mother dearly, Izzy. It's unfortunate she found her that day. What happened once you all arrived at her house?"

I pat my watery eyes with a tissue. "As we approached the front door, I heard murmurings from my siblings speculating about Mother's death, and it confirmed that Father did not share any further details during the ride over. Mrs. Wilson invited us to sit in her living room and disappeared into the kitchen to make iced tea. Slowly, we took off our jackets and plopped down on the sofa and chairs. Two calico cats jumped on my lap and startled me back to reality that life moved on regardless of our situation. I rubbed their fur, and the soft purring brought a brief comfort. Father rubbed his forehead and paced in the foyer." I stop and linger on the memory of the horrible news.

"It's okay, Izzy. Don't stop now."

I take a sip of coffee. "I watched every move my father made. His eyes darted around the room like a laser light beam. He clenched his fists together, then bolted into the living room and told us Mrs. Wilson arrived at the house around noon for their weekly lunch date and found Mother in her bedroom. Feeling no pulse, she called 911, and they rushed her to the hospital, but she'd already passed away. Father broke down into tears and my siblings knelt beside him trying to offer comfort. I remained motionless. Roger scowled at me. After Father gained composure, he continued sharing that Mother died from a self-induced overdose of prescription drugs."

"Did you know she was taking medication?"

"No, and none of my siblings knew. After receiving hugs from my sisters, Father announced he was leaving to prepare funeral arrangements. Despite Roger's insistence on joining him, Father asked Roger to stay and take care of us girls. My three siblings clamored around him asking why Mother would do this, and if she'd left a suicide note. I remained seated, numb, and terrified, wondering if I should speak up. Father quickly interrupted their questions and advised everyone to calm down. He mentioned police investigating the house, possibly finding a note but he was currently unaware of one. He glanced at me, and for the first time, we locked eyes, which I interpreted to mean, stay quiet. Genuine concern showed on his face, so I refrained from sharing what I saw last night or my conversation with Mother. My family couldn't handle more devastating news. I carried the burden in silent isolation, letting my father manage the situation, and curious to see what he would do next. Like countless times before, he left. I wondered if we would ever see him again."

"Did your father come back?"

"Yes. But not until the following day. He phoned Mrs. Wilson later that evening and told her he needed to get some things from our house, and he would sleep on the couch. Upon hearing this update, my sisters appeared stunned. They questioned how Father could sleep alone in the house where Mother just died and leave us with Mrs. Wilson. Roger jumped to his defense, as he always had done, assuring us Father had valid reasons for his decisions. Without thinking, I blurted out accusations that our father never put us first, and my siblings turned to me with bewildered looks. My timing was bad. I retracted my harsh words, excusing my emotional outburst. Everyone became silent and subdued. The assumption that Father abandoned us to be with his other family instead of offering comfort sickened me. How could someone be so cold? He was a wicked, deceitful man, Counselor."

"I'm sorry, Izzy. This is painful, but please keep going."

With a deep inhale, I close my eyes and tears flow. I lower my head, keeping my eyes closed, and continue.

"The next day, we awoke from a restless night to face an overwhelming nightmare. The aroma of crackling bacon didn't negate the harsh reality that our mother was not coming back. Shannon and I stumbled to the kitchen to join Roger and Abbey already at the table. To my surprise, Father walked through the front door. At that point, I became a numb observer and shut down, which was a blessing in disguise. Losing my mother, managing the burden of knowledge about my father—no other way to deal with the pain. We were tight siblings, and they deserved the true story, but not from me. Meanwhile, back to Father's entrance. He joined us in the kitchen, kissing each sibling on the forehead, but I flinched with his touch. Roger noticed my reaction. Father patted my head instead and said he'd like to speak to us in the living room once we finished our breakfast. My siblings rose and hustled into the living room. They hadn't touched the meal, anyway. I withered in my chair."

"Did you join them?"

I open my eyes and look at the counselor. "Mrs. Wilson pressured me to go and promised to reheat the food. Out of respect for her, I found a seat away from Father to avoid eye contact. I tried to imagine what he would say, thinking he would never tell us the truth. Then, the unthinkable happened. It's a surreal moment to have your mother commit suicide one day and your father deliver the ultimate betrayal the next."

I try to focus on the present. My heart throbs like a sharp, stabbing pain, and tears flow. Reliving the next scene is far more painful than expected. Bent over, holding my stomach and my heart simultaneously, I rock forward and backward, trying to ease the pain. I'm a mess. Should I leave our session? The counselor stands, hands on my back, and my rocking stops. He stands over me with a tangible strength and I'm calm.

"You're okay, Izzy. Take your time. Remember the reason you are here. It's time to heal the past and live the life you crave. But there's no rush."

"Not sure if I can keep going."

"If a better way to heal your past sorrow existed, we would grant it. I'm not leaving your side."

"I believe you."

"Don't give up now. Lean on my strength to move beyond the pain."

I nod quickly and choke back my tears.

"Father pulled a side chair to the coffee table in front of the orange-and-yellow sofa where Roger, Abbey, and Shannon sat on the edge of their seats. I chose the matching velvet recliner to the right of my siblings. Father choked up as he tried to speak. Roger interrupted, assuring him it was okay, and wanted to understand why mother would take her own life. Roger's words gave Father the grace to collect himself and start again. His words delivered a shock almost as devastating as the news from yesterday."

I grip the counselor's hand tightly for strength.

"He started by telling us he never suspected Mother was suicidal. He said it didn't fit her character, but she struggled with depression and used her medication to end her life. Tears rolled down his face, and he looked away from us. I'd never seen my father fall apart or express so much emotion. He seemed like another person. As we exchanged surprised glances, Roger inquired further about her depression. We were not aware of her mental health issues, but given her private nature, it was understandable that she didn't share her struggle with her children. Despite knowing about her discontentment with Father's weekly travels and her frequent crying, suicide came as a complete shock to us.

The counselor raised his hand for me to stop. "The grip of depression was severe, Izzy. Your mother dealt with constant turmoil as a foster child, and she experienced horrendous events that haunted her daily.

She didn't want to relive the pain of her past and burden her family, so she suffered internally in quiet isolation, trying to manage the pain through medication."

"I was naïve. At seventeen years old, hearing about her secrecy compounded the uncertainty and betrayal."

"I understand. What happened next?"

"Father dropped his head and mumbled he never wanted this to happen. Lifting his head, he gazed at us for several uncomfortable moments. Then he blurted out that he'd been living a lie, and we deserved the truth. Although I imagined the next words out of his mouth, it didn't soften the blow. I was frightened, predicting everyone's reaction. Then Father said four penetrating words that obliterated any remaining bond among the five of us. He had another family."

Looking intently at the counselor, I clench my fist to my mouth and cannot continue. My body trembles as the rage rises from my feet to my face. I stand and turn my back to the counselor to release a gut-wrenching scream. A horrid shriek too embarrassing for anyone to see, even the counselor. After each exhaustive breath, the screams weaken until there's nothing left.

The counselor moves closer, resting his hand on my shoulder. A loving sensation pours through my body like a thick layer of warm honey oozing down my throat. It fills every crevasse hollowed by the elimination of deeply mangled sorrow. God's pure love replaces the dark hole in my heart, which was previously filled with rejection, guilt, and shame. I savor the moment. He continues his gentle touch on my shoulder a while longer. Through the pain of swollen eyes, I peer up into his radiant stare. The tears lessen. I'm okay.

"You did it, Izzy. The guilt, loss, and suffering you endured from your mother's death is over. Dealing with your father's betrayal was the next step towards your ultimate healing.

"Thank you. I am lighter, and the darkness is fading. During the meltdown, I'm struck by the intense anger I had buried toward my mother for leaving us. I'd always attributed any rage felt to my father. Why would she choose to leave her children behind? The answer hit me. Her decision, not the consequences, had nothing to do with me or my siblings. Just like the suitcase ride with Father. In her desperate hour, I doubt she could think clearly about the future of her children when she took her life. I believe she didn't mean to hurt us. She loved us. Instead, I believe she only meant to escape her unbearable pain."

He grips my shoulder. "You're very astute. I am so proud of you and your progress."

"Thank you, sir. The answer came from your teachings. You showed me that my father's choice to leave every week had nothing to do with my actions, even though the consequences of his decision affected everything for me and my family.

"You're correct. Choices made from selfish motives always have negative consequences."

"It's clear now. I couldn't repair the outcome. However, it's regrettable that my response to this disaster caused decades of lingering misery. A lesson I'll never forget."

"Good. Now, let's continue your story after your father delivered the shocking news about his other family."

I close my eyes and exhale slowly. "Despite watching my father kiss another woman at the diner, the news struck like a thunderbolt. I hoped he would explain away the kiss as an innocent misunderstanding. I was wrong. Red in the face, Roger slowly stood and asked Father to repeat himself. After the second confession, Roger pointed his finger and shouted at him. Had our mother found out? Father hesitated. Roger screamed the question again, and he admitted she learned about his affair yesterday."

I glance at Duke trying to fight back the tears.

"Keep going, Izzy."

I swallow the lump in my throat. "Roger flew over the coffee table airborne, lunging at Father's throat, and threw him to the floor with his fists whirling. Father covered his face to avoid the punches, but there were red marks. My sisters screamed. They clung to each other on the couch, pleading for Roger to stop. I sat frozen. Roger climbed off, pointed at the door, and ordered him to leave. Father begged to let him explain. Guilt-ridden, I held my breath and prayed Father wouldn't tell them it was me who told Mother. Roger refused to listen and shoved him out the door. Roger turned and put his fist through the entry wall. I rushed to the sofa and latched on to my sisters. They trembled.

"Mrs. Wilson rushed in, appearing terrified by the outburst, and asked what had happened. We couldn't speak. The news was too much after losing our mother just hours ago. Roger told her to call our father and ask him what happened. He asked her to watch over us while he took a walk to calm down. Mrs. Wilson nodded while hugging us on the couch. I'd never seen Roger lose his temper. Not once. He became our father and fierce protector that day."

My arms fall limp in my lap. Telling the story is heavy. The pain of guilt and disappointment sinks in from such a devastating outcome.

"How do you feel, Izzy?"

I wrap my stomach. "Queasy. I still wonder if Father knew I exposed him. Maybe she called him at work to confront him, and he confirmed the affair. If so, did she tell him who informed her? Since I haven't spoken to him since that day in Mrs. Wilson's living room, the answer remains unknown."

The counselor raises his hand. "Wait, you haven't spoken to your father since you were seventeen?"

"No, sir. And I don't intend to."

"And you told no one other than your mother about witnessing your father at the restaurant?"

"Correct. I swore never to reveal what I saw at the diner after the catastrophe involving Mother. Not even Jacob. I should have wiped the scene from my mind and buried the skeleton. I couldn't handle it if my brother and sisters hated me and blamed me for Mother's suicide. If my siblings had knowledge of it, they would undoubtedly confront me. Even though Father tried to reconcile with us over the years, none of them have spoken to him since then either."

"So, your father lost all of you when your mother died."

I look away. "He made the choice long before Mother committed suicide."

The counselor sighs heavily. "Please continue the story."

"Roger instructed Mrs. Wilson to phone our father and tell him not to contact us ever again or attend the funeral. A few days after her death, we held a private funeral service in a neighboring town to protect our privacy. Since Mother didn't have any family members, it was just us kids, along with Mr. and Mrs. Wilson. Roger hired a security guard to stop Father from entering the funeral home. I recall sitting in the front row with my sisters staring at my mother lying peacefully in a shiny white coffin covered with Stargazer Lilies, Mother's favorite flower. The familiar fragrance filled the room. She used to put bouquets of lilies on the hall entry table. Behind me, there are fifty empty seats, and I realize how unpredictable life is. Her death was not the expected outcome for someone so young. People who loved and admired her should have filled those seats. My heart ached for her fateful decision, the one I initiated."

The counselor scoots forward and pats my knee. "I'm so sorry, Izzy. Her service sounds lovely. I'm curious if your father showed up. Did he?"

"I don't think so. If he did, Roger kept it to himself. Each of us took a turn saying our goodbyes to Mother. I remember her skin looked flawless. The lines of loneliness and sadness erased with tranquility. Her dainty body fit perfectly in her favorite pink gown. Her ballet shoes nestled beneath the blanket as a symbol of her life's passion and sacrifice. After the viewing services, we drove to the cemetery. Rain gushed over the limousine windows so thick it was impossible to see the road. We sat in silence, listening to the downpour and rapid screeching of windshield wipers. Which now explains why I change my windshield wipers when hearing the slightest squeak.

"The drive seemed endless. Once we arrived, giant black umbrellas circled my mother's casket. Among the whimpers, I heard a car door close from behind. Concerned it might be our father, I glanced over my shoulder, trying to avoid anyone's attention. Father leaned against his car door at a distance in the gushing rain without an umbrella. He looked pitiful. We locked eyes, and for a split second, empathy consumed me. When he peered at his shoes, reality replaced empathy with rage that settled in for good. And then he was gone. Thankfully, no one else spotted him, and I never mentioned it."

I let tears flow freely, embracing their cleansing power without wiping them away.

"You're doing great. Did he try to make contact after the funeral?"

"Oh, yes. He called Mrs. Wilson every day and asked to speak with me, but I refused. She said he wanted me to live with him, and I became so upset, she never mentioned it again. He tried contacting my siblings too, but they never responded. The days, weeks, and months following Mother's death were a blur."

"Where did you live?"

"Mr. and Mrs. Wilson offered to be my guardians until I turned eighteen and asked me to live with them to finish high school. Father consented, I assumed. Without them, I wouldn't have survived my senior year. After a few weeks off from school, I dreaded seeing my classmates. It was brutal. Everyone avoided eye contact or speaking to me. I understood they were clueless about what to say and remained silent. Even Misty. I felt like an outcast, and piling on my internal guilt, each day was dreadful."

"How did you cope?"

"I kept to myself and focused on earning straight A's. It paid off getting into college, and I tried to block the events from my mind. The time with the Wilsons was a marvelous blessing. I learned more about my mother in one month than my seventeen years as her daughter."

"Like what?"

"Mrs. Wilson lived in the same foster home as Mother for their last two years of high school. That's how they met. They became best friends. Since Mother never mentioned how they became acquainted, I assumed they became friends at the country club much later in life. Mrs. Wilson told me the foster parents became overwhelmed with too many children and demanded her and Mother serve as co-parents. She said the foster parents were verbally abusive, but they didn't get physical like some of the previous foster parents. My heart sank when I learned about the abuse. They plotted to run away and marry their prince charming. Mother ran to the dance studio during her free time. Mrs. Wilson said she danced around the house instead of walking, constantly honing her skill."

"Your time with Mrs. Wilson sounds precious. Your mother's childhood fueled her determination to become a professional ballet dancer. It kept her going, and she succeeded. Through her ambitions, she became an acclaimed dancer, a remarkable mother, and a devoted wife. The heartbreak of abandonment took its toll."

I stare at the ground, thinking about the theme of abandonment that we share. Such irony. "You're correct. So how could my father betray her for so long?"

"Izzy, that's a fair question only your father can answer. He made some serious mistakes, and he's suffered for those decisions. More than you can imagine. Which brings us to the last phase of healing your sorrow."

"The last phase, are you serious?" Could this mean I'm getting close to reuniting with my family?

He leans forward with a serious look. "It requires forgiveness."

I bolt from my chair, pacing. My face flushes hot, and my body stiffens. "I can't. How could anyone treat their family this way? Seriously, how could they? And then expect us to forgive and forget? He wanted another family. Well, he got one. I'm sure they lived happily and glad we were gone. He's the reason my mother is dead."

The counselor stands. "It's okay to feel this way."

"You're darn right."

"I'm not asking you to forgive your father yet."

I stop pacing. "What? Then who?"

He pauses. "Yourself."

I'm motionless, as though paralyzed. Duke buries his head between his paws. I lock my gaze with the counselor. "I'm unsure which is harder to forgive, me or my father."

He gestures for me to take my seat. "Let's find out."

CHAPTER 15

Forgiving Myself

"Izzy, do you want to stop the session or continue?"

"Let's keep going. I'm on the last stretch."

If I had known the extent of my suffering and the grip of these mind traps, I doubt I would have agreed to stay. How much longer here? And me, forgiving myself? What does that look like?

"Counselor, I must admit, I'm not feeling confident about this last phase."

"Why?"

"I don't believe I have the right to forgive myself. I've lived with guilt for so long. First for telling my mother about Father's affair, and then leaving her alone to commit suicide. It's part of who I am. I robbed my siblings and Mrs. Wilson of more time with our mother."

"The only reason it's part of who you are is because you buried the guilt deep within instead of facing the situation. So, yes, that dark sadness lives in your soul. Isn't that what you prayed for God to remove?"

I hesitate to answer. "Never thought about it that way."

"I'll cut to the chase. You're afraid of losing familiarity. That's what you mean when you say it's part of you."

"I don't understand."

"When mind traps run this deep, they become part of your comfort zone. It sounds odd because it's painful and sad. Yet, over time, the mind links familiar thoughts to comfort."

I stare at my hands folded neatly in my lap. "Yes, the thought of letting go of my guilt makes me extremely uncomfortable. I deserve to feel bad."

"That's a lie you've told yourself for decades. You deserve to be free."

"I want the pain to end. Sometimes I understand why my mother chose death."

"Izzy, you trusted me to walk with you and face the darkest hours of your mother's suicide. You survived and you're better for it. Do you agree?"

"Yes. That's true."

"So why resist the idea of forgiving yourself and your father if I promise you the same reward? Liberated from anger, sadness, shame, guilt, and regret. Aren't those reasons why you're here?"

"Whoa. My father too?" I comb my fingers through my hair.

"Will you trust me, Izzy?"

I can't deny his accuracy. And what about my family? I must get back to them. It's time.

"You would make a brilliant lawyer, sir. But there's something else."

He winks and pours more coffee. "What is it?"

"Despite sounding ridiculous, releasing guilt for disclosing Father's second family to Mother reveals the humiliation of my decision."

"It's okay. Just say what you think."

"If I forgive my father, he gets away with betraying and abandoning us, and I won't allow it. As if everything he did is okay. He doesn't deserve forgiveness."

He squints, tapping his cheek. "Do you deserve God's forgiveness?"

My eyebrows squeeze together. "What?"

"You heard the question. Do you deserve the sacrifice Jesus made to forgive your sins?"

"Come on. It's different."

"How so?"

"I'm not perfect. I've made mistakes and sinned. Still do. No, I don't deserve it and neither does anyone else. But I would never hurt my family the way my father hurt us. There's no comparison."

"Do you believe God forgives all sin regardless of how horrible?"

"You're not being fair, Counselor."

"It's a reasonable question."

I frown. "Okay, fine. Yes. I believe God forgives all sin if we surrender our life to Him and repent."

"Excellent answer. Do you think God would forgive your father's sin if he asked?"

I pause, kicking a pebble. "Based on God's promises, I must admit, He would forgive my father."

"Even though he doesn't deserve it?"

"No one *deserves* God's forgiveness. So what? Why do I have to forgive my father if God will?"

"To release your sorrow."

"I don't understand. How does forgiving my father link to my sorrow? Punishing him is all I have left." I fold my arms and look away.

"Your sorrow lives in a world of sad stories. You dwell on past hurts brought on by your father's choices of neglect and betrayal. You believe punishing him for the pain he caused creates justice, but you're still hurting, so where is the justice? Serving this madness weakens your soul and robs you of living the incredible life you have with Jacob. You're stuck in the mind trap of unforgiveness."

"Another mind trap?"

"Yes. I said they intertwine."

"You did."

"Until you release the burden and forgive, you'll continue living from a distorted view based on your wounded past." He pauses. "Who's really being punished?"

My head drops in silence. I could never pinpoint it, but he just described the way I've felt my entire life. I experience the world from the view of a hurt toddler and teenager, waiting for the next sting to trigger the wound that feeds my sorrowful nature. A cloud of melancholy hangs over me, believing someday I will have joy, but someday never comes. I am trapped living in the duality of a genuine good life plagued by the past that won't allow me to enjoy it.

"Izzy, what are you thinking?"

"You perfectly described the unexplained sadness. I'm understanding where it's coming from. How do I release the burden?"

"Through grace."

"Grace?"

"Yes. Think about your children. When they made mistakes, even big ones, did you punish them forever to ensure justice, or did you extend a second chance through forgiveness?"

"Of course, I forgave them with lots of second chances. But their mistakes didn't come close to what my father did."

"You choose which sins are forgivable?"

"You're tricking me. You can't compare the sins of my father with the sins of my children."

"Didn't you just say God forgives all sin, including your father's, regardless of the severity?"

"Yes."

"So, if God in all His magnificent glory can forgive, shouldn't you?"

I stand and stare at the counselor, trying to let his words sink in.

"Take your time."

I take my seat. "I get it. But my father's deception is not okay."

"Correct. God's forgiveness doesn't eliminate the consequences of anyone's sin. There's no denying the significant damage surrounding your father's reckless actions. No one escapes God's judgement. However, there is nothing you or your father can do to bring your mother back or change the decisions your father made. It's done. Instead, you choose your response to life's situations."

I keep fighting this. What am I so afraid of? I slump back in my chair. "I want to be free."

"As a starting point, let's focus on forgiving yourself audibly."

Tears stream down my face, but I'm determined to get the words out. After a big gulp, I blurt it out. "I forgive myself for sharing the dinner scene with Mother and abandoning her in her bedroom that fateful morning. If I could fix it, I would."

The counselor places his hand on my shoulder as I weep. "If you can accept it wasn't your fault, please say it aloud."

I struggle to speak through the sobbing. Mrs. Wilson told me about

Mother's battle with depression when they lived in the foster home. I can't deny the truth, but the desire to keep the pain inside holds back my tongue. Then it releases.

"It wasn't my fault. I didn't want to leave her that morning, but she insisted I go to school, so I obeyed her. Her childhood pain wasn't my doing. I didn't betray her or cause her to kill herself."

"Although learning of your father's infidelity added to years of mental suffering, he didn't kill your mother. She had a choice to live and move on with her life. She chose not to."

"True. I just wish she had talked to someone like Mrs. Wilson. Even Mother's best friend didn't suspect the level of her torment."

"How do you feel now?"

I close my eyes and catch my breath. "Like a gigantic boulder lifted from my shoulders. I didn't realize how much guilt weighed until now." We look at each other and I wipe my nose.

"Good. The key is to never reclaim the guilt. Can you do that?"

"I don't want it back."

He pats my back and sits in his chair. "I'm proud of you. You accomplished the first step."

I sip my coffee, sensing a penetrating peace about the day Mother died. For the first time, I realize it doesn't matter who is to blame. She's gone. Being tangled up with my role in her death and my father's betrayal, I never grieved properly. Guilt overshadowed my loss. I miss her.

"Counselor, I'm just being realistic. Choosing to forgive myself is one thing. Forgiving my father is unimaginable."

"I understand but, tomorrow, we face the unimaginable together."

How can I forgive a deceitful man like my father? I'm desperate to see my family, but I fear being stuck here forever.

"You need a break, Izzy."

I stand with my arms folded. "I agree. See you tomorrow?"

The counselor rises and gives me a tender look of compassion. "I'll be here."

"Thank you, sir. Duke, lead me to the bungalow."

Duke barks and I follow him. Once we reach the labyrinth, he makes a sharp left turn and runs ahead of me. He's going the wrong way.

"Duke, wait, where are you going?" He keeps running. I chase after him fearing I will get lost. We pass a row of tall pine trees expertly aligned and manicured. He darts sideways through an opening, and I speed ahead to follow.

Once inside, I drop to my knees and gaze at the magnificent beauty. Must be a million butterflies flittering within a massive glass conservatory encompassing the most incredible botanical garden. I wipe my brow. The humidity is tangible, but the temperature is unchanged.

"Duke, where are you?" He pops out of a huge purple butterfly bush and sits in front me panting. I kneel and scratch his furry cheeks.

"Good boy. I'm not sure why you brought me here but I'm blown away." He licks my face and thumps his tail on the ground.

"Yuk." I giggle and use my shirt to wipe my face.

He leads me on a winding trail of smooth cobblestones in a variety of earth-tone colors. Tall pink hollyhocks line the path along with daylilies, colorful flower bushes, and sunflowers. Too many to describe. The fragrance of sweet florals blended with a hint of fresh herbs tantalizes my senses. I stop and inhale the aroma.

Duke stops at a section where Milkweed dominates the area. He nudges me toward a tree with probably hundreds of cocoons lining its branches. With my eyes fixed on one cocoon, I stare at the unattractive coating holding the beautiful creature captive. The butterfly must feel safe in its tightly wrapped barrier. Kinda like me.

Immediately, the cocoons begin opening and a sea of Monarch butterflies surround me. I stretch my arms sideways, and countless butterflies cover each arm. They are weightless.

Duke barks and twirls around but they do not budge. I laugh uncontrollably.

When I quiet down, a brilliant blue butterfly lands on the tip of my nose. I jerk, but it doesn't flinch. Must be twice the size of the other Monarchs. Not sure what to do, I freeze. The wings gently flow as the creature rests in place.

I receive an impression in my mind saying, *Izzy, you can break free from bondage too and become the beautiful creature God created.* My eyes bulge like they could pop out of my head. A tear trickles down my face.

I watch the blue butterfly leave my nose and disappear into the garden. One by one, the rest of them fly from my arms. A euphoric sensation rushes through my body.

I lower my arms and comb Duke's back with long strokes. He sits and pushes his gigantic body against my leg delicately. I believe it's his way of sharing a hug.

I hear you, Lord. Can I truly break free from my cocoon?

CHAPTER 16

Forgiving Father

I awake in a cold sweat. Jacob and the kids consume my thoughts. I hyperventilate. Is this a panic attack? Duke stares at me with his head on the edge of my bed, whimpering. I rub his forehead, and my breathing normalizes. Each morning, I say a quick prayer. Perhaps today I need more than a brief encounter with God. I need full-blown assurance. Honestly, I don't think I can survive. *Oh, Mother. I understand your heart.*

The pink velvet chaise lounge by the armoire looks inviting. I grab a matching faux fur blanket and cozy up on the chair. Peaceful time with God is what I need. I close my eyes, and my mind refuses to relax. How can I stop the chatter? Instantly, an impression enters my mind. *Be still and know that I am God.* It's Him. It's a reminder to surrender, so I do. Through prayer, I give myself to the Lord, asking Him to lead my life. All of it. My mind is empty. I lie there quietly for a long while, enjoying the sweet serenity of His loving presence.

I pick a lovely floral dress, and Duke and I walk to the sanctuary. My body feels like I'm walking on air. Yet, the heaviest challenge awaits me. Am I capable of forgiving my father?

Arriving at the sanctuary, the scent of Stargazer lilies overwhelms me. A welcome surprise. Fragrant lilies, Mother's favorite, line the path

153

to our quaint sitting area. I soak in the nostalgic aroma and spot a large blue Monarch from the butterfly garden atop my chair. Could it be the same one? I rub the gold key necklace to be sure it's securely fastened and tiptoe toward my oversized chair, trying not to scare the gorgeous creature.

I lower into my chair cautiously and the butterfly hops to my shoulder, giving a few flutters for another day of potential transformation. A welcome gesture. Duke curls up in his favorite spot, and I hear whistling from the counselor who is approaching the sitting area.

I wave. "Good morning, sir."

"Good morning, Izzy." He grins sheepishly and stands over the table between us to pour coffee. He hands me a pink paisley cup. Pink? I shrug and shake my head.

"Counselor, you can predict today's outcome, so hopefully, cheerful whistling is a positive sign."

"I'm whistling because life should be joyful and celebrated. Once we clear out those mind traps, you will understand. Perhaps you'll whistle too."

"I sure hope so."

"Me too. Ready to face the last boulder?"

"If you're serious, I suppose."

"I'm not much of a prankster, am I?" We chuckle.

"No, sir."

"Let's dive in. We already laid the groundwork that forgiveness doesn't eradicate your father's actions and choosing to be estranged can't change the consequences of those actions. Do you agree?"

"I guess so."

"No one lives free from pain, tragedies, or disappointments. The key is how we respond."

"Got it."

"This is where free will matters most. You can continue dwelling on the casualties caused by your parents' choices and keep expanding the negative effect through the punishment of separation, or you can extend grace and forgive. Your choice."

"It's not that easy."

He pauses. "Do you understand the consequences of your choices since your mother's death?"

"What consequences?"

"For starters, the lack of reconciliation with your father is an endless tragedy that far exceeds your mother's death and his infidelity? Not to mention depriving your children of a grandfather." He blows on the steaming cup with one eye closed.

My mouth drops open. "How can you say such a thing?"

"Because it's the truth. By holding yourself hostage to the pain and suffering for decades, you added to the casualties of her death and your father's betrayal."

"You're defending him?"

"Not at all. I'm pointing out the never-ending pain from events occurring decades ago, and you can end it. Reconciliation is the ultimate answer."

I grip the armchair. "But he chose another family."

"I'm not defending his transgressions, we are addressing your role in the aftermath."

"You said I needed to forgive him but never mentioned reconciliation. What are you suggesting?"

"First, forgiving your father here with me. To release the entire burden and end your part in the mess, you must forgive him directly before it's too late."

"What? You expect me to reconcile with him now? After all these years? There's no way." I stand and pace as he keeps talking.

"The day your mother died, your father lost a wife and four children. You lost two parents and never properly grieved the loss of your mother until now. You never grieved the loss of your father at seventeen. Instead, you've allowed anger and guilt to replace grief."

"To my knowledge, my father is alive. Why would I grieve?"

"Since you were six, your father's time with you was minimal. You lost any remaining interaction with him the day your mother died and choose to never speak to him again. Most people might consider your decision rational by human standards. But God's ways are not your ways."

I stop pacing and stare at the ground. "Is it necessary for me to forgive him and instigate a relationship after decades of no contact? Haven't I been through enough because of him? Besides, he's not asking for my forgiveness."

"True. Forgiving him will set you free. To reconcile with him brings redemption."

I sigh. "I can't do it, Counselor."

"Izzy, you asked to be free from your miserable mind trap. This is the way. Don't you want to find out if he's changed?"

"What? How could a man like that change?"

"With God, anything is possible. I understand you're still angry, but ask yourself this question. What purpose does this endless punishment serve?"

"Endless punishment? That's how you see it?"

"The consequences of your father's lifestyle decisions and betrayal resulted in losing everyone he loves. No question, he made monumental mistakes. The consequences of your response to the tragic events compounded the pain and cost you a relationship with your father, a grandfather to your kids, and crippling sorrow. You can't replace those lost years."

I pull the gold key back and forth on the necklace chain for an awkward silence. Is this conceivable? "What would I say? I can't drift into my father's life expecting to be Daddy's little girl."

"Is it possible that you hunger for a father and daughter relationship like the one every little girl dreams about?"

I'm ready to defend myself but unable to speak. His face becomes blurry through my water-filled eyes, and I'm stunned. After swallowing a few lumps in my throat, I continue.

"Oh, my goodness. Is that what I'm doing? Still craving the fairytale father and daughter relationship? How pathetic."

"You tell me."

I glance at the clear sky. "I hate admitting the truth. Even when he was home on the weekends, the mysterious phone calls kept him from us. Father talking to his girlfriend right in front of us sickens me. I can't see him." I push back and close my eyes in silent disapproval.

"Let's focus on working through the pain you feel, and let God reveal whether you meet and reconcile. Sound good?"

I linger on the mental images of Father's neglectful behavior and my desire to have been Daddy's little girl. A lost opportunity. How do I move beyond the pain of my past? Thoughts of my family remind me why I'm here. Returning home is my goal. I open my eyes and flop my hands in my lap.

"Let's do this before I chicken out. How?"

"The same way we confronted the trauma of your mother's death. What's the worst outcome you can imagine by forgiving your father and meeting with him?"

I huff. "I'm stuck on the belief that I'm letting him off the hook."

"Still?"

"I must be honest."

"Fair enough. Why do you think you're choosing a false belief?"

I play with a string in the chair's fabric. "Control."

"I urge you to accept the truth in knowing he's not off the hook, and start over."

"Give me a second. I've never thought about seeing him again."

"Take your time."

"He'd make excuses and wouldn't accept responsibility for destroying our family."

"Is that truly the worst? Dig deep, Izzy."

Sitting back in my chair processing, I try to visualize the scene with him. What is my greatest fear? Is it an embarrassing confrontation? Then it hits me as the vision focuses on me riding my father's suitcase down the hallway.

"He rejects me again. I don't want to give him any more opportunities to disappoint me. I couldn't bear the pain."

"Ah, I think we reached the core of the layers. You assume his rejection and you're terrified of the painful disappointment."

"You nailed it."

"And if your father is not in your life, he cannot hurt you, correct?"

"Right. I'm in control."

"Then why are you still hurting? You haven't seen him in decades."

I stare at him with a flushed face. "Good point. Why am I?"

"You're avoiding the actions necessary to eliminate your pain. Imagine your soul like a reservoir overflowing with polluted and stagnant water. No more room. We must empty the polluted reservoir and refill it with pure fresh water."

"How?"

"Surrender the dark past to God, become empty, and make room for a bright future, like what we've been doing all along. Forgiveness will open the floodgates to flush out the toxic water and let the new, freshwater flow to cleanse the mind trap."

"I understand. My reservoir stinks." I give Him a slight grin. "I must laugh at myself, Counselor. Otherwise, I will sit here and bawl, as usual."

"Humor is the best antidote. Soon, everything will be okay."

"I trust you. Tell me what to do next."

"Empty your toxic reservoir by accepting and owning the truth through the mind trap method you labeled. Not erase any wrongdoing by your father. That's impossible. Accept the past at face value and allow room for new beginnings."

"Okay. Let's empty the polluted waters."

"I like your enthusiasm. Before we begin, realize a life is never void of sadness or disappointments. You will have more, but you will manage them from a healthy adult viewpoint versus the wounded child. Am I making sense?"

"Perfect sense."

"Good. Your father admitted his affair and betrayal to you and your siblings. He asked you to live with him and tried to speak with you and your siblings for years following her death. You cut off communications and haven't spoken to him since your mother's death."

"I'm sorry, but it sounds like you're defending him again?"

"I'm simply stating the facts. Have I said anything untrue?"

I peer at the ground with my arms crossed. "No."

"Okay. Among the disappointments in your life, most of your experiences are pleasant. Dare I say, even happy?"

"Yes." I unfold my arms.

"Izzy, can you accept your past as is, including the good, the bad, and the messy?"

"I want to." I chew on my lower lip. "It sounds good in theory, but is it realistic?"

"It's your choice. You control your suffering more than you realize."

Taking some deep breaths, I pause for an extensive silence, taking it all in. He's speaking the truth. I can't deny it. If I acknowledge the lies and own the truth, there could be hope for my future back home. I'm sick of feeling miserable inside. It's time.

"Before our time together, my life seemed so fragmented and messy, like you said. I couldn't see the truth through the pain. I admit you've helped me organize the memories, and it's becoming more rational and clearer each day."

"That's great. Perhaps the reservoir is draining?"

"I think the stench might be weakening." We chuckle.

"Do you accept the truth?"

"I do. I'm not saying my reservoir is empty yet, but it's insane to believe lies once exposed, right?"

"I wouldn't advise it." He scratches his head as if he's holding back.

"What is it, Counselor?"

"I have one more truth to share regarding your father."

I lean forward. "What is it?"

"He loved you the minute he laid eyes on you, and he's never stopped."

My eyes well up, and I'm too choked to speak. After my throat clears, I stammer. "Whoa. I would love to believe you, but I can't."

"What would convince you?"

I glance around the garden. "I guess hearing it straight from his mouth."

"Precisely. That's why it's imperative for you to meet with him."

"Ugh. I walked right into that one."

He raises one finger. "Before you visit him, I have a favor to ask. It's very important."

"You're already assuming a visit? And what favor?"

"I want you to visit your Aunt Maggie's home and ask her to share your father's letter stored in the hat box wrapped with turquoise paisley material. Once she hears those words, she will hand you a letter to read before meeting with your father. Go to her house to read it. She should not bring it to you."

I inch to the edge of my chair. "Wait, what letter? What does it say? Did you say paisley box?"

"Yes. You'll find out everything once you retrieve the letter. But you must follow my exact instructions. That's all I can share." He leans back in his chair and smiles.

"Unfair. You sound certain I will see him."

"I'm sure of many things, Izzy."

Is this really happening? He believes I'm going to visit my father and read a letter. It sounds absurd. Everything he's taught me so far is true and life changing. I must stay open-minded.

"I need time to process everything I've learned. I'm concerned it won't stick, and I can't help wishing I had this knowledge years ago. Imagine how different my life would be."

"It doesn't matter. Always look forward and never look back. Keep learning God's ways and share my teachings with others to bring God glory. The pathway to joy develops through an intimate relationship with the Lord and by leaning on the Holy Spirit's guidance daily. Will you look forward and keep growing?"

"I will, Counselor. Thank you."

"My pleasure. Once again, I'm impressed with your progress. From this day forward, you can enjoy your life with renewed energy, gladness, and overtime, free from those dreadful mind traps."

"Am I finished? Can I go home?"

"Not yet. There's more to discover about mending your marriage with Jacob."

I lower my head. "So close."

"You don't want to miss the secrets of a successful marriage, do you?"

"Certainly not. I've come this far. Thoughts of reuniting with Jacob and restoring our love affair from college warm my heart. I can't wait."

"Excellent. The secrets will surprise you."

"I'm not surprised." We stand and Duke stands and stretches his legs. "Care to walk me to the bungalow, sir?"

"I'm always delighted to walk with you, Izzy."

We mosey to the bungalow in silence. My mind sizzles. Could

tomorrow be our last session? Will I see my beloved family soon? My heart sinks with thoughts of Jacob. Whatever secrets the counselor has, is it too late to save our marriage?

CHAPTER 17

Isabelle's Fate

JACOB

Startled by a loud buzzer, I jump to my feet. The clock reads 6:17 a.m. Medical staff rush into Isabelle's room, pushing me out of their way. What is happening?

"Mr. Beckham, please wait in the hall."

"What's going on?"

"Please go."

I wander toward the door as the team uses defibrillators on Isabelle's chest. Is this it? Am I losing her? I cover my mouth and look for Nurse Wanda. I notice her limping toward me with a concerned face. She approaches me and ushers us into the waiting area around the corner.

"Wanda, what's going on?"

"Isabelle is flatlining and they are working to revive her. Wait here and pray. That's what she needs most." She turns to leave, but I pull her arm back.

"Are you kidding me? I want to be with her."

"Listen to me, Jacob. Let them do their job. She's in expert hands."

"Why now? What changed?"

"Her heart rate is weakening, so we've been monitoring her closely throughout the night."

I rub my forehead. "You should have wakened me."

"Why? Worry and lose sleep all night? Let's pray she comes out of this."

We pray for several minutes. Then Isabelle's doctor approaches us with a look of relief. I hope I'm reading his face correctly.

"Doc, is she okay?"

"She pulled through this time, but I'm concerned about her weak heart rate."

"Oh, thank You, God." I bend over, blowing out puffs of air.

"Mr. Beckham, it's good news for now, but I'm not sure she will survive the day. The brain swelling is the same, but she's too weak for surgery. My advice is to notify your close family members. I'm so sorry."

I cover my face and pray silently for God to intervene. "She's a fighter. She will overcome this. Give her more time."

He nods. "We are doing all we can."

"I am confident you are."

"I'll check on her later."

The doctor backs away and exits. He doesn't know Isabelle the way I do. No one does. She will wake up and recover. Wanda grabs my shoulder.

"Come on, let's go see her."

"Thanks, Wanda." I hurry to Isabelle's side, peering over her mangled body. I lean over and kiss her forehead, and her eyes twitch. I blink to be sure my eyes are not tricking me.

"Wanda, did you see that? Her eyes twitched."

Wanda moves closer to Isabelle. "Did her eyes open?"

"They didn't open, but I saw movement. Is she waking up?"

"Child, don't get your hopes up. It's probably reflexes from the electric shock."

"Could be, but they flinched right after my kiss. Not a coincidence."

She chuckles. "Then don't stop kissing her. Everything helps. I'll keep watching for eye movement and inform the doctor."

"Good."

I linger by Isabelle's bed, waiting for her eyes to flinch again. Could be God's signal to keep my faith alive. I should call Isabelle's siblings and share this latest update. The one I dread calling is her Aunt Maggie. I reach in my pocket for my phone, but I am distracted by Travis and Katie entering the room. A welcome sight.

"Hi, Dad, how is she today? Any changes?"

"Hi, kids. Unfortunately, I have some sad news."

Katie gasps and I recap the morning's events with them. They rush to their mother's side and Katie grabs a tissue. Travis caresses Isabelle's arm as they speak positive words over her in an emotionally charged moment.

"Mom's stable. I'll step out and call Uncle Roger and your aunts with the status."

"Okay, Dad," Travis says. "We'll watch over Mom."

Luckily for me, the waiting room is empty. I place the first call to Roger and share the news. He offers to call Abbey and Shannon, so I agreed with tremendous relief. I need extra energy for Aunt Maggie. I ring her number.

"Hello, Jacob. How cute, your face pops up on my phone screen. How's my darlin' Isabelle doing?"

"Hi, Aunt Maggie. I have some news."

"Oh, good Lord, don't tell me she's gone. It's too soon."

"No. No. I'm sorry. She's still with us but we had a scare this morning. The medics revived her, and she's stable now."

"What a relief."

"It certainly is."

"On God's green earth, I can't imagine why this is happening to our precious Isabelle. Can I see her?"

"That's why I'm calling. Even though I believe she will wake up and recover, the doctor recommended I call her closest relatives. She's very weak."

"Honey, I'm so glad you did. This is awful. Let me call Phyliss and tell her I can't make the Peachtree Pastries fundraiser because I need to see my baby Isabelle. They will understand. I'll be there this afternoon. You hang in there."

"Thank you. Drive safely."

"I will, sugar. Bye now."

I end the call and close my eyes. *God, give me strength.* Where is He? A few seconds later, I'm reminded to check on Isabelle. Entering her room, I'm greeted with smiles from both kids.

"Travis, what's going on?"

"Her eyes are moving."

"Did they open?"

"No. But they are moving around. Is she waking up?"

"I saw her eyes twitch earlier. Let me get Wanda." I sprint toward the nurses' station, but she's not around. Another nurse approaches me.

"Mr. Beckham, I'm Nurse Dottie, can I help you?"

"Yes. Come quick."

We approach Isabelle's room as I explain the eye movement we saw. The nurse bends over Isabelle and lifts her eyelids with her fingers. She waves her hands across her face, almost shouting Isabelle's name. She doesn't flinch or look directly at the nurse. Just a blank stare.

"Dottie, what do you think?"

"Mr. Beckham. I'm sorry to disappoint you, but she's not responding. It's common to see eye movement during a coma state. Occasionally, eyes open with a blank stare, but no focus or speech. It's not a bad sign either, so let's stay hopeful."

Katie turns her back to us, sniffling. Travis pulls a tissue from the box and hands it to his sister.

I stiffen and stare at Nurse Dottie with a desperate look. "She's coming back to us. I feel it in my bones."

The nurse's eyes soften, and her lips curve into a gentle smile.

I frown and place my hands on my hips. "I don't need your pity. We need a miracle."

"I didn't mean—"

"It's okay, Dottie. I understand." The nurse scurries out of the room. I pace beside Isabelle's bed and stare at her bruised face.

"Your Uncle Roger and Aunt Magie are on their way here. It won't be long." I ask the kids to stay with their mother for a while. They agree.

Travis steps in front of me. "Where are you going?"

"I have an idea that might help bring your mother back."

"What is it?"

I smile widely for the first time in days. "You'll see. Watch over your mom, and I'll be back as quickly as possible. Please, call me if anything changes."

I grab my jacket and lunge through the doorway to the elevator. I hit the down arrow repeatedly. Why didn't I think of this sooner?

CHAPTER 18

A Bad Dream

ISABELLE

Startled, I rise out of a deep sleep, a bad dream. No, a nightmare. Reaching under the covers, I touch my legs and wiggle them. Grabbing both shoulders, I release my hands and count ten fingers. I'm okay. Sucking in the pure air in the room, I exhale. I am alive and uninjured. I blink a few times. What a terrible dream. Or was it?

Perhaps I had a glimpse of my body's condition when I return. Broken legs, or worse, paralyzed. With so much focus on healing my soul, the need for physical healing back home escaped me. Oh, my gosh. How could I be so naïve about the potential harm caused by heavy tree branches? I need to speak with the counselor. He will tell me the truth.

I shimmy into faded jeans, throw on a white t-shirt and call for Duke. We sprint to the sanctuary. My mind is frantic. Did the counselor assure a full recovery or just waking up? I don't remember.

Arriving at the garden spot, I rest one hand on the back of my chair, trying to catch my breath. Duke pants and sips water from his bowl nearby.

The counselor arrives shortly after us. "Izzy, what's wrong? It's not even morning yet."

I try to speak, still catching my breath. I hold up one finger.

"Please sit. Breathe deeply and tell me what's happened."

"I had a terrifying nightmare that my body was in critical condition back home, with severe injuries from the fallen tree, maybe even paralyzed. I saw myself lying in the hospital bed unconscious and sensed I wouldn't walk again. Is this true? Will I recover and walk again?"

"I'm so sorry about your scare. Upon your return, you will awaken from your coma, but that's all I can reveal."

I jerk back. "I could be paralyzed?"

"It's a possibility."

Staring at the ground, I struggle to think. My mind is swirling with terrible thoughts of the accident and my family wondering if I will wake up. Panic sets in.

"I want to go home now, Counselor. I need to know if I'm going to wake up crippled."

"Izzy, you may return whenever you wish, but you will miss the remaining insights about your marriage. Are you sure?"

I pace the area. "I'm scared."

"I understand. I presented the consequences, and your choice to stay has been a blessing. Now, you're assuming the worst-case scenario about your physical condition. Truth is, you don't know the outcome."

"The dream seemed so vivid."

"Have you had other lifelike dreams?"

"Yes. Except I hadn't considered my physical recovery until the realistic nightmare. More uncertainty awaits me."

"You can't predict what tomorrow brings. God doesn't promise a flawless, pain-free life to anyone."

I take my seat. "True. I expect to have injuries from the accident, and it must be serious if I'm still unconscious. I'm frightened. Why can't you tell me if I'm going to walk again?"

"I'm sorry. I can share certain details, but you must discover the outcome on your own. Remember our discussion about trials being an opportunity to grow closer to God?"

"I do." I stare at the sky with my hands limp in my lap.

"God is with you, regardless of the outcome. He will never leave you. Are you still interested in returning home right now?"

"We're supposed to talk about restoring my marriage. I need that. If I leave, it's out of fear, not the right reason to go back. I can learn more from you, Counselor."

"Well, I'm never short on life lessons, am I?"

I release my pent-up emotions with a heavy sigh. Somehow, he provides what I need to hear, giving me courage. "I'll stay."

"Good."

"I haven't slept long. How did you know I was here needing your guidance?"

"I'm always aware. It's understandable to be concerned, since this is a rare circumstance. But let's talk about reactions. With reason, you assumed the worst outcome with your physical condition, and we've already established this as your typical thought process."

"Yes. Instinctively, I run through the worst-case scenario by defining multiple outcomes and play out in my head how to respond."

"Is that useful?"

"It's automatic. The chatter in my head helps me plan and prepare for the worst. My imaginary outcomes rarely take place, so I waste time thinking about fictional situations. Afterwards, I'm relieved because the worst outcome didn't happen, yet I'm frustrated for worrying over nothing."

"Then, why do it?"

"I feel smart and in control by anticipating upcoming disappointments."

"Were you able to control those outcomes?"

"No. Most situations turn out fine and nothing like what I conjured up."

"Do you use this approach for every situation?"

"I think so. I use it when challenges crop up at work, vacation planning, family situations, and the kids' college life."

"So, imaginary drama in your head causes the stress, correct?"

I tap my cheek. "I guess. It sounds silly when you put it that way."

"It's not silly, it's a reckless mindset."

"Oh great, another mind trap?"

"Not a new one. This thought pattern links to the rejection mind trap because the trigger is potential disappointment, an emotion linked with rejection. During your early years, your mind associated disappointment with the same pain as rejection. In the worst-case scenario, you might not feel rejection, but sensing potential disappointment prompts your mind to release a similar thought pattern of false beliefs used as a coping mechanism to avoid pain. Plus, giving you a false sense of control."

"It sounds complicated, but I'm following."

"Do you remember our discussion when we uncovered the rejection mind trap and misinterpreting your children's view of you and Jacob?"

"I'll never forget it."

"Good. What emotion triggered the misinterpretations of your children's thoughts about you?"

"Insecurity because I wasn't good enough."

"And when you expect a challenge or obstacle, what is the emotional trigger?"

"Disappointment by feeling let down."

"And when both emotional triggers occurred, what happened in your mind?"

"I created false ideas and lied to myself."

"That's correct. And what is the antidote for ending false beliefs and negative thought patterns?"

"The truth."

"You've got it, Izzy. And how do you apply the truth?"

"I use the mind trap method. First, I pray for awareness and for God to reveal the negative thought pattern. Second, I disrupt the pattern by challenging the lies. Third, I replace the lies with the truth."

"Good. Every time you sense worry and start creating worst-case scenarios, ask yourself if you're dealing with reality. Are you evaluating facts or worrying about non-existent experiences? That's the question."

"I will try, but it's so automatic it's going to be difficult to identify."

"Be patient, Izzy. It takes time to break unconscious habits, but now you are aware of the choice to either experience phony mental imagery or live according to actual events. If you choose truth, you will only manage genuine challenges and disappointments. Why add unnecessary issues when there is already enough trouble in your day?"

"Yeah. It's illogical."

"Remember, the Holy Spirit always reveals the truth. Relying on God's strength and becoming closer to Jesus enables the truth to flow automatically."

I lift my finger in the air. "Yes. Patience and God's strength. A killer combo."

I'm in awe of the counselor's knowledge. The intensity of his confidence and friendship ooze from his presence today. I press my heart with watery eyes. I'm blessed.

"Your dream left you panicked about your physical condition. How do you feel about it now?"

"Whoa. Give me a minute to process."

"Take your time."

I sit for a few moments in the thinker position. "A healthy mind seeks reality and handles what is true. With God, of course."

"Impressive. Am I sitting in front of the same person? You arrived frazzled, yet now you're calm and courageous. Did the information about your accident change?"

I look at the ground with my arms limber. "No, sir."

"Splendid. You should return to the bungalow for a complete night's rest."

"I suppose."

Reluctant to leave, the counselor persuades me, and Duke nudges my legs with his nose. I'm eager to discover the secrets that could save my marriage. Thoughts of Jacob serenading me beside the stream in college enter my mind. I stop and close my eyes to zero-in on the memory. It seems like yesterday.

"Izzy, are you coming?"

"Yes, sir."

A little longer, I must be patient.

CHAPTER 19

The Anchor

JACOB

After a quick ride to the house, I drive back to the hospital, park the car in the high-rise garage, and race to the elevator. Through the hallways, medical personnel stare at the large object I'm carrying in one hand with a few sharing warm looks and smiles. I wonder if they understand the power of this instrument. Finally, reaching Isabelle's room, I'm greeted with a compassionate look by Roger seated next to her bed, holding her lifeless hand.

"Roger, it's so good to see you." I stretch out my hand.

"You too, Jacob." He stands and gives me a giant bear hug, ignoring the handshake. I'm a tall guy, and he's a head taller. Roger is a successful venture capitalist and dresses like he just stepped out of GQ magazine. Despite his height, Isabelle resembles Roger the most with similar ginger hair and freckles. I wish we spent more time together.

"Roger, did you reach Shannon and Abbey?"

"I did. They're coming together tonight."

"Great. Aunt Maggie is coming this afternoon."

"Oh, boy."

"I know. I will do my best to keep her calm."

"Good luck with that." We chuckle as he points at my guitar. "Getting the band back together?"

"Very funny. I thought the guitar might help stimulate something. Maybe if I sing to her like I used to, she will recognize my voice and come back. Hey, I'm grasping at straws here."

He pats my shoulder. "Not at all. I think it's a great idea, bro. I've heard the college creek story at least fifty times."

I lean the guitar against the wall. "I should have been doing this since day one. The idea hit me after almost losing her this morning. You been here long?"

"About thirty minutes. I haven't seen a nurse yet, but the kids said her heart rate is still extremely weak."

"Yes. The doctor is deeply concerned and so are we. Where did Travis and Katie go?"

"They just slipped out to give me a moment with Sis."

"Good. Spend some time with your sister, and I'll be back shortly. I'll track them down and grab coffee. Want some?"

"Sure. But am I holding you up from singing?"

"It's okay. Hearing her big brother's voice is good medicine."

I leave Roger and head toward the hospital café. Despite our problems, I reflect on my incredible life with Isabelle. It can't end.

"Dad, over here." I look to my left and Travis waves me over.

"How are you guys holding up?"

"We're okay. Just giving Uncle Roger some time with Mom. Where did you go?"

"I went home to get my guitar." My face warms.

"Awe. Dad, that is so cute. Mom will love it." Katie lightly claps her hands with teary eyes. The unknown outcome is taking a toll.

"Thanks. It might be silly, but that song by the trout stream bonds us together. I'll try anything to waken her."

Travis shakes his head and smiles. "We're aware, Dad. We've heard the story a thousand times."

I purse my lips. "It can't hurt, Travis."

"Totally agree. So, what are you waiting for?"

"I'm giving your uncle some private time."

Katie touches my hand. "Dad, he will understand."

"I guess, you're right. Why wait any longer? Please get coffee for Uncle Roger and me, and I'll meet you back in the room."

"We got this. Go, Dad." I salute the kids and race to Isabelle's room. Nurse Dottie scowls at me like a teacher scolding a student running through the halls. Wanda's head rises above the computer screen with wide eyes.

"Jacob, what are you up to?"

"You'll see, Wanda. I mean, you'll hear."

"Child, I wonder about you."

Roger is putting on his coat as I enter her room. Good timing.

"Sorry, Jacob. I got called back to the office. Raincheck on the coffee?"

"Of course."

"My heart breaks seeing my little sister like this. I hope she senses I'm here."

"I think she does."

Roger leans into her ear. "I love you, sis. Please come back to us." He kisses her forehead and hovers over her for a tender moment. He turns to me, and we hug like football players before the big game and say our goodbyes.

I close the door behind Roger, grab my guitar, and clear my throat. Do I still have the magic touch? With butterflies in my stomach, I sit beside Isabelle's bed. It's like college all over again. I tune the guitar, stalling. My fingers fumble with the strings as the creekside memory syncs with the melody in my head.

The first lyrics are shaky as my vocal cords warm up. In no time, I tap my feet and belt out the original love song dedicated to my sweet Isabelle. I'm so enthralled, I don't hear Wanda shouting my name, but I feel her sharp tap on my shoulder and stop.

"Jacob, are you crazy? You can't play that loudly in ICU." She stands back with her hands on her hips.

"I'm so sorry. I got carried away."

She waves her finger. "This is new. What's this about?"

"I'm serenading her with our special song. Maybe following my voice will guide her back. I wrote this song for Isabelle and sang it to her in college. She loves it."

"Is that right?" She rolls her eyes and smiles. "Child, you are quite the charmer. I'm going to do you a favor."

"Really?"

"Yes. Lower the volume and keep singing. I'll cover you if anyone complains."

"You're the best, Nurse angel." I raise my hand for a high-five. She slaps my hand and steps out. This time, I sing quietly, close to Isabelle's ear for an hour, with no reaction. Not a single eye twitch.

I hear a knock and rest the guitar in my chair. Aunt Maggie pokes her head through the door and enters with her arms extended.

"Oh, for pity's sake, look at you. Give me a hug, sugar. You must be exhausted." We embrace and she squeezes me like she's making fresh orange juice. I pull back unable to breathe, holding her palms.

"Aunt Maggie, thank you for coming so quickly. It's a long drive from the Georgia coast."

"Are you kidding me? Wouldn't miss seeing Isabelle for anything. How are you holding up?"

"Best I can."

"You are a charming husband, and that girl adores you."

"And I adore her."

She taps my cheek. "You two are so precious. I can't believe this is happening. It's just awful."

"It's a nightmare."

I take her coat and gesture for her to sit next to Isabelle's bed, removing the guitar. Aunt Maggie prides herself as a traditional southern belle wearing a frilly full-length dress and a floppy hat. Looks like she just left church or a photo shoot with *Southern Living*. She's the real deal. Her fried green tomatoes and peach cobbler are the best I've ever tasted. Despite being overly dramatic, she has a tender heart and loves Isabelle like a daughter. I'm glad she's here.

"Oh, my good Lord, look at her just lying there not moving with her broken bones and bruises." She covers her face.

"Can you handle this?"

She waves her hanky at me. "Don't worry, I'm a tough old bird."

She blows her nose. "I just feel terrible. The last time we spoke, we had a little argument. I need to apologize if she can hear me."

"What about?"

"I was meddling again. Every time I bring up her daddy, she gets furious with me. Although it's not in my nature to sit by and say nothing, I should butt out. It's hard watching my baby brother and his kids still separated and hurting. I'll keep praying for restoration."

"Isabelle never mentioned this."

"Believe me, it's a quick conversation. I try to convince her to meet with him, she says no, end of story. Because of her sensitivity about the past, I don't mention it often. Wish I'd kept my mouth shut the last time."

"She doesn't talk about her father or her past with anyone, to my knowledge. It's a forbidden topic."

"Not surprised. I keep praying for a miracle meeting someday. If she would just listen, things might change. My baby brother is different now, but little miss Isabelle won't hear me out. I love her dearly, but she can be stubborn."

She pulls a tissue from the nightstand and pats her eyes. I rest my hand on her shoulder, and she taps it.

"Please take your time with her, Aunt Maggie. The doctors say she can hear us, speak freely. I'll check in later."

"Thank you, sugar. I won't be long because I can't drive after dark."

"I'll step out into the waiting area to give you some privacy."

"No need to leave, sugar. I prefer you stay."

"Okay, no problem." I glance at Isabelle, expecting eye movement. Nothing. Her heart rate is the same according to the digital monitor. My head drops and I sit near the door to give Aunt Maggie space to speak with Isabelle. I glance at my guitar. What did I expect? A miraculous awakening from one song? What a fool.

Aunt Maggie's voice escalates. "Isabelle, please wake up. Your family is deeply worried, and life would change drastically without you. The last time we spoke, I upset you and I'm so sorry, sugar. Oh, my lucky stars, you heard me. Jacob, come quick."

Aunt Maggie stands and waves her hands. "Isabelle's eyes are moving."

I join her alongside Isabelle's bed, but the movement stopped.

"Say something, darlin'." Aunt Maggie says.

Nothing. I caress Isabelle's swollen cheek. "Her eyes flinched and moved around earlier, but according to the medical staff, it's normal with coma patients."

"Oh, what do those fancy doctors know? Her eyes twitched when I spoke to her. It's a sign from God she's coming back. I know it, Jacob."

"Me too. I feel it in my bones, so I'm not giving up either."

"For heaven's sake, no. She's a fighter and if anyone can pull through this, it's our Isabelle. Never give up."

I place my hand around her shoulders and apply a gentle squeeze. She looks up. "Thank you. I needed that today."

She blows her nose and points to my guitar.

"How sweet. Are you singing to her?"

"Yes. Just thought of it today. So far, no reaction."

"Well, you keep singing your little heart out. I believe she hears you."

"I will."

"I'm going to hurry on home to beat the sunset and leave you two lovebirds alone."

"So soon?"

"I must. Are the children here?"

"Yes. Travis and Katie are in the hospital café on their laptops. I'm sure they'd love to say hello. Isabelle's critical condition is taking a toll on them, but they are real troopers. I'm proud of them."

"As you should be. They are wonderful kids. I'll stop by on my way out."

I help her with her coat, and she pauses for one last look towards Isabelle. She rests her hand on my crossed arms. "Keep praying, sugar. She's in God's hands."

"You bet." I receive another intense body squeeze before she leaves the room.

Love birds? More like strangers. I sit beside Isabelle contemplating. If the tree hadn't fallen, would we be meeting with divorce attorneys or walking in the park eating chocolate ice cream? The last twenty years are a flurry. We lost ourselves separately with demanding careers and active kids. But, when I tried to fix it, nothing seemed to make her happy. Even if she awakens, is it too late for us?

I grab my guitar and sing quietly to avoid another reprimand from Nurse Wanda. After several minutes, I break for water and relieve my parched throat. When I turn around, Isabelle's eyes flutter.

I press her arm. "Isabelle, are you coming back?"

Marriage Secrets

ISABELLE

My throbbing head wakes me. I touch the right side of my chin, pinpointing the source. I toss the covers open, sit upright and leap out of bed to peek in the full-length mirror beside the armoire. After a few soft taps on the bruise, it fades into my skin. It vanishes. Am I hallucinating? I search for Duke. Where is he? I call for him, and he strolls into the bedroom with perked ears. Thank goodness he's here.

I've experienced serious emotional distress but never physical pain during my time here. I sense another urgency to see the counselor, so I race to get ready and ask Duke to lead us to the garden sanctuary.

Morning dew blankets the landscape, and I rub my naked arms briskly. Dew? Something has changed. I lose sight of Duke and take a shortcut. When rounding the corner of the labyrinth, I run smack into a scrawny elderly man, knocking him over. I gasp and then bend over to help him up.

"Oh, I am so sorry, sir. I'm in such a hurry and didn't see you coming around the corner. Are you okay?" I hand him his derby hat.

He stands and brushes off his trousers. "It's okay, Isabelle. I'm fine."

I take a few steps back. "How do you know my name? Who are you?"

He gives me an awkward grin. "We all know. Besides, I helped design this place specifically for you. Forgive my impoliteness, name's Bernard, but folks call me Bernie. I'm in charge of the grounds and gardens. It's an absolute pleasure to meet you."

He holds out his hand. After a long stare, I reach out to shake his. He gently rolls my hand over, kissing the top like I'm a queen. With flushed cheeks, I jerk my hand from his.

"It's nice to meet you, Bernie. You're telling me this magnificent place is solely for me?"

"Uh, yes. I expected you knew."

"The counselor is the only person I've seen here."

"I'm honored, but it's my fault we bumped into each other. By now, I should have reached the other side of the labyrinth. My timing got messed up, that's all. Please forgive my oversight."

"It's all right. Meeting another person is a treat. Besides, I'm the one who should apologize. I took a shortcut and plowed into you. I'm a little out of sorts today."

"No harm done, and I'm sorry to hear that."

I grin. "I'm feeling better now, meeting with you."

"Well, I'm glad. We try to stay out of sight, so you can focus your precious time on the counselor's messages. Quiet, intentional time with Him is the number one priority. Needless distractions and chatter from others offer no value when interacting with Him."

He pats my arm. "You have a team of invisible cheerleaders working around you, and you don't even realize it."

"That's kind of you to say. Tell me more about this place."

He bows and then places the derby hat on his head. "I'm sorry, I must get back to tending the gardens. You run along. The counselor is waiting. I'm so glad to have met you, Isabelle. We're all praying for you."

I hold up one finger. "Wait."

And before I can blink, he disappears. What's happening today? So many inconsistencies. My reaction is to worry and start thinking about negative reasons for these anomalies. Now, I have the tools and knowledge to focus on the truth and actual events. I examine my arms. I'm not harmed or in trouble, so I should keep moving about my day. It will unfold as planned.

Duke's bark echoes in the distance. I follow his barking to catch up. Am I being tested? A thought prompts me to resist old habits and renew my mind. Then I will be able to test and discern what God's will is—His good, pleasing, and perfect will.

God's ways overpowered my typical panic. I saw a bruise on my chin and watched it vanish. Previously, I'd be in a frenzy, but I'm confident there's a logical explanation. My headache is gone, so I'll keep going.

Duke comes into view and dashes towards me, then halts. He jumps, placing both paws on my shoulders, licking my face. I giggle while petting his back until he drops. He seems relieved to find me and, no doubt, part of my cheerleading squad. I gaze at the sky and thank God for Duke's companionship. We rush to the sanctuary.

We arrive at the garden sanctuary. Duke trots ahead, but I pause under the rose-covered trellis and rub my fingers over the engraved sign. The customization of this extraordinary place sinks in, and I notice the counselor already seated in our white comfy chairs. He's always here when I need his wisdom, regardless of the hour.

"Good morning, sir."

"Good morning."

The counselor's appearance is flawless, and his expertly styled silver hair glistens. He's wearing a baggy, white linen shirt and matching pants. Still, no shoes. I suppose certain things must remain a mystery.

I scratch my head. "Strange morning. Woke up with a headache, found a bruise on my chin, but it disappeared when I looked in the mirror. On my walk here, I bumped into Bernie by the labyrinth."

The counselor bends over the table between us and pours coffee into the most exquisite paisley cups yet. He hands me a turquoise and pink paisley cup and saucer. I turn the cup around admiring the intricate detail and take a sip.

"Bernie is a fine chap."

"Yes. A true gentleman."

He offers me a plate of fresh berries and a warm chocolate croissant. Somehow, He knows I missed breakfast at the bungalow, and my favorite foods appear. I take a bite of the flakey croissant which melts on my tongue. I lower my eyes briefly and reopen them.

"Why did I feel pain, see bruises, and experience the temperature change this morning?"

"You're on the final stretch, maybe your return home is approaching?"

"To see Jacob and the kids would be incredible. I hope today is the day."

"Your progress will determine your path home."

We sip coffee and my stomach flips with thoughts of my return. I gaze at Duke and the counselor as reality sinks in. Is this our last day together? I can't imagine being apart from them. My heart skips a beat and tears well up as I peer around the garden sanctuary. I press on my heart.

"Bernie said he helped design this entire place exclusively for me. Is that true?"

"Yes. I explained your surroundings on the first day. Why are you surprised?"

"I misunderstood. Even though I haven't seen anyone else, I assumed others are meeting in private spaces with their counselors on the same property."

"No. This wonderland is one-of-a-kind, created for our special time together."

"So, the lavender fields, butterflies, rose gardens, crystal waterfalls, and the magnificent mansion you call a bungalow, all for me?"

"All for you."

"Why the extravagance? I would be thankful meeting in a stodgy conference room."

"God adores you. He wanted to surround you with exquisite and familiar things to make you more comfortable. It's not a burden."

My eyes well up and I cover my face. I cannot imagine why God would shower me with extravagance.

"I don't deserve this. Especially after learning about God's ways. How can He love me when I've been so neglectful of Him?"

"When you delight yourself in the Lord, He gives you the desires of your heart. You delighted in Him through your desperate prayers and by sticking it out with me. He met you at that precise moment, regardless. Walking with God is a continuous journey, not a one-off event."

I play with the gold key necklace. "Why me? Why don't others receive this gap in time?"

"Why do you assume others don't?"

My eyes bulge. "Because I've never heard of this experience before."

"When tragedies happen, God might use the situation as a wake-up call to reach His children, especially under extreme circumstances like yours. You pleaded for help, and He responded His way."

I lower my head. "I've been lazy with my faith. Uncommitted."

"Has that changed?"

"You bet. He certainly got my attention."

He smiles wide showing his pearly white teeth.

"Never forget. Your ultimate father is Father God in Heaven. If you can grasp the genuine distinction between your earthly father and God above, it will transform the way you view both. Perhaps help strengthen relations with your biological father."

"Back to my father? We don't have a relationship, so I doubt that."

"We shall see." His smile forms into a sheepish grin, and I roll my eyes.

"I find it strange how I've said the Lord's prayer countless times and never thought about God as my *literal* Father figure. Just in reverence."

"That's fine. Because every lesson we've discussed comes together, pointing to one core belief and action."

"Please, tell me."

"God must be first in your life. Think about the way Jesus refers to His Father in the gospels. The reality of the Lord addressing His Father in human form comes to life. Although never perfect like Jesus, your role is to function in the image of Christ and interact with your Heavenly Father the way Jesus did. Do you see?"

"Wow. I do. Jesus demonstrated how to be God's children." I tingle all over. The power of God as my ultimate Father takes root. I have a loving Father, regardless of the outcome with my biological one.

"Izzy, once your heart and mind grasp the magnitude of this belief, you'll live according to God's grace and His will."

"I'm realizing that." I tap my heart. "You're the best teacher. That's what you meant about the need to adjust my priorities, right?"

"Yes."

I flinch. "How do I ensure God is first in my life?"

"Assess your life. Evaluate the individuals, activities, and places consuming your time."

"I see. Kids and work demand most of my attention, leaving Jacob behind."

"See the issue?"

"Yes, but I don't want to neglect Travis and Katie."

"On the contrary. Soon, you'll find every relationship growing stronger and more intentional because you shift to God's ways. With Him positioned as Lord over your life, surpassing all others, His love fills every void and crevasse that even the finest earthly fathers could never supply. Even though you're estranged, your biological father served an important purpose. He brought you into the world and provided for you growing up. Because the past separates you, your life lacks the role of an earthly father in your adulthood. The good news is, he's still alive to provide a greater role. Aren't you being too harsh?"

I fold my arms.

"Izzy, you still have time to develop a relationship with your earthly father if you choose."

"You're stuck on that?"

"I won't let it go. Besides, you promised to visit Aunt Maggie and read your father's letter. You wouldn't break a promise, would you?"

"I thought discussions about my father ended. What about my marriage?" I scowl.

He raises an open palm. "Patience. God wants you to experience seeing your father through godly eyes. You must trust me on this. I'm reiterating the importance of considering a second chance to start fresh with him and see what happens. Are you open to the idea?"

"I'd do anything for you, Counselor. My father's words on paper will decide any next steps, but I promise to pursue his letter even though I doubt a reconciliation is possible."

"Fair enough. One more thing before we get to the chief topic."

I perk up. "Marriage secrets?"

"Indeed. Always remember that regardless of what happens with you and your father, you always have God in Heaven as your Ultimate Dad. That's His promise."

"The same thought hit me earlier, and I'm glad you're confirming it. From the family home movies and our sessions, recognizing the distinction of my earthly father in a more human-like perspective helps." I hesitate. "But it's strange."

"What is?"

"Besides you, only Mr. Merriweather and Aunt Maggie, Father's sister, have encouraged me to reconcile with my father. Isn't it odd that both play a role in this gap with you?"

A sly grin spreads across his face. "Maybe."

"Years ago, Mr. Merriweather asked about my parents. I gave the usual curt reply, saying my mother passed away when I was young, and I hadn't spoken to my father since. Of course, he asked more questions, but I abruptly cut him off. Anyone who asked about my parents quickly realized it was a topic to avoid. But not Mr. Merriweather. He pried and encouraged me to contact Father, saying I should give him another chance. Out of respect, I listened."

"It sounds like Mr. Merriweather cares about you deeply and offers wisdom only a few possess. Take his words to heart. And your aunt?"

"Aunt Maggie is an outrageous character, and I love her. Over the years, she's been relentless about a reunion with my father. I cut her off quicker than Mr. Merriweather. She means well."

We sip our coffee, and thoughts of Mr. Merriweather overtake me. I visualize his impromptu visits eating warm peach pie and listening to his soothing voice. He never left our cottage without mentioning my father. He was brave. I pause for an extended time rubbing my top lip. The counselor waves his hand, gaining my attention.

"Izzy, it's time we move on and reveal the secrets of successful marriages. I've already shared the most important one."

"Did I miss it?"

"No. It's God positioned in the number one spot, but Jacob comes second."

My eyes pop. "Before the kids?"

He scoots to the edge of his seat. "When you and Jacob married, you entered a covenant with God, and the two of you united as one entity. You still love him, don't you?"

"Yes. But it's not the same."

"You prayed for restoration, so you want to stay married, correct?"

"More than ever. Because of our sessions, I'm a new person. Even though we're both guilty of detachment over the years, I recognize how my past interfered in our relationship."

He nods slowly. "Imagine a marriage even better than your honeymoon period."

I slap my leg and laugh. "Are you serious?"

"I'm not a comedian."

We both chuckle and sip more coffee.

"That's true, sir. But you're witty."

"Thank you. Back to your marriage. Each of you spent boundless energy on growing your careers and creating a beautiful life for your children. Kudos on parenting." His hands interlock. "But we're not looking back anymore. Look ahead by seeking God's direction and reunite in a godly marriage. Which means both of you align in your rightful positions second to God."

"We didn't prioritize our marriage God's way, and now we're stuck."

"Are you? Your life is always moving ahead."

I sit upright, staring at my wise counselor. His teachings change everything. Jacob and I are only stuck if we continue the same old, flawed patterns.

"You're right. We have a way out of this rut. Please tell me what to do next."

"You treat Jacob the way God would treat him."

"How? I'm not God."

"Do you remember the morning when the Holy Spirit prompted you to read scripture?"

"Yes. It was in the book of Malachi."

"On those pages God revealed His unconditional love for Jacob."

"I'll never forget the intense encounter and the grace God revealed for Jacob."

"He wanted you to feel His love and acceptance for Jacob. As you gain knowledge about God's ways, your capacity for grace, love, and acceptance will flourish."

"It sounds lofty."

"Selfishness rules every person until surrendering to Christ weakens it, replacing it with a desire to serve others first. Like Jesus did. With a deeper surrender, you'll love and serve Jacob in a way you never understood before, and you'll gain much joy doing it."

"Doesn't that make me less independent and weak?"

"Was Jesus weak when He served the people? Did He depend on His Father?"

My eyes nearly burst. "Heaven's no. I didn't mean to imply that the Lord is weak. The concept struck me as antiquated with me serving Jacob by today's standards."

"Whose standards?"

"Society's?"

"God is not of this world and don't assume it's a one-way street."

"What do you mean?"

"The best example of a godly marriage is two servants in love. When each spouse wants to serve God first, naturally, they serve each other. Equal contributors joyfully nurturing the sanctity of their marriage."

"Why?"

"Because that's God's way, and it brings joy to His children. When applied, it works. Don't you realize God knows what's best for you better than you?"

"It's hard to wrap my head around this concept."

"When you activate the teachings of Jesus, you rise to a much higher standard, and I can prove it to you."

"How?"

"Allow me to use a relatable example. Why are you an exceptional sales executive?"

I stiffen my posture. "People say they can rely on me. I will move mountains for my company, team, and clients to help ensure their success. I'm available around the clock, and I love surprising them with their favorite things."

"Sounds familiar. What types of things?"

"Recently, I gave a co-worker concert tickets for his extra efforts on a tight deadline. Sometimes I hand out gift cards from the local coffee shop to show my gratitude. If a colleague has a concern or family matter, I arrive early or stay late to listen and offer support. Stuff like that."

"There you go. Think of Jacob as the most valuable client you can't lose or disappoint. Perfection doesn't exist but applying this principle will produce the results you both desire."

"Whoa. A lightbulb just exploded in my head. Is it that simple?"

"It depends on the attitude of your heart."

I stare at my feet, hesitating. "If Jacob doesn't reciprocate, then what?"

"Who are you ultimately serving, Izzy?"

"You said Jacob."

"Jacob is second. Who are you serving first?"

"God?"

"Exactly. If you serve God first, you succeed. Bar none. The shift takes time to absorb and don't expect instantaneous change. With practice and focus on bringing glory to God as your primary motive, the best Izzy appears."

"The best Isabelle. I like that."

"The world reflects your deeds. You've heard the expression, 'you reap what you sow.'"

"Yes."

"When you smile at strangers, what happens?"

"Typically, they smile back."

"It will be identical for you and Jacob. Even though you drifted apart, I bet Jacob already expresses love through acts of service, right?"

"He doesn't engage as much, but he still brings me coffee every morning when he's home. While I sit and read in the evenings, he builds a fire in the fireplace. Sounds trivial, yet it's important to me."

"He's a good man. With God as your priority, you can reunite stronger than ever. Based on your proven foundation of love, you don't need to worry. It's your anchor."

I lean forward. "The anchor. I almost forgot."

"Izzy, God doesn't sit by waiting for others to love Him first. He just loves."

My mouth drops. "That's true."

"Never forget this. Even though it's expected to be a two-way street, it only takes one person to put God's character in motion, so trust me, you can do this. Before long, you and Jacob will be madly in love again."

"I would give up anything for that to happen."

"You did."

I jerk, believing I hear music. "Did you hear that?"

"Hear what?"

"Music. It's subtle, but I hear someone in the distance playing a guitar and singing. Don't you hear it?"

"I do now. It's lovely."

I shriek, touching my cheeks. "It's Jacob. He's singing 'Sweet Isabelle.' The love song he wrote and sang to me back at college."

The counselor stands beaming with his arms outstretched. "Izzy, is it time?"

His eyes flash the most exquisite white light. I stand before Him as if paralyzed, and we embrace. Then he whispers in my ear. "Always look forward. You're never alone again."

We release. He kisses me on the forehead, and we face each other holding hands. Duke nudges my right elbow, and I stroke his head. He whimpers. Then I squeeze my eyes shut, clutching the gold key around my neck and pray for courage. I open my eyes.

"Yes, Counselor. I'm ready to go back to Jacob. I want to go home."

CHAPTER 21

The Return

I can't open my eyes. What's happening? The constant chatter and buzzer noises need to stop. My head throbs like a jackhammer. What happened to Jacob singing and playing the guitar? I want to see him, but I don't hear his voice or sense his presence.

"Isabelle, sweetheart, can you open your eyes? It's Nurse Wanda."

The chatter intensifies.

"Isabelle, this is Dr. Abbot. If you can hear me, open your eyes, or squeeze my hand."

Voices repeat saying my eyelids show signs of rapid eye movement. Why can't I open them? Instead, I try to move my hand holding his.

"I felt some movement from her hand. I think she's coming back," he says.

The cheers are deafening. My eyes water and tears trickle down my cheeks.

"Oh, my gosh, she's crying. She's coming out of it. Mom, can you hear me? It's Katie."

"Mom, it's Travis. Can you hear us? Please open your eyes."

Hearing their voices soothes my entire body. I want to reach out and hug my children, but I can't move. Where's Jacob? I'm stuck. Am I going to wake up?

"Darling, it's me, Jacob. Please come back to me." His voice cracks, and I feel his touch on my right hand. My eyes flutter for a few seconds and I open them. I gaze upon the man I love staring back at me with tears flowing down his cheeks. He smiles and leans in to kiss me. My eyes flicker from the bright lights, and I try to focus. A man in a white coat is waving his hands, and I can make him out. Must be Dr. Abbot.

"Okay, everyone. This is incredible news, but I need to check her vitals. Nurse Wanda, please clear the room."

"Yes, sir."

I don't want my family to leave, but I can't speak.

"Isabelle, it's Dr. Abbot. You've been in a coma for several days. I'm thrilled you're waking up, and we need to make sure you stay with us. Fight to stay awake. If you hear me and understand, please squeeze my hand."

Struggling to make any movement, I give my best squeeze.

"Great job. The next several hours are crucial."

The doctor checks my heartbeat and presses my abdomen while giving orders to his team. He asks Nurse Wanda to stay with me, and the rest of them scurry out the door.

"Hi sweet Isabelle, It's Wanda. I've been with you since the accident, and I'm going to take good care of you, girl. Now, try to stay awake for us. Jacob and the kids will be back shortly. When the doctor asked, I had to push Jacob out. That poor man."

Wanda's warm and comforting voice calms my nerves, much like the counselor's. She's blurry, but I see a plump round face with short dark hair, and I sense the strength in her touch. My throbbing head reminds me of the fallen tree that crushed my body. Am I paralyzed? I try to feel every inch, wondering which body parts still function and if they ever will. I can't move my legs or lift my arms.

My heart races. *Stay calm, Isabelle.* I close my eyes, remembering to focus on the actual event, but in this case, reality seems dire. I breathe in and a sharp pain pierces my ribcage area. Not a good sign. My mind shifts to thoughts of the counselor sitting in my peaceful garden sanctuary. The memory is comforting and sad. Jacob and the kids quickly return. I open my eyes and their faces relax. Jacob leans down stroking my hair and kisses my cheek.

"You're going to be okay, my darling. We've been worried to death, but I never lost hope. Prayers were answered. I can't tell you how relieved I am you're awake."

My heart slows to a normal pace after hearing his words. On her tiptoes, peering over Jacob's shoulder, Katie moves forward and Travis steps into my view. Travis looks away, touching the corner of his eye.

Katie takes my hand in both of hers, sporting a bright blue fingernail polish. I stare into her watery green eyes. She looks thinner. Her sleek brown hair falls around her face, flowing down her shoulders. I notice dark circles under her bloodshot eyes. I bet she hasn't slept well for days.

"Mom, I've missed you so much. Really . . . really happy to have you back. I love you."

Travis stands beside his sister with his hands in his pockets, politely waiting for his turn. I glance at him and see a younger version of Jacob —the same tall, slender stature, wavy light-brown hair, and stunning blue eyes. Tiny lines beside his eyes reveal the stress, despite his lingering tan. They've endured a lot. Katie kisses my cheek and steps aside so Travis can have my attention.

"Mom, you look more beautiful than ever." His face softens, and he smiles widely, showing his pearly white teeth.

Jacob raises his hand. "I agree."

My attempt to laugh turns to agony, and I clench my eyes shut with a muffled groan. Travis continues.

"Oh, I'm sorry. Even though you love hearing that, I didn't think about laughter causing more pain. Mom, I love you, and I'm thrilled you're awake."

My son has the best dry sense of humor. I can't speak with the breathing apparatus covering my mouth, but a flow of tears slides down my cheeks revealing my joy. Believing it wasn't possible to love my kids more, somehow the love has deepened. Jacob nudges his way between our kids, standing united while dabbing tears with tissues. The concern on their faces is obvious. Am I going to make it? Nurse Wanda enters the room, and I notice her limp.

"Don't worry, folks. My shift just started, so I'll be right by her side all night monitoring her vitals. As the doctor mentioned, these next few hours are crucial. Y'all should go home for a while and return later. I promise to call if anything changes."

"Come on, Wanda. There's no way we're leaving her side. Don't even try."

She gives us a wink. "You are a dear, but stubborn man. How about you kids?"

"We just got her back." Travis said. Katie stands beside her brother, nodding.

Wanda raises both hands. "All right. If you all need anything, I'm your girl."

Jacob moves around the bed to Wanda and places his hand on her shoulder. "She's in the best hands. Thank you, Wanda."

She folds her arms. "Anything for you, Jacob. You are fierce like a bull, but I like you. Isabelle is one special lady. No doubt about that."

"She sure is."

Wanda limps out of the room, promising to check in regularly. Her compassionate eyes and warm smile assure her commitment and the playful exchanges between her and Jacob ease my frantic mind. She's a blessing. When I can, I'll thank her for watching over me and my family.

Jacob whispers in Travis's ear. "Take Katie to get us coffee."

I watch them leave arm in arm. The closeness between them melts my heart. So badly, I want to tell them how much I've missed them and hug them tight.

Meanwhile, Jacob pulls a chair beside my bed and touches my cheek. I close my eyes, soaking in his tender touch. My eyes bounce around the room and ceiling eager to share the counselor experiences with him. When will they remove the breathing tube? My legs are immovable when I try kicking them. Attempts to clench my fists are futile. I want to scream.

Jacob rubs my bare arm. "It's okay, Isabelle. Try not to get worked up. I love you."

My body tingles from the waist up hearing those words from his lips. I close my eyes and let the tears flow. He reaches for a tissue and dries my eyes.

The room is quiet as he caresses my hair. At random times, he spontaneously sings a soft melody and my mind calms. He's back. The same guy I met in college. The one who understands me better than anyone, including me. Our future isn't clear, but the thought of divorce is inconceivable.

Wanda enters the room a few times, trying not to disturb our precious reunion. She grins at Jacob and slowly limps to the nurses' station in line of sight. I am safe.

Several minutes pass and the kids return with coffee. I shut my eyes, visualizing the paisley cups and drinking coffee with the counselor. I miss Him. Travis pulls up a chair next to his dad. Jacob stands and gestures Katie to sit, then excuses himself from the room. They catch me up on their college life and their enthusiasm normalizes my dire condition momentarily. Travis talks about his entrepreneurial classes and projects while Katie shares stories about parties and football games. On the topic of classes and exams, Katie avoids eye contact. It must be rough looking at me, bruises and bandages cover my body. I'm a mom again. I hope my eyes reveal how relieved and proud I am right now.

Jacob stands in the doorway and listens while holding a white Styrofoam cup. He blows on the steam and beams. Our family is whole again.

A few hours pass, and Jacob prods the kids to say goodbye. Each one touches my hand, then walks to the door, stealing a few glances behind. "Be back soon, Mom," they echo. Jacob hugs each child and reclaims his seat beside my bed.

Being positive and upbeat couldn't hide the distress they've endured. The shuffled hair, wrinkled clothes, and dark circles are dead giveaways. They will help me through this nightmare, but at what cost? Will I walk again? I'm tormented by the unknown condition of my body. I can't speak and ask questions, so I hope Dr. Abbot returns soon to share his prognosis.

The mental fogginess fades, and I scan the room, spotting Jacob's guitar in the corner. He notices and asks if I'd like to hear a song. I squeeze his hand as tightly as possible. He sings his love song to me until his voice becomes hoarse, and his words motivate me to keep fighting. I pray for God's strength.

Lucky for Jacob, Dr. Abbot enters the room grinning, followed by Nurse Wanda and a line of medical personnel carrying clipboards. Dr. Abbot places his hand on my arm, and a medic offers him a clipboard.

He takes it, and I stare at him wide-eyed and eager to hear an update on my situation.

"Isabelle, I reviewed your vital signs and test results. They show a remarkable improvement for the brief time you've been awake. That's good news. Based on the results from our test, I'm going to remove the ventilator to see how you breathe without it. Squeeze my hand if you understand."

I squeeze with all my might.

"Hmm. Your strength is better already. Let's remove the apparatus."

Jacob is on the opposite side of my bed, holding the guitar, then places it on his chair. He takes my hand. I close my eyes as the medics work to remove the tubes keeping me alive. It's creepy to think about. Once the tubes are out, I try to speak through gurgling sounds.

Dr. Abbot presses my arm. "It's okay. Take your time."

I manage a raspy whisper. "Thirsty."

He pours a cup of water and places the straw in my mouth. "Go ahead, take a sip."

The lubrication on my throat is a welcome relief. It's raw. I'll never take water for granted again. I hope he can hear me whisper.

"So much pain."

Jacob squeezes my hand tighter. Dr. Abbot hands the cup to Wanda, picks up the clipboard, and flips the page. He folds his arms, dangling the clipboard by his side. He leans in and delivers the shocking news.

"Isabelle, you're lucky to be alive. You suffered a severe blow to your entire body. We stopped the brain hemorrhage in time for you to survive, but we need to run more brain scans to check for any remaining swelling or permanent damage. Your body endured multiple fractures, including five broken ribs, a shattered femur bone in your left leg, and a right broken ankle. You also have multiple fractures in your left arm and a broken shoulder. We performed surgery on your left leg and shoulder and they're looking good, but you'll need follow-up surgeries to ensure full usage, along with long-term physical therapy. Over time, your ribs will heal. Since your arm and ankle fractures are clean breaks, they will heal faster. Truth is, you're going to suffer intense pain for a while, but your future looks positive."

"Am I paralyzed?"

The doctor flinched then touches my shoulder. "Goodness no, Isabelle. You can't move because multiple casts confine you. Despite significant bruising, there's no harm to your neck, back or spine. You're very lucky. This could be much worse."

I rest my eyes and thank God. The relief is overwhelming. I recall the terror when I believed the worst about my condition. It's not my best day, but at least I will walk again. The pain snaps me back to reality.

"My head. It's pounding."

"That's expected from the head trauma. I'll increase your pain medication and order a series of tests. Let's stay positive and hopeful about the findings."

"Okay."

"You have a long road to recovery. I like the results, but the next several hours remain critical. You need to stay awake. Can you do that for me?" He smiles brightly, reminding me of the counselor.

"Yes, I'm not leaving."

Everyone's laughter helps lighten the mood.

"Looks like your humor is intact. An excellent sign. We're going to leave you with Nurse Wanda, and I'll stop by in a few hours to check on you."

"Thank you."

"My pleasure, Isabelle. Get some rest."

He pats my hand again and gives Jacob a firm nod. With hands on his hips, Jacob drops his head and shoulders, letting out a deep exhale. He rubs his fingers through his hair and moves to the doorway with his back to me. He's been through torture. As the medical team leaves the room, the gravity of my injuries sinks in, but the heavy weight of uncertainty lifts. Imaginary drama would consume my thoughts without the counselor's wisdom. I'm at peace. It's going to be difficult, but a full recovery is possible. The accident is an opportunity to get closer to God. The concept crystallizes.

Jacob walks back to my bedside slowly. He looks at me with tired, bloodshot eyes and messy hair. Still incredibly handsome, he lifts my hand.

"Isabelle, I can't express how terrified I was about losing you.

Waiting for you to wake up has been excruciating, not knowing if you would. I don't know where to start, but I love you and never want to lose you. This experience is a wake-up call for me."

My heart leaps as tears stream down my cheeks. My voice is still hoarse, but I must speak. "Oh, Jacob. I never stopped loving you, and I don't want to lose you either."

He looks up. "God, thank You for bringing her back to me." He lowers my hand and leans over, kissing me with his sweet soft lips, and for a split second, I'm giddy. I clinch my eyes and grit my teeth. Jacob's eyes widen.

"I'm sorry. Did I hurt you?"

"No, I love kissing you, but the pain is unbearable."

"I wish I could take your place."

"I understand. I can't wait to tell you everything that happened during my coma."

"What do you mean?"

"The counselor and our time in the sanctuary."

He hovers over me with a serious stare. "Counselor? What sanctuary? You must be hallucinating from the pain medication. Rest, Isabelle. You can tell me everything tomorrow."

The stress on his pale face worsens. I've burdened him too much, without considering the potential reactions from Jacob and others to my supernatural experience. Will he believe me? I should consider this carefully. Besides, I doubt my voice could handle the time required to tell the stories.

Should I tell anyone? Maybe the sanctuary wasn't real and just a lucid dream.

CHAPTER 22

The Recovery

Startled by the sound of curtain rings sliding on the metal rod above my head, I open my eyes to Nurse Wanda smiling at me. Her brown eyes exude compassion, and her warm hand on my forehead comforts me.

"Rise and shine, buttercup. It's your favorite nurse. Looks like your vitals are improving by the hour, and your face is a little less swollen."

It might be the pain, but I miss the sessions at the sanctuary. My experience in the magical garden is surreal. Was it simply a dream? Wanda is a ray of sunshine, but I miss the counselor and my normal body. My head is throbbing, and my throat feels like sandpaper when I swallow. Still, I'm grateful to breathe without a ventilator.

"Good morning, Wanda. Where's Jacob?" My voice sounds scratchy.

"He just stepped out for coffee and hazelnut creamer. He said it's important to you, but I think it's important to him. Despite his lack of sleep, the man refuses to leave your side. I gave up arguing with him days ago because he's been so upset. He loves you so much, girl."

"Jacob slept here?"

"Every night."

"Oh, my."

Wanda points to a chair. "He slept in that recliner. You should see the lousy green chair he tried to sleep in for the first two days. After he refused to go home, I rounded up two muscular fellas to bring in that oversized recliner from the waiting room so he could stretch out. Good grief, a man his size can't sleep well in a little chair. But he never complained. Not your Jacob. I made sure he had a fluffy pillow and a soft blanket. When Travis and Katie are here, he takes a short walk. That's it."

I attempt to smile with swollen lips. "Thank you for looking after him."

"It's my pleasure. I was on emergency duty the day of your accident. I've seen plenty of upset husbands, but your man was a wreck. Since then, I've been watching over him and your kids. Such sweet kids. And Jacob is one smart, determined man, and very protective of you. You're lucky to have such a beautiful family who loves you so much."

"Yes. I'm very blessed." My eyes well up.

"You got that right. Is there anything I can get you before I leave my shift? Nurse Erica will take over for me, and I'll be back this evening. She's a doll, you'll love her."

"I'm okay. Thank you."

"You're welcome. If you can't tolerate the pain, push the nurse's buzzer. Before I go, I'll see if your man found the hazelnut creamer."

She shakes her head chuckling and limps out the door. Tears trickle down into the corners of my grin. I look around for a tissue when Jacob walks in proudly displaying two Styrofoam cups of coffee steaming with the aroma of hazelnut. His bright smile quickly fades and rushes to my side.

"What's wrong, Isabelle?" He places the cups on the serving tray and hovers over me.

"I'm okay. These aren't tears of pain. You brought coffee. That's so sweet, and you added hazelnut, my favorite."

"I love bringing you coffee, and Wanda found hazelnut creamer hidden in the cafeteria. How are you doing?"

"Wanda said my vitals are improving every hour. A good sign."

His face lights up, appearing less pale and strained. "It's an excellent sign. You'll get through this, Isabelle."

He looks thin in his red golf shirt and khaki pants but less redness in his eyes. I'm relieved to see him put back together with neatly combed hair and fresh clothing. A clear sign he's optimistic about my recovery.

He holds the coffee cup, and I sip through the straw, letting the hazelnut flavor rest on my tongue before swallowing. A delightful treat. I breathe in the scent of Jacob's crisp, masculine cologne mixed with hazelnut, and thoughts of mornings at home warm my entire body. Even though he's a strong, confident man, I'm concerned about the effect on him from the accident.

"What about your work, Jacob? Wanda said you've been here almost every waking hour."

"Under control. George, at the law firm, insisted I take a temporary leave of absence. Jerome is handling my cases until I return. He's a fabulous lawyer. I'm lucky to work for a firm that believes family comes first."

I want to weep but hold back to avoid more pain. Jacob leans over to grab a tissue, careful not to bump my wounds. As he wipes my tears, I feel powerless. I can't move my legs and can barely lift my right arm. My independence is shattered.

For the last several days, I confronted deep emotional pain, and now I face extreme physical suffering. Without the counselor's teachings, I'd crumble, believing it's too overwhelming. Now I'm equipped to tackle my physical battle the same way I battled my internal mind traps. Through God's strength, these outward wounds will heal as well.

"Jacob, poor timing yesterday, but I need to share what happened after the accident and where I went."

He pulls up a chair beside my bed, touching the top of my hand. "You mean the hallucination from the medication?"

"I'm not hallucinating, and I need you to hear me out."

"I'm listening."

"When I was unconscious, God took me to a special place. He called it a gap in time."

Jacob lowers his head, then raises it with a serious expression. "We almost lost you. Did you have a near death experience?"

"I'm not sure, because it wasn't Heaven. It was a place created especially for me with all my favorite things. It was magnificent. Each day, I met with the counselor who taught me about God and how He works in our lives."

"Whoa. A counselor?"

"He said he was an old friend sent by God to be my guide."

"Isabelle, I'm not sure if it's the medication or you had a vivid dream, but I think you should rest."

I close my eyes and reopen them. "No. It's not the medication or a dream. It's real, Jacob. You must believe me. It will save our marriage."

"Our marriage? You talked to a total stranger about us?"

I scowl. "He's not a stranger. Listen to the entire story."

Jacob shares an awkward grin. "I'm going to ask Dr. Abbot to check on you. I'll be right back."

Jacob bolts from the room. He doesn't believe me. Hearing me describe the experience makes me question. Was I dreaming? The crystal waterfalls and gemstone walkways surrounded by lavender fields and glorious gardens seemed so authentic. Duke, Bernie, and the counselor. Were they real? How can I be sure? I scan my aching head for proof and then it hits me. The letter. If Aunt Maggie has the letter from my father in a turquoise paisley hat box, the experience must be real. Jacob and Dr. Abbot enter the room with concerned faces.

"Good morning, Dr. Abbot."

He stiffens, holding his clipboard behind his back. "Good morning, Isabelle. Good news, you're showing more signs of improvement. I believe you're safely out of the woods with the critical period, but we will continue monitoring closely for a while before I move you from ICU."

"That's incredible." Jacob throws his fist in the air, declaring victory.

The doctor examines my heartbeat, throat, and abdomen, then continues. "Your husband tells me you had an intense dream during the coma. Are you feeling stressed about it?"

"Stressed? Quite the opposite. It wasn't a dream. The experience healed my soul, filling me with powerful strength and courage that will help me through this recovery and my entire future. I can't imagine lying here without this new wisdom."

He pauses and tilts his head. "Okay. It's fine to hold those thoughts if you believe it helps your recovery. Sounds positive. Research shows some patients dream during a coma, others do not. Don't worry either way. Rest for now. Soon, you'll be going downstairs for the brain scans we spoke about. Your progress is excellent. Keep it up." He pats my arm.

"Thank you, doctor." He doesn't believe me either. Jacob stands with his arms folded.

What did I expect? Everyone jumping up and down, eager to hear about my divine encounter with God? They're just relieved I'm alive.

Dr. Abbot and Jacob step outside the door and talk. I'm sure Jacob wants confirmation that I haven't lost my mind. Then I recall the counselor's teachings about positioning God and His ways first and quickly realize my selfish impatience can wait. My husband's endured enough. He doesn't need the uncertainty about my mental stability on top of my physical state. That wasn't my intention.

Just then, an impression pops into my mind, a phrase saying it only takes one person to put God's character into action. Those are the counselor's words. I sense his presence. Sharing my experience with others right now is unnecessary. Maybe once I recover, Jacob will be more open to listening without the fear of my mental stability. Regardless, it's between God and me. And just like that, I proved God's perfect will again. Before the accident, I would be desperate to tell everyone in sight about the encounter to pursue their opinions and validation. I don't need their approval anymore. God approves.

I observe Jacob shaking Dr. Abbott's hand as the doctor turns to walk away, and Jacob reenters the room alone. The relief on his face is obvious from the doctor's consultation. I want him to grasp my incredible journey with the counselor, but his well-being is a higher priority. He sits and presses my hand against his cheek. "Are you okay, Jacob?"

"Yes. The doctor reassured me it's normal to have dreams that seem real, but let's not discuss the dream in front of the kids. Okay?"

"Of course, Jacob. I'm sorry to cause you more stress. Maybe we can talk about it later but not in front of the kids. My recovery will take a long time. Months, but it's okay."

"Isabelle, you're so calm. I expected a different reaction from you. Heck, you're consoling me. According to Dr. Abbot, we should expect anything from the aftermath of a traumatic event like this. I just wasn't prepared."

I move my eyebrows up and down. "It's the new me. No one prepares for unexpected events like this. I agree with Dr. Abbot. We should expect anything, including miracles. I can't predict the outcome of my recovery, and I realize it's going to challenge me in ways I can't comprehend right now. But with God, all things are possible."

Jacob perked up with a smile. "You're right. He brought you back to us. Prayer works."

"It sure does."

Jacob squeezes my hand. I wish we could hug. His loving eyes remind me of our wedding day when we exchanged vows. It's impossible to think of us drifting apart when we're so bonded right now. But is it temporary because of the accident?

Meanwhile, Travis and Katie arrive with a vase of Stargazer lilies and a get-well balloon attached. As the rich pungent fragrance fills the room, I think of Mother. She's with me. Travis leans down to kiss my cheek.

Katie fusses with the flower arrangement and speaks. "Mom, the bouquet is small because they're super strict about keeping your room clutter free. I needed approval for a few lilies. Once you move from intensive care, we can shower your room with gorgeous flowers and spoil you for once."

"Katie-bug, the flowers are perfect. Thank you. Please don't bother with more stuff. All I need is my family here."

Katie leans down to kiss my cheek. "Okay, Mom."

Thankfully, her dark circles have faded, and it's reassuring to see her wearing her favorite urban style clothing that compliments her athletic body so well. Her makeup is meticulous, accentuating her green eyes. I'm glad. With her shiny brunette ponytail in place, Katie looks like herself again.

I gaze at Travis. One would think he's a Marine by his stance. Equal to Katie, he's put back together today with his classic button-down shirt untucked over dark jeans. I'm biased, but he could easily be a male model. I wonder about the future mates God has selected for my precious children.

"That's a spiffy shirt, Travis."

"Thanks, Mom. As usual, divert the spotlight away from yourself. How are you feeling?"

Travis stands beside my bed and holds my hand.

"I'm doing better. The doctor was here earlier with positive news, and they're running more brain scans today."

"I'm relieved."

I notice a gurney approaching my open door. "Looks like I spoke too soon."

"Knock, knock. Isabelle Beckham?"

"That's me."

A petite medical technician checks my digital monitor and leans over with a warm smile. She appears so young. "It's time for your scans. Let's take you downstairs for a quick ride."

"I'm ready."

"Mom, I'll take Dad and Katie downstairs and grab an early lunch. I doubt if Dad made time for breakfast, as usual." Travis nods to his dad and Jacob chimes in.

"Everyone gives me a hard time." Jacob leans over me. After a brief pause, we share a light kiss. He moves back, and we gaze at one another like smitten teenagers.

The technician coughs politely. "We need to get you downstairs for those scans, Miss Isabelle."

"Yes. Let's go. I'll see you all later."

Jacob grins and leaves with the kids waving goodbye. He seems fearful to leave my side. I was skeptical that Wanda embellished Jacob's devotion. He's the prince charming I remember from our college days.

After the tests, I'm back in my room alone, staring at the ceiling in silent prayer. I ask the Lord for courage, physical healing, and a cheerful outlook. I confess to God being frustrated and frightened, but I depend on Him. My mind and body relax. Nurse Erica enters my room, and the quiet time ends.

"How are you feeling, Miss Isabelle?"

"A little better today."

"I have a special request. We only allow immediate family to visit patients in the intensive care unit. But there's a sweet elderly gentleman who comes every day checking on Jacob and the kids. He spends time in our chapel down the hall. Now that you're awake, I think it's okay for him to see you, if you agree."

"Who is it?"

"His name is Mr. Merriweather."

Tears roll down my smiling face. "Of course. I'd love to see him."

"Oh, he will be thrilled. Should I bring him in now?"

"Now is perfect." Thoughts of my precious neighbor were frequent during my gap experience. I can't imagine the tree crushing his frail body. The branches had to fall on me.

Before the tree fell, inner bruises and brokenness polluted my soul. Now I lie gazing at real fractures and wounds that visually represent the purification of my mind. Uncanny.

"Okay, I'll be right back."

"Wait. Before you go, I'd like to see myself. I haven't thought to ask for a mirror."

"Are you sure?"

"Yes. Mr. Merriweather hasn't seen me yet, like my family. I want to prepare for his reaction. Seeing me in this contraption in a partial body cast is shock enough."

"Very well." Nurse Erica reaches inside a nearby drawer and pulls out a hand mirror. She slowly lowers it, revealing my face. Staring in the mirror, my mouth drops open. I didn't realize the massive swollen eyelid was contributing to my headaches and blurred vision. My face looks like it lost a fight with a bad tattoo artist. I shut my eyes and seek God's strength. I can sense His presence, reassuring me that these scars will also heal.

"Okay, Miss Isabelle. Have you seen enough?"

I blow out my disapproval.

"I'll bring him in now, okay?"

"Please do. I'm ready." That was a fib. Mr. Merriweather is tender-hearted, and I bet he's consumed with guilt over the accident. I need to suck it up and be strong for his reaction. About five minutes pass, and Mr. Merriweather shuffles through the doorway and stops. He looks fragile, gripping his cane, but as usual, he's dressed to the nines. He covers his mouth with his handkerchief.

"Mr. Merriweather, it's alright. I look much worse than I feel. Come on in. I'm so thrilled to see you."

Nurse Erica leans down and whispers in his ear, but I can't hear. He nods, and she guides him to the chair by my bed, where he sits trembling. He blows his nose into a crisp, white handkerchief.

Nurse Erica kneels beside Mr. Merriweather with her hand on his shoulder. "Will you be okay, sir?"

He waves his handkerchief, nodding. She slips out of the room, giving me an empathic look as she slowly closes the door behind her.

"Mr. Merriweather, I'm relieved you're not hurt too badly, and I hear you've been visiting the hospital daily, checking on Jacob and the kids. Thank you, but I'm concerned about you driving this far."

His hands shake, trying to hold back his emotions, but he can't. He sobs. Soon, his hands relax, and he regains his composure.

"I'm so sorry, Isabelle. It should be me in that bed, not you. Reuniting with Rosemary in Heaven would be just fine with me."

From my swollen face, I push a look of compassion the best I can.

"Please don't say that. It wasn't your time. I'm surrounded by wonderful doctors and nurses here. Though it may take a while, I'll recover."

"You're so brave. God made an exceptional lady when He created you. The last several days have been a living nightmare for your family. You can't imagine the stress of uncertainty about your return. But here you are. Praise God for your homecoming. Being here, sharing my support is the least I can do. You saved my life, for goodness' sake."

He holds the hanky over his mouth again, crying.

"Mr. Merriweather, you owe me nothing. You're a godly man. What if I told you God used this accident to heal my soul? Would you believe me?"

He lowers the handkerchief with wide, watery eyes. "You have my attention, child. What do you mean?"

"It's a long story, but during my coma, I went to an enchanted place —not Heaven—and met with a man who called himself Counselor. He claimed God sent Him to help heal my soul from past pain and teach me the ways of Jesus. He called it sanctification. We faced my darkest hours when my mother committed suicide, and he asked me to visit my estranged father. If I hadn't saved you, I would have missed the greatest gift of my life."

He sits quietly for a moment. "That's an unusual experience. Maybe a dream?"

"Please don't mention this to Jacob. In my excitement, I tried sharing the story with him, but he became distressed about my mental stability because of the head trauma. I can't pile on more. Please believe me, the experience was real. When I'm well enough, I can prove it."

"How?"

"The counselor mentioned a letter written to me by my father. He said my Aunt Maggie has the letter stored in a turquoise paisley hat box at her home, and if I ask her for it, she will give me the letter. He gave specific instructions for me to visit her home to retrieve it. Unfortunately, it will take time for me to travel."

"Why not call her and ask about the letter?"

"Still foggy. I hadn't thought about a simple phone call."

"I can't explain why, but I believe you. The supernatural powers of God are far beyond our understanding. Who am I to question Him? Your story is safe with me, and I'm honored you shared your divine encounter. During Rosemary's passing, it became clear that every trial is an opportunity to become closer to God."

My mouth drops open. "Where did you hear those words?"

"From the Holy Spirit when Rosemary died. It was such an unbearable trial for me. I loved her so much. Still do."

"I know you do. Strange, the counselor said those exact words to me during one of our sessions."

"Well, you said he taught the ways of Jesus, so it shouldn't be a surprise. Perhaps the Holy Spirit is speaking to us right now. You believe He's always there, don't you?"

"I'm starting to."

"Well, believe it because it's the Truth of God. Will you visit your father, Isabelle?"

I pause. "It depends on his letter, if it exists."

"I hope it does, and I'll continue praying you choose to visit your father. My gut says you two need each other."

"Aside from Aunt Maggie, do you realize you're the only person with enough courage to mention my father more than once?"

His snickers. "I'm not surprised."

"Why does it matter to you whether I reconcile with my father? You haven't been shy over the years to voice your opinion."

"It's important to me because it's important to God."

"How do you know?"

"I never told you, but the Holy Spirit prompted every one of those conversations at the lake cabin. It was uncomfortable for me, but He wouldn't let me ignore the nudges to take you a peach pie and bring up your father. I can't explain it. Funny thing is, you've never mentioned his name."

"His name is Sam. Sam O'Sullivan."

He gasps like he's seen a ghost and grabs the chair.

"What's wrong?"

After a long silence, he stares at the ground, hesitating to speak. "I knew a Sam O'Sullivan well. He was my neighbor about ten years ago, before we moved to the lake house. Where does your father live?"

"I'm not even sure if he lives in the same state."

"Well, back then, we lived in a small suburb west of Atlanta. Rosemary didn't like the traffic, so we moved. I lost touch with Sam after that, so I don't have his address."

"Interesting. Can you imagine if my father was your neighbor too?"

My mind races. Of course, there's more than one Sam O'Sullivan. Don't be silly. But what if it's true?

"It would be a remarkable synchronicity, Isabelle."

"It sure would. Describe the Sam you met."

"He was a severely broken man with a lot of problems. When we met, he was near death because of too much alcohol. I didn't think he would survive, but we kept praying for him. Eventually, he found peace in the Lord and turned his life around. He attended church with us until we moved to the lake."

I interrupt. "Mystery solved. There's no way my father came to Christ and goes to church. Oh well, it was a stretch."

"Are you sure?"

"Trust me. My father is the most deceitful, selfish man on earth. It's not him."

"Okay. If you say so."

"By the way, thank you for caring enough to share your wisdom and encouragement about reconciling with my father. You couldn't tell, but I was listening."

He glances down. "I must admit, I didn't want to talk to you about your father."

"Why not?"

"It was awkward, remember? Every time Rosemary baked a peach pie, the Holy Spirit prompted me to carry that pie to your cottage and mention your father. I was being obedient to God's request, that's all."

"Really?"

"Yes. I used to beg Rosemary to stop making peach pies or choose another fruit, but she wouldn't listen. Not sure what God was doing. Maybe I was planting His seeds."

"I loved those pies." Thoughts of sweet Rosemary in her colorful apron always sharing a kind word or delicious dessert warm my heart. Then it hit me.

"Wait, you were putting God first and following His ways, even though I made it uncomfortable for you. His love in action."

"You got it. It might be uncomfortable sometimes, but it's the only way to live."

"I'm still learning. I'm taking your wise advice and calling Aunt Maggie the first chance I get. First, I must convince Jacob."

"You're a sharp cookie and you will figure it out. Keep me posted."

"Thank you. I will."

His knees creak when he stands, wobbling to grasp his cane. He grips the bed railing, smiling broadly with puffy eyes. The shock of my condition wore off.

"Isabelle, I'm so thankful you survived the weight of those fallen branches. You're a brave lady, and I'm eternally grateful to you for saving my life. I guess God's not finished with me yet. I'm going to skedaddle so you can rest. Thank you for seeing me and sharing your divine encounter. I'll continue praying for a complete recovery. If you need anything, just say the word."

"Your support means the world to me and my family. Release any guilt about the accident. Trust me, when those heavy branches fell, it granted me a new life."

"I pray that's true. See you soon."

I watch Mr. Merriweather leave the room with more vigor in his stride. My heart is full. God is everywhere if I pay attention.

Now, I must convince Jacob to hear my story and help me call Aunt Maggie about the letter. It's the only way forward. Question is, does it truly exist?

CHAPTER 23

Real or Lucid Dream

After a week under intense supervision in ICU, I'm moved to a much quieter and larger room with lots of windows. The fragrance of lilies and roses of every color fill the room. My beautiful surroundings remind me of my lovely sanctuary. I miss Duke and the counselor terribly.

Jacob continues fussing over me except for a few hours at home. I held off calling Aunt Maggie but it's time. Once he is more comfortable with my progress, I'll mention the gap experience again. Will he listen this time?

Dr. Abbot's decision to scale back the pain medication is agonizing. Rough week. Still, I'm full of positive encouragement from my family's love and support. Several close friends and colleagues trickle in to visit or send flowers. I'm blessed. Roger and his wife are coming today, and Shannon and Abbey will stop by later this week. I hope they bring their kids.

I sense our sibling bond strengthening through this crisis, along with the outcome of my internal healing. Our interactions are light-hearted and more genuine without my guarded walls and pricks at my insecurities. A noticeable difference. I can't help wondering how they would react to the counselor's teachings. All four of us need healing since we've been in denial about our mother's death and severed ties with our father.

In the present moment, I scan the room observing nurses and paramedics rushing down the halls. Until now, I've been fortunate with exceptional health. Aside from visiting others in the hospital periodically, medical facilities are foreign spaces. Now, unfamiliar people surround me, and I sense the motivation to activate God's character. Every person and encounter are new opportunities to inject kindness and compassion. I wonder if God understands the difficulty when my entire body lies in agony. I think of Jesus on the cross, and I close my eyes remorsefully. A level of excruciating torture I can't fathom in my physical suffering.

Interrupting my thoughts, Dr. Abbot enters the room for his routine check-up. With the brain scans reporting no permanent damage or swelling, I focus on follow-up surgeries and rehabilitation.

"Good afternoon, Isabelle." He stops and smells the flowers lining my windowsill. You've built a fan club."

"Hi, Dr. Abbot. My family spoils me because I'm crazy about flower gardens." Even more so now.

"You're a lucky lady. Your positive outlook is exemplary, which is probably why you're progressing above average. I'm a straight shooter, so the next several months will be challenging, but I'm optimistic about a complete recovery. You're on our miracles list."

"Do you believe in miracles?"

"I've witnessed too many unexplainable recoveries to disqualify miracles as an option."

"I bet you have. Thank you for everything."

He pats my good shoulder. "My pleasure. Keep up the magnificent work, and I'll see you soon."

As the doctor leaves, Jacob walks in. His face is fuller, and his color is back to normal. My face lights up when he smiles at me.

"Isabelle, unless you're adding makeup, your bruises are fading quickly. Each day is a step closer to bringing you home. I can't wait."

"Me too. You're so thoughtful. I mean, look at these flowers."

His cheeks flush. "The kids insisted. They're amazing."

"Yes. I miss them but thrilled they left for college. They've missed so much because of me."

"That reminds me. We need to talk about Katie."

I flinch. "What is it? Is she okay?"

"She's fine, but . . ."

"What?

"Never a good time, but you should know. She's failing her classes."

Stunned, I didn't prepare for this news. "I can't believe it. She hid this from us?"

"Yes. Her college advisor called. We agreed to a leave of absence for Katie due to your accident, and she's going to sit out this semester. She flew back to pack her things and move back home."

"A college dropout. That never occurred to me."

"Not sure she will drop out; just taking a break to sort out her future. She's confused. Don't worry, everything will work out for Katie and please let me handle this. You have enough on your plate."

"Okay. I trust your judgment."

He does a double take. "Really? You're not freaking out and taking over?"

"No, Jacob. That was the old Isabelle. I'm a new person because of my experience."

Jacob pulls a chair close to my bedside and wraps his hand around mine. He stares at me with thoughtful eyes.

"Shifting topics, Isabelle. I want to plan another trip to the lake cottage for next fall. Only this time, you won't be driving without me. Plus, I hired an arborist to inspect every tree on the property, even Mr. Merriweather's. His walks to Rosemary's gravestone should not include dodging trees."

"Once again, you're a thoughtful man, Jacob."

"Whatever. It's ambitious with your surgeries and rehabilitation, but we need this trip. We were not in a good place, and I won't hide from it. Almost losing you changed everything, especially my perspective about life and our marriage. Our next weekend at the lake cottage will be a momentous occasion—not to rekindle our marriage, but to celebrate the love we've always had. We never stopped loving each other, did we?"

Tears stream down my face. "No."

"We just got lost in the chaos. It's sappy, but I'm tired of holding back my feelings. I will ensure you're never uncertain about our love again."

The tears keep coming, and I'm speechless. Staring into his handsome blue eyes, I try to figure out how we got lost. *Look forward, Isabelle.*

"There's more."

"What?"

"No more traveling out of town. I have a new work schedule. The firm is fine with me taking local clients only. It means fewer hours so I can help you through recovery, and after that, we can go to Paris, and visit the kids at college more often. What do you think?"

Jacob keeps wiping my tears, and I can't quit smiling. "I think it's perfect."

He beams. "You're going to get sick of me pampering you."

"Jacob, that's impossible. I'll never get sick of anything you do. We both need to adjust priorities. When I'm able to work again, I'll cut back too. Thank you for being so supportive. I think planning another trip to the cottage is brilliant. It gives me something to look forward to and motivate my therapy."

"That's the spirit."

"Speaking of spirit, I need to talk to you about my dream again. I mentioned nothing to the kids, as promised. However, I shared a little with Mr. Merriweather."

"Isabelle, why?"

"I'm not crazy, Jacob. My brain scans are normal, so please hear me out. I need you to believe me. Mr. Merriweather was so distraught, blaming himself for my injuries, I had to tell him the truth."

He squints his eyes, leaning in. "What truth?"

"I believe the tree branches fell on me instead of him for many reasons. Someday, I'll tell you everything. When I arrived at the lake cabin for our weekend together, I cried out to God in desperation, asking Him to restore our marriage and heal the pain from my past. He answered my plea with a supernatural experience during my coma."

He pauses from wiping my face. "What?"

"I know it sounds ridiculous, but God used the coma as a temporary gap in time, saying it was the only way to gain my attention."

"You don't normally talk about God. It's wonderful, of course. Anyone facing death probably goes through some sort of spiritual shake-up. Don't you think it was just a lucid dream like virtual reality?"

"I believe I can prove it with a phone call."

"A phone call? To whom?"

"Aunt Maggie."

"Aunt Maggie?"

"I know."

"How is she connected to this?"

"Please keep an open mind. It's going to get more bizarre."

Jacob sits back in his chair and crosses his arms. "I'm listening."

"My sessions with the counselor included confronting my past and healing the sorrow I've carried since Mother died. He aided me in confronting her suicide and my never-ending contempt for my father. God started purifying my soul, but additional steps are necessary to free myself from the mind trap of unforgiveness."

"Mind trap? Come on, Isabelle."

"I'll explain that later. He said I need to forgive my father completely. Which means I must visit him and attempt reconciliation. Uncertain about doing it or even wanting to, but I long to be rid of this torment."

Jacob stands with interlocked hands on his head. "Isabelle, are you listening to yourself? Your father? The same man we're not allowed to speak of, and you haven't seen since you were a senior in high school? And what torment?"

I clench my teeth. "I'm not excited about the idea either, but he mentioned a letter."

He throws his head back. "A letter?"

"Yes, a letter my father wrote to me that Aunt Maggie has stored in a turquoise paisley hatbox at her house."

Jacob lets out a roaring belly laugh. I bet he hasn't snorted like that since college. "Isabelle, I'm sorry. This is nuts. What are you thinking? This is not like you."

"Even to me, it sounds crazy, but I must find out if the letter exists.

If it doesn't exist, Aunt Maggie might think I'm a little kooky, but that's no big deal. It's a harmless request and will prove whether this is a fantasy or the truth."

He pauses as though searching for a valid rebuttal. "I suppose a phone call couldn't hurt anything. Especially if it ends this nonsense."

"We'll see. Keep in mind I didn't commit to visiting my father. I need to read the letter first. I promised the counselor I would."

"Who is this counselor again?"

"He said God sent Him to be my advocate and teach me God's ways, and He did. Truly, we worked through my toxic thinking brought on by my father's neglect, betrayal, and the trauma of Mother's death. So many issues needed healing."

He leans over the bed with desperate looking eyes. "After everything we've been through, this is too much."

"I wouldn't be asking if I didn't believe it was true. If the letter exists, we drive to Aunt Maggie's house to read the letter. Isn't it worth a call to see if the letter is real?"

"I think the big red cedar shook up your redheaded obstinance, and I'm going to lose this debate, regardless. I'll help you make the call on one condition."

"Anything"

"Acknowledge the encounter as a lucid dream and never mention it again."

"Deal. And my hair is auburn. I'd hug you if I could, even after your snarky joke."

Jacob stands and pulls out his phone. "Let's call her now to finish this."

"Great. Can you dial her number and hold the phone to my ear?"

"Way ahead of you. It's ringing."

Jacob holds the phone next to my ear with his other hand on his hip. I catch him rolling his eyes. This is it. The moment of truth.

"Aunt Maggie? It's Isabelle."

"Hi, sugar. How are you feeling? It's good to hear your sweet voice. You gave us all quite a scare. Jacob says they moved you out of ICU, and they're calling you a miracle woman. Look at you."

My face warms. "Yes. I'm doing better each day. Thank you for driving so far to see me. You didn't have to."

"Oh, good gracious, of course I had to. You're like a daughter to me."

"Thanks again. There's another reason I'm calling."

"Dear Lord, more bad news?"

"No. I'm calling about a letter."

"Letter. What letter?"

"I'm curious if you have a letter my father wrote to me stored in a turquoise paisley hatbox." I clench my teeth and wait. Jacob leans into the phone to hear the verdict. The phone is dead silent. Jacob shrugs. Aunt Maggie stutters but gets the words out.

"Did you say hatbox? I can't believe my own ears. When did you speak to your father?"

"I haven't spoken to him since the day Mother passed. Nothing's changed. It might sound weird, but I believe you might have a letter I'm supposed to read stored in an old hatbox. Does this make sense to you?"

After a loud thud, I clinch my eyes shut. Jacob pulls the phone away from my ear, and I motion him to hold it back again. He holds the phone close enough for both of us to hear.

"Aunt Maggie, are you there?"

She stammers. "I'm sorry. I dropped the phone, sugar. That's impossible. How on God's green earth did you find out about the letters and my hatbox? Even Sam doesn't know where I store those letters. I'm the only one."

My eyes seem to bug out of the sockets. It's real. Jacob's face fades to white.

"Wait. You said letters. You mean there's more than one?"

"I'm not supposed to be talking about this. I promised him— he's my brother, for goodness' sake."

"Please, Aunt Maggie. It's important."

I hear a heavy sigh on the other end.

"Yes. One for Roger and each of you girls. Despite my disagreement, I swore on a stack of Bibles to keep the letters secret until your father's death. How did you get this information?"

"During my coma, I had a supernatural encounter with God. It was so real that I thought it was worth confirming. I won't tell my siblings. Promise. This is between you and me and no one else, especially Father."

"Isabelle, could it be?"

"How else?"

"I've been after you for years to meet with your father and give him another chance."

"I am aware, but no meeting. I want to read the letter first."

Another long silence on the phone. "I don't break promises. Especially with my baby brother. Despite his distant mistakes, he's dealt with enough misery."

"I'm sorry to put you in this position. I'm just following instructions. You trust in God, don't you?"

"What kind of wackadoodle question is that? You know I do. I might regret this but reading his letter could be the only hope for y'all."

"So, you'll let me read it?"

She huffs. "He wrote you kids lots of letters after your momma passed. You didn't read a stinkin' one of them, did you?"

"I didn't, Aunt Maggie. I can't change the past."

After another long pause, the phone stays silent. Jacob's ear is on top of mine. We wait.

"Oh, sweet Jesus. All right. If there's a chance to reunite Sam and his kids, it's worth it. I'll bring the letter over this week."

"Oh, no. I must visit your house. Not sure why, but it's part of the instructions from God."

"Oh, for pity's sake. Really? How long until you're able to travel?"

"Probably two months and that's aggressive. I'll be in a wheelchair."

"Can you hold off that long?"

"Aunt Maggie, I've waited this long. What's a few more months? It's important I do it this way. Trust me."

"All right. The letters will stay snug as a bug in the hatbox until your arrival. Call me when you're ready, and I'll make strawberry shortcake with my secret biscuit recipe. You take care of yourself, and I'll be praying my heart out for a full recovery. Anything else, sugar?"

"No, that's all, and thank you. I'll be in touch. Goodbye, Aunt Maggie."

"Goodbye."

Jacob pulls the phone back and ends the call. He stares at me with humongous eyes. "Isabelle, I can't believe it. It's true."

"I can't rationalize it, but God made it happen. Once I tell you the complete story, it will blow your mind."

He smacks his forehead. "Oh, it's already blown. Tell me everything."

I want to jump up and down so badly, but my body is immoveable. "I will. Thank you, darling."

"Now, you have two big motivators for your recovery. The lake cottage trip and the hatbox letter. The day you're physically able, I'll drive you to Aunt Maggie's house."

"Thank you. Couldn't do this without you."

Two months later, after multiple follow-up surgeries, I'm hitting rehabilitation goals early. The mystery of my father's letter inspires me to approach physical therapy as an adventure versus laborious exercises. I won't get my hopes up speculating what Father might have written, but the time to visit Aunt Maggie is drawing near.

CHAPTER 24

The Hatbox Letters

The past few months have been incredibly challenging. Even though it's temporary, adjusting to life in a wheelchair is no picnic, along with constant visits to the hospital for surgeries and rehab while Jacob juggles the needs of his local clients at the law firm. He's a trouper. In the past, I didn't appreciate his self-assurance and positive attitude enough, but now I do. He never complains. All uncertainty about Jacob's love for me and my significance in his life has disappeared. Our anchor is steadfast.

The recovery process tests my independence, a constant reminder that God is in control. For this stubborn redhead, full surrender takes practice, but I'm getting there.

Despite the surprise setback of Katie skipping a semester of college, her presence and support around the house are welcome blessings. Encouraging Katie to explore her passions and actively listening to her, rather than imposing our expectations, creates better results. She dreams of being an investigative journalist. From our discussions, she realizes that attending a huge university far from home is a misguided fit. Too overwhelming. Since journalism requires a degree, she's evaluating more intimate colleges in Georgia. I'm giddy thinking about frequent trips to visit Katie over coffee.

My heart breaks when she describes feeling inferior, recognizing my negative influence. *Look forward, Isabelle.* Gratitude quickly overpowers guilt, since I can teach Katie important lessons shared by my counselor. My attention shifts to Katie walking toward me, carrying a purple plastic bag.

"Mom, I found this wedged beside the washing machine while cleaning the laundry room. See the hospital logo?"

"Oh my. What's in it?

"Not sure."

Katie empties the bag, which includes the jeans I wore the day of my accident. She slides the jeans out, holds them upside down, and a gold necklace falls to the floor."

I shriek, "My gold key necklace."

She quickly kneels to grab it and drops it in my right hand. Tears well up. I hold the long chain staring at the shiny ornate key.

"Are you okay, Mom? Should I get Dad?"

I nod and Katie sprints to Jacob's home office. A few minutes later, Jacob runs into the room with Katie, his face pale.

"Isabelle, what's wrong?"

"Nothing. Everything is perfect. It's time to visit Aunt Maggie."

"Why now?"

I dangle the necklace in front of me. "Remember the gift from the counselor I mentioned? This is it. He said it would unlock the ultimate mystery to end the last bit of sorrow from my past."

With his mouth almost hitting the floor, Jacob takes the necklace staring at the gold key in his palm. "Unbelievable. Yes, I remember. It never occurred to me that the necklace came home with you."

"Funny. Me either."

"I'll grab your phone. It's time to call your Aunt Maggie."

Katie touches my shoulder. "It's beautiful, but what's going on? Who gave this to you?"

"Soon, I will tell you everything. For now, will you please clasp this around my neck?"

"Of course."

She fastens the necklace and pats my shoulder. "Thank you, Katie."

"You're welcome. If you're okay, I'll finish in the laundry room."

"Never better."

I rub the familiar key, thinking about what it unlocks. Is it merely symbolic or the key to a tangible item? Can't wait to find out. Jacob walks in carrying my phone. He presses in her number, and I place the phone next to my ear.

"Hello." I love the sound of Aunt Maggie's voice—animated, loving, and strong.

"Aunt Maggie? It's Isabelle."

"Oh darlin,' how are you doing?"

"My recovery is ahead of schedule, but our visit is right on time. I'm eager to read my father's letter. Will you be home this Friday?"

"Super. Let me check my calendar."

"Take your time."

She hums an old-time hymn to the background music while I wait.

"You're in luck. I make chicken biscuits and blueberry muffins for my Bible study group that morning. I'll be free after 10:00 a.m. Does that work?"

"Perfect. I bet they love your homemade biscuits and muffins. The best in the south. Let's plan around two o'clock, considering the long drive."

She giggles. "You're too sweet. Two o'clock it is. I assume Jacob's driving."

"Yes. I'm healing well, but I'll be in a wheelchair for a while."

"Oh, good gracious. I can't get over that big tree falling on you. You're lucky to be alive. I've been praying, though, and the good Lord is working."

I look up and give Jacob a wink. "We look forward to seeing you on Friday."

"Same here, sugar. I'm making your favorite treat."

My eyes bulge. "Strawberry shortcake?"

"That's right."

"Sounds yummy. See you soon."

"Goodbye, sugar. Drive safely."

I hand the phone to Jacob to end the call. He kneels beside my wheelchair, touching my arm.

"Are you sure you're up for this?"

"Never been more certain about anything."

"Okay, then. I'll take care of the van and the trip details."

I stare into his ocean-blue eyes and clutch his arm. "Thank you. I can't imagine life without you."

He grins. "Me either. We're in this together."

Friday arrives, and Jacob helps me into the van equipped to handle my wheelchair. We head to Aunt Maggie's house. Thankfully, the highways are smooth, so I don't expect too much jostling around with my healing body. Still, Jacob insists on putting cruise control lower than the speed limit to avoid any sudden moves. He's so protective.

My palms are sweaty, and my stomach churns like I'm going to the prom. What's wrong with me? It's just a letter. If I don't like what it says, I can give it back or throw it in the trash. Jacob interrupts my thoughts.

"Are you nervous, Isabelle?"

He must be reading my mind. "About a piece of paper?"

"Come on. What do you think it says?"

"Despite that letter consuming my thoughts over the last few months, I don't want to create false fantasies."

"Says the new and improved Isabelle." We both laugh.

"Yeah. The counselor taught me to tackle each moment at face value and stop creating imaginary drama about life's events. Every time I started creating worst-case scenarios about the letter or even good thoughts, I stopped myself. It's been incredible practice."

"Maybe that's why he insisted on visiting Aunt Maggie instead of a delivery."

"What do you mean?"

"The counselor expected your recovery period and your inability to drive for months, allowing you time to retrain your thought patterns."

"Hmm. I wonder. Are we almost there?"

"One more mile. You can wait in the van until I get everything unloaded to bring you in."

"Don't worry, I can't maneuver alone, but I'll be walking on crutches soon."

"With your redheaded determination, I'm sure you will."

I scoff. "It's auburn."

Jacob glances my way. "That's right. My ginger spice." We both roar.

Humor soothes my queasy stomach, and my hands stop sweating. I recall Duke's nudges when I felt nervous. I miss his furry face.

"Jacob, what do you think about getting a Harlequin Great Dane and naming him Duke?"

"Let me guess, more advice from the counselor?"

"No, this idea is all mine."

"Not surprised. I think we could use a little Duke in our lives."

"Trust me, he won't be little for long."

Casual chit-chat helps the last mile fly by, and I embrace the simple pleasures among the daunting unknown ahead.

Arriving in front of Aunt Maggie's house opened a floodgate of memories. Her house looks smaller. I recollect Roger leading my sisters and me as we snuck around the back to pick wild raspberries off her fence row and played baseball in the field next door until dusk. Nothing's changed. Although modest, Aunt Maggie's house is a solid stone with rich history. The curb appeal is still impressive, with manicured bushes and topiaries. Something she and I have in common, our love for botanical gardens. She would have flipped out seeing the magnificent landscapes in my special sanctuary for my meetings with the counselor.

I notice Aunt Maggie poking her head out the front door, standing on the top step, smiling and waving us in. She dries her hands on a familiar floral apron worn and faded and cinched tightly around her thick waist. Could it be the same one? She's still wearing a bun, usually tucked underneath her floppy hat, out of sight. I doubt anyone except Uncle Ivan has seen her long, gray hair. Even at a distance, she radiates warmth and compassion. No wonder I admire her. She cups her hand over her eyes to block the sun, extending another energetic wave at the windshield, where I sit patiently for Jacob's assistance. Then her loud southern accent echoes through the neighborhood.

"Do you need some help, sugar?"

"Hello, Maggie. No, I'm good. Give me a few minutes to assemble Isabelle's wheelchair, and we'll be right in. Thank you."

She dabs her forehead with her hanky. "No rush. I've got fresh coffee on, and my homemade strawberry shortcake in the oven. It's been a banner year for strawberries."

"Fantastic. Be right in."

Jacob mastered the art of wheelchair transportation by clocking his time getting the chair out, assembled, and me in it. The man is so competitive. It certainly contributes to his success as a lawyer and helps us stay upbeat about my condition. Besides, I complain enough for both of us.

Jacob lifts me out of the van and cautiously into the wheelchair. I stare at decades of weathered sidewalks which play havoc on wheelchairs and sore bodies. Looks like one of the worst in this little coastal town. Approaching the front steps, Jacob scoops me in his arms like a knight escaping with a princess. He carries me to the kitchen table and lowers me onto a fluffy pillow. Is he showing off?

The aroma of fresh-brewed coffee and soothing vanilla fill every air pocket of her home. Oh, how I've missed her baking. Aunt Maggie faces the oven window checking her shortcake. Now that I'm closer, I swear it's the same apron she wore thirty years ago. Aside from more wrinkles and rolls, she's the same stout woman I remember. When she turns around, she covers her nose and mouth as her eyes scan my injured body. She waddles to me and stops, hunched over with her hands on her knees.

"Isabelle, look at you. Oh, my goodness gracious, that tree sure did a number on you, didn't it? I am so sorry you're going through this. But I'm glad you're here." She kisses my forehead.

"Hi, Aunt Maggie. It's wonderful to see you too. I'll recover eventually. I'm progressing better than normal, they say."

With hands on her hips, she straightens. "I'm so happy to hear that. Those fancy Atlanta doctors sure know their stuff, don't they? You're in excellent hands."

I nod. "Yes, ma'am."

"Jacob, you sit right there next to Isabelle. Would you like a thicker cushion too? I thought Isabelle could use one."

"No, thanks. The chair is fine."

"Okay, then. The shortcake is almost ready, so let me pour you both a nice steamy cup of coffee. I bet the long drive wore you out."

I shift in my chair trying to get comfortable. "Thank you. I think the butterflies in my stomach kept me awake. Not sure about Jacob."

"I'm fine too. Been a while since we've been to the Georgia coast and enjoyed the country drive. I'm a southern boy through and through."

I wink at Jacob while Aunt Maggie fusses with the coffee. I scan her home, reminiscing. The décor hasn't changed since the seventies except for the newer carpet and freshly painted walls. Same off-white with fall color accents. The classic cherrywood cabinets are still flawless, with a well-kept sheen and the matching corner hutch stuffed with Avon decanters is still the same. I snicker. As the most frugal one in the family, I admire her financial stewardship and high-quality style.

She pats her forehead with a napkin. "Isabelle, those butterflies in your stomach must be because of the letter. We'll get to that shortly."

Aunt Maggie places a cup of coffee in front of Jacob and me.

"Yes, ma'am. I can't imagine what my father wrote."

"No, you can't. He's different from the father you remember. Totally changed."

"With all due respect, I find it hard to believe." As the last word rolls off my tongue, remorse overtakes me. I stare at my cup thinking about my journey with the counselor and how much I've changed. Jacob nudges me gingerly with his elbow and gives me 'the look.'

"I understand, Isabelle. You'll have to see for yourself."

"You're right, Aunt Maggie. I should be more open-minded."

She raises her brow and points up to my left. I strain my neck, careful to avoid pain, and behold, sitting atop her antique buffet table like a trophy was the most exquisite and uniquely shaped hatbox wrapped in gorgeous turquoise and pink paisley fabric. I gulp. The fabric is the same pattern as the counselor's shirt and the last set of cups.

"That's the one."

Aunt Maggie signals Jacob to retrieve the hatbox. Jacob carefully places the delicate box in front of me. The pattern is lively and loud, with tiny beads expertly crafted into the design. I try to open the lid with one hand, but the latch appears to be locked. Jacob fiddles with it and confirms it's locked.

Aunt Maggie perks up. "Don't worry, sugar. I forgot the key. Before we continue, may I indulge you with the tale of this fortunate hatbox?"

I pause, hesitating. "Sure. We'd love to hear it."

The oven buzzer goes off. "Oh, for pity's sake, the shortcake is done."

Jacob gestures to Aunt Maggie to stay seated. "Don't get up. I'll handle the shortcake while you continue your story."

"Thank you, sugar. That's sweet of you."

I motion for Aunt Maggie to keep going.

"Okay. Daddy, I mean your late Grandpa Finn, gave this hatbox to your late Grandma Millie after returning from the war in 1944. Before boarding the train station in London, a stranger approached him frantic about wanting to switch tickets. The stranger needed to return home to his wife sooner, who was expecting a baby, but his train left a day later. He told your grandpa he didn't have anything to offer except this lovely hatbox in exchange for his ticket. Your Grandpa Finn didn't give a hoot about a hatbox, but he was a big softy and agreed to the trade."

I sip my coffee. "How interesting. Then what happened?"

"The stranger thanked him and went on his way. Your grandpa didn't have money for an overnight room, so he planned to sleep on a bench in the train station. After finding a clean bench, he opened the lid and then slammed it shut. No hat. He looked in the box again and noticed a small rip in the silk lining. When he poked his finger through the hole, he felt something. When he stretched it further, he pulled out a gold key. The latch key for the hatbox. Relieved, he wondered if anything else hid beneath the lining. He dug a little further through the rip and pulled out a twenty-dollar bill. He said it was a lucky charm. He found nothing else."

"Twenty dollars?" Jacob finishes cutting the shortcake and takes his seat.

"Yes. Today, that's worth around three hundred."

"Oh, wow."

"It gets even better, sugar. He booked a room, ate a fancy steak dinner, and went shopping for the finest hat to surprise your Grandma Millie. He found a bright pink felt hat wrapped with a paisley silk ribbon. The next day, he boarded the train, arrived home, and presented the lovely hatbox with the most elegant hat inside to Momma. She loved it so much, she wore it out."

I glance at Jacob listening intently and I smile. "What a beautiful story."

She raises her hand. "There's more. He read in the newspaper that the train he originally planned to board derailed, but thankfully, no one was injured. Even though he couldn't confirm it, he believed the gentleman that traded the hatbox arrived home safely to be united with his newborn child. That's why I stored those letters in the hatbox, hoping it reunites your father with his kids."

I squirm and peer down. "You're ruthless, Aunt Maggie."

She ignores me and shimmy's forward.

"Since your grandparents are gone, I'm the only one alive with the secret. Momma passed it down to me as the oldest daughter, and I swore to keep the hatbox hush-hush. They were superstitious and wanted it to stay with a female in the family. Someday, I'll pass it down to your cousin Elizabeth. Momma kept it hidden in her closet all those years, and now it stays covered in my closet. I'm a stickler with confidentiality but there's no explanation except God's supernatural power. Still, it's killin' me to break a promise to my baby brother. I pray it helps."

I peer at Jacob, our eyebrows raise, and we grin.

"Thank you. Your story is safe with us. I miss my grandparents and our family reunions at the lake cottage."

"Me too, sugar. Let me fetch the key for the hatbox. I keep it in a different spot. One cannot be too careful. I'll be right back."

Aunt Maggie disappears into the hallway as we enjoy our coffee, quietly absorbing the bizarre experience. It's nice to reminisce with her, but why did the counselor insist I come here? Was it to hear the hatbox story or perhaps Jacob's right about needing the time to practice retraining my brain? Jacob pulls his chair closer to me and inspects my shoulder sling.

"Is this too much, too soon?"

"No, I'm fine. I'll sleep on the ride home, but the extra pillow helps."

Aunt Maggie returns with her hand on her pale cheek, appearing bewildered. "Oh, good gracious. I can't believe it. The key is gone. I searched everywhere."

Without realizing it, I play with the gold key around my neck. Jacob points to the key with big eyes. I stop and look down. Could it be? Jacob quickly stands to unclasp the necklace. Aunt Maggie moves closer.

"What is it, Jacob? What are you doing?"

"Just a second, Maggie. I think Isabelle has your key."

Aunt Maggie shrieks. "What? That's impossible. It's been here forever."

Jacob releases the chain, and I hold up the gleaming gold key. "Does it look like this?"

She screams, waving her hands in the air. "Oh, my Lord. It's just like mine. What is happening?"

I place the key in the latch, and it fits. Aunt Maggie keeps both hands on her cheeks, and Jacob rocks on his feet. With my heart beating furiously, I turn the key, and the hatbox lid opens.

"Oh, my lucky stars. This is a miracle." Aunt Maggie fans her face, taking in deep breaths. Jacob claps once while my mouth gapes open. Inside the box, there's a stack of four letters tied with a red ribbon. I reach in and pick up the letters. The first one is for Roger. Jacob helps me flip to the bottom and pulls my letter from the pile, holding it in front of me. In perfect penmanship, it reads *Isabelle*.

"Do you want me to open it for you?"

"Let me hold it first."

Jacob hands me the letter, places the remaining three back in the box, and closes it. Then he helps Aunt Maggie back to her chair, still fanning herself. I pray she doesn't pass out.

You'd think he just handed me a nuclear bomb. Beads of sweat crop up all over my body. I stare at my handwritten name on the letter thinking about the counselor's teachings on grace and forgiveness. Thoughts shift to the suitcase ride and the restaurant scene involving Father and his other family. My face flashes hot, then I hear an impression in my mind saying, *look forward, the past no longer serves you, Izzy.* I flinch and drop the letter. The counselor is still guiding me. And I hear another impression saying, *you're never alone again because I will never leave you.* Tears roll down my cheeks and Jacob moves closer.

"Isabelle, this was too much. You're not ready."

"I'm fine, Jacob. Holding the letter just hit me hard."

"Are you sure you want to keep going? You don't have to."

I nod. "I want to move forward. Please open the letter."

"Oh, good Lord. Just open it, sugar. I couldn't guess what it says. He never told me."

Jacob pops the seal open and slides the letter out, flattening the creases. I hold it with my right hand.

"I'm standing right here until you finish the letter. If it's too upsetting, I'm yanking the paper out of your hands. Deal?"

"Deal."

"It's okay, sugar. He wouldn't write anything to cause you more pain. Go ahead and read it."

Whatever this piece of paper holds will change my life forever, and it scares me. If it's filled with excuses and blame, will the bitterness choke out my soul's healing? That's the risk. Another impression enters my mind, saying *every action has risks and consequences.* I sense His presence and ease into my chair. The biggest risk is living with the mind trap of unforgiveness forever. I close my eyes and ask God for His strength and courage. It's time to discover the contents of this letter after decades apart.

Dear Isabelle,

If you're reading this letter, I must have perished. Which means I left the earth carrying a heavy heart, knowing the pain I brought into our family. This letter is not about excuses because I have none. The reasons for my actions cannot wipe out the destruction or bring your mother back. Instead, this letter speaks of the unexpressed love I had for you. For that, I am deeply sorry. If given the chance, I would treasure every moment spent with you.

The man writing these words is not the same guy you called Father. Instead, I'm the man you deserved to have as a father. Back then, I was nothing more than a selfish coward. I wrote this little poem just for you, Isabelle. I hope you like it.

IF I COULD GO BACK...
I'd see every smile as God's little treasure.
Ensure you felt loved overflowing with pleasure.

I'd offer my shoulder to use as your guard.
Fight off your battles when things get too hard.
I'd attend school programs and chaperone dances.
Protect you from boys with too many glances.
I'd delight in your cartwheels and long auburn hair.
Buy you a pony to ride at the fair.
I'd laugh at your jokes and notice your fears.
Give you warm hugs and wipe away tears.
I'd share all my wisdom and offer my guidance.
Equip you for life and protect you from crisis.
I'd offer your hand to the gentleman you marry.
Be the best grandpa to the babies you carry.
I could go on until the page is all spattered.
But I can never replace the family I shattered.

No words or poems can fix the pain I caused or regain the lost years of separation. Along with the little girl, I missed a relationship with the woman you've become. I'm confident you are one precious gem. Remorse and regret filled each passing day. But at the end of those days, my guilt and shame didn't change the past. I could only change myself, so I did. I hope you're enjoying a beautiful and blessed life with a family who adores you. I loved you the minute I laid eyes on you, and I never stopped.

I love you,
Your Father

Jacob is doing his best to stop my tears from smearing the ink on the page. Aunt Maggie hands him one tissue after the other. Stunned, I sit at the table quietly. My mind swirls with conflicting chatter, trying to convince me my father couldn't have authored this letter, but my urge is to choose the truth over the lie. I believe my father wrote these words, but I don't recognize this person. Jacob leans over to check my breathing.

"Isabelle, are you okay?"

I stare at the letter. "I'm confused. His words are beautiful and heartfelt, but I don't know this man."

Aunt Maggie sits upright with her shoulders back.

"Well, of course you don't, sugar. Your father changed. I'm his big sister and I'm still amazed. He's a new man. It started several years ago, after that dreadful accident."

"What accident?"

Interrupted by a knock, Aunt Maggie squints toward the front door.

"Well, who on God's green earth could that be? I'm not expecting company today, except you two. Probably a pesty solicitor. Hold on, and I'll get rid of them."

Aunt Maggie leans and stretches, her eyes squinting more intently toward the door, then waddles quickly through the kitchen. I'm facing the other direction and hear murmuring between her and a man. Then Jacob utters the words I never expected. I tremble.

"I heard Maggie call him Sam. Isabelle, I think your father is at the door."

CHAPTER 25

The Reunion

Could it be my father at the door? It's killing me not being able to twist around and look. Did Aunt Maggie invite him here? I can't imagine her tricking me. Jacob fidgets while Aunt Maggie stays with the visitor.

"I'll find out who it is. Be right back."

"Okay, Jacob."

The murmurs turn to an audible whisper between the three of them. I can't take the waiting, so I call out for Jacob. With pounding footsteps, he approaches.

"Isabelle, I can't believe this. It's your father. He's right outside."

I'm queasy. "Are you serious?"

"Dead serious. Do you want to see him?"

I pause and my mind scrambles. "Yeah. No. Maybe. I don't know."

"Your Aunt Maggie is having a meltdown. His visit was unexpected. I'm sure of it."

I hear an impression on my mind saying, *you have a choice, Izzy, faith, or fear.* I blink several times attempting to think straight.

"I choose faith."

"What?"

"It's fine, Jacob. Assure her it's okay and let him in. This needs to happen."

"Are you sure?"

"Yes. I want to see him. But hurry before I chicken out."

"Okay. I'll be right back."

The impressions coming to my mind are clear. It's the counselor guiding me forward. *Don't look back.* And with that, my shoulders ease. The day will unfold precisely as intended. I'm living in the present, facing an actual event. No need for imaginary drama when every day brings enough trouble. The freedom of living in God's will permeates my soul. With God, I can face this. Jacob walks into the kitchen, resting his hand on my right shoulder, and whispers.

"Isabelle, your father's coming in. Are you okay?"

"I'm not sure."

"Now you're scaring me. Your Aunt Maggie is freaking out."

"I'm good. She will be fine. Bring him in."

Jacob studies me, pats my shoulder, and walks away. Aunt Maggie comes around the other side of me with teary, puffy eyes.

"Oh, sweet Jesus, Isabelle. I was not aware he was coming. You must think I set this whole thing up. I wouldn't. He said he felt an urge to see me. That's all."

"Of course, you wouldn't. I'd like to see him."

"Okay, sugar. I'll send Sam in, and we'll sit in the living room. Holler at us if you get upset."

Nothing prepared me for this moment. It's like ripping off a Band-Aid. You view the rip as too painful, but after one swift tear, it's all over. Then I look up and hear my father's voice.

"Hello, Isabelle."

Standing before me is a man I barely recognize. Holding on to the image of my father as a young man, I didn't expect the wear and tear of the aging process. Still fit and distinguished, but less flashy. His attire is sharp, yet modest. The icy demeanor etched in my mind from childhood melted. His eyes are warm and appear humble. Approachable.

I nod toward a chair across the table, holding back any emotion. "Hello. Have a seat."

"I'm so sorry about your accident. Are you healing up, okay?"

"It's a long process, but I'll be back to normal soon enough." I try to stiffen, but the sling makes me immovable. I couldn't run away if I tried.

His eyes briefly lower before returning to meet mine. "What a pleasant surprise. I assure you Maggie didn't tell me about your visit or knew about my unannounced appearance."

"I believe her. But why did you choose today?"

"It's strange. I never leave work early on Fridays like most of my co-workers. I felt an urge to leave the office at noon and take a long drive on this sunny day. Maggie popped into my mind. It's been a while since I've seen her, so I stopped by the nearby farmer's market and picked up fresh peaches and the apple cinnamon bread she likes. And here I am. Shocked to see you and Jacob, but I'm thrilled. He seems like a nice gentleman and is certainly protective of you." He shares an awkward grin.

Peering down, I sip my coffee. My mind searches for what to say.

"There's more coffee behind you, along with Aunt Maggie's famous strawberry shortcake. I'd get it for you, but as you can see, I'm immobile."

"I'm fine, but thanks for offering." The long silence is deafening. "Look, Isabelle. I understand your surprise and the overwhelming situation. Plus, you must be sore and tired. If you prefer that I leave, I understand. I'll depart a fortunate man with this chance meeting."

I pause and look up at him. "I read your letter."

"My letter?"

"The one you gave Aunt Maggie to hold until you passed away."

He jerks sideways. "But I'm not dead. Why would she do that?"

"Please don't be mad at her. It's a long, crazy story, but I learned about the letter on my own. Since I knew about her secret hiding place, she felt compelled to share the letter early. Roger, Abbey, and Shannon are not aware or involved."

"I'm not upset, just confused. How did you find out?"

"During my coma —"

"Coma?"

"Yes, I assumed Aunt Maggie told you I was in a coma after the cedar tree accident, and during the coma, I had an experience. Let's just say it was a supernatural encounter, and someone I trust told me about your letter and its whereabouts."

He raises his eyebrows and leans forward. "Wow. Sounds like a near-death experience."

"Not quite. I doubt you'll believe this, but I met with a counselor claiming to be sent by God to guide me. During my time with Him, He told me secret things, including your letter and where Aunt Maggie hid it. She's the only one aware of the secret hiding place. That's why she agreed to share the letter early. She couldn't explain away my knowledge and thought it might help."

He rubs his chin. "It's an outlandish story, but if God is involved, I can't deny it either."

I squeeze my brows together. "So, you believe me?"

"Why wouldn't I? Out of the blue, I get a nudge to visit my sister, and now I'm sitting across the table from my youngest daughter, who read the letter that was sealed until my death. He has my attention."

I stare at his letter. I can't believe the author is my childhood father. He never would have expressed himself like this. I'm dumbfounded.

He stretches his hand forward. "Since you read it, what did you think of the letter? I meant every word."

I breathe in deeply and exhale. "It's touching. I avoided all expecta-tions, but it shocked me." I pause briefly and toss the letter aside. "Frankly, I don't know the man who wrote those words. After so many years apart, it's difficult to comprehend."

He glances at the kitchen floor. "I know. We're strangers. I mean, look at you, you're a grown woman now. Still beautiful. Same auburn hair and sharp green eyes. So many years." He forces a grin.

"Thank you. You look good too, but you're a different person."

He sighs. "I take your words as a tremendous compliment. And the exact words in my letter."

"But how could you change so much?"

"Are you familiar with the phrase, with God, all things are possible?"

My mouth almost hit the floor. "More than you can imagine."

"Isabelle, God changed me. I'm glad to admit I'm not the same person, and I wouldn't be alive without divine intervention."

"I can relate. Aunt Maggie mentioned you started changing several years ago. I didn't believe her until seeing you now. Am I prying, or do you mind talking about it?"

"I don't mind, but it might be difficult to hear."

"Why?"

He swallows hard and pauses. "It involves my second wife and daughter."

The hair on my neck rises, and my face is hot. I try to squirm, but I'm a hostage to my injuries. It's futile. The impression on my mind says repeatedly, *faith or fear.* I close my eyes and pray silently for strength and reopen them. "Please tell me. Your life is a blank slate since the last time we spoke."

"Okay. Just stop me if it's too much."

I pull a tissue from the box. "I will."

"About a year after your mother passed, I married the lady you saw at the diner."

I gasp. Mother told him.

"You knew it was me that told Mother?"

He nods and lowers his head. "Yes. She told me that morning when she called my office to confront me. I hated myself for putting you in that position. It was cruel and unfair."

I grab more tissues and dot my eyes. "You told no one?"

"Of course not. It wouldn't change the outcome and only add more pain to a devastating situation. Our secret is bound between us forever."

"Thank you. Please continue your story."

"My second marriage lasted twelve years until a fatal accident."

I straighten. "What happened?"

"My wife and daughter went to the shopping mall to buy new clothes. On their way home, a semi-truck driver fell asleep at the wheel, they believed. He crossed over the median and hit their car head on. They died instantly." He closes his eyes and drops his head.

I gulp, taken aback by the shock, and stare at the top of my coffee cup. I'm speechless. The awkward silence lingers like a heavy cloud. He stares at the table. It's inconceivable to comprehend losing a child. Plus, losing a second wife at the same time. It's too much. I struggle to find any words. Nothing could prepare me for such news.

Nothing comes out when I try to speak. I take another gulp. "I'm so sorry. What were their names?"

He clears his throat. "Priscilla. My daughter's name was Tiffany. I'm better now. Truly."

Tears roll down my face and I wipe my cheeks with a tissue. I have no words.

"Isabelle, it must be difficult taking in so much in one day. I'm not sure this is a good idea considering your health. Would you like some water?"

"Please." He hands me a glass and I take a drink. "Thank you."

"Should I keep going with the story about how God changed me?"

"Yes, please."

"All right. Losing your mother and the separation from you all, plus losing another family, was too much. The mental anguish is inexplainable. To cope, I convinced myself I deserved it. I hurt too many people, and it was my turn to pay through mental torture. Everything made sense by inflicting a life sentence of self-punishment."

"I can't fathom losing one of my children. There are no words."

"I pray you never do. Losing five children is unbearable. Words from others trying to console me made it worse, forcing me to shut out those closest to me, like Maggie. I hated myself so much, positive words felt like daggers."

Self-loathing sounds familiar. "What happened to you?"

"The coward in me turned to alcohol to blur the mental clarity of my mistakes. After too many missed days and failing performance, I lost my job. Not working enabled a non-stop drinking binge and my money ran out. I was one day away from homelessness when a stranger knocked on my door. He saved my life."

"How so?"

"That evening, I drank enough to kill three men. I didn't care if I lived anymore and expected that night to be my last. I ignored the knocking, assumed it was my landlord, and waited for him to leave. The pounding got louder. He wouldn't quit, so I yelled for him to go away and threatened to call the police for trespassing. He shouted it was urgent, a matter of life and death. Hearing that, I dragged myself off the floor and staggered to the front door. Opening it, I questioned the short but fierce man about the emergency, and he said, sir, you are the emergency."

"Wow. Who was he?"

"My neighbor. I'd never met him before, but he said he watched me carry boxes of liquor into the house every day. When he took out the garbage, he noticed an excessive number of empty bottles in my trash bin. I scolded him for being nosey and later thanked the Lord for sending someone who cared. He had a gut feeling I was in trouble. So that same night, he dragged me out of my house, shoved me into his car, and drove me to an alcohol rehabilitation center. Too intoxicated to fight, I went along with it, admitted myself, and stayed ninety days. Evicted from my home and nowhere to go, the rehab offered me a book-keeping job for room and board plus meals. I gladly accepted. A humbling experience is exactly what I needed. He chose a Christian-based recovery center, and I thank the Lord again for my neighbor's wisdom."

My mind races for a proper response. Deep compassion overrules my old instinct of anger and resentment. I hear another impression saying the words, *grace, Izzy*. I'll keep listening.

"Keep going."

"Because of a stranger's kindness, I was given a second chance. During my time at the center, my neighbor and his wife picked me up every Sunday for church. I wasn't a godly man, and my view of church equated to TV evangelists soliciting money. I thought they were all scoundrels."

"I remember."

"In the beginning, I went to church out of respect for my new friend. After all, he saved my life, and I could never repay him. About six months in, I started listening to the sermons instead of fighting it. I joined a men's Bible study along with my Alcoholics Anonymous meetings. Over time, I fell in love with God's Word. By His grace, God healed me and I'm a new man."

Familiar skepticism creeps in, but it's weaker. The evidence of his story is undeniable. Do I believe him or fall back to my old ways of distrust and guarded walls? I close my eyes and call on the counselor for wisdom. An impression forms in my mind, saying, *choose to believe the truth and the lies will fade away.*

"Are you okay, Isabelle? Is this too much?"

I open my eyes. "I'm sorry for your losses. Believing you again seemed impossible, but I do. I'm relieved you're alive."

His mouth quivers. "Thank you. That means the world to me. I hope my story didn't upset you too much considering the history. I welcome opportunities to bring glory to God, but it still tears me up." He pauses. "Your mother, and all of you, are mentioned with honor in my testimony."

We both exhale at the same time. Empathy for the new man in front of me consumes every vessel. I can't stop it. The thought of me adding to his punishment for decades sickens me. I'm nauseous. I receive another impression repeating the words, *your life is always moving forward. Don't look back.* I thank the counselor in silence. He's right. Nothing good comes from living life stuck in the past, reliving the pain through punishment.

I raise my hand. "Wait a minute. Your neighbor? What is his name?"

"Otis Merriweather, and his wife, Rosemary."

If I could move, I would fall out of my chair. My mouth gapes open. "Do you know them?"

"He said he lived next door to a Sam O'Sullivan, but it just hit me. Otis and Rosemary Merriweather are neighbors at the family lake cottage."

He startles. "Really? I can't believe it. I haven't been there since . . ."

I interrupt the awkward moment. "Rosemary passed away several years ago. It was tough for Mr. Merriweather."

He lowers his head. "Oh, no. Poor Otis. I should have been there for him. They will always be my guardian angels. When they moved away, we lost touch. I miss him."

"He's doing well." I pause. "Funny thing, he used to encourage me to reconnect with my father. Until recently, I never mentioned your name, so he never knew it was you. The irony is uncanny."

"No doubt, Otis is one of God's anointed vessels. Wherever the

Lord places him, you'll see the hand of God in action. Rosemary too. She was a force for good."

"I agree. Special people."

Another pause lingers.

"Isabelle, thank you for listening. But I feel bad. I've done all the talking. If you don't mind, please tell me about your life."

I hesitate, staring at the yellow plastic flowers on the table. "I would like that. But it's getting late, and I shouldn't overdo it."

He stiffens. "Of course. I understand, and I'll be praying for your healing."

"Thank you." I tap the side of my water glass, stalling. "Perhaps we can plan another time to get together."

He sits upright with an eager look. "Isabelle, you name the date, and I'm there."

I swallow the enormous lump in my throat and my eyes well up. "How about tomorrow?"

He leaps out of his chair and bends on one knee beside my broken leg. Tears gush down his wrinkled face. He presses my cheeks, and we lock eyes. Then he says the words I've yearned to hear since I was a little girl.

"Isabelle, I love you. I've always loved you. Can you please forgive me?"

I break down, stammering to get the words out. "I forgive you, Dad, and I want to be in your life from this point forward."

"Me too, Isabelle. Me too."

He hugs my head carefully among my contraptions. I sense the love he's always held for me. It's marvelous.

The last boulder lifted. Through God's grace, we are free, and through forgiveness, we are redeemed. Now I understand what the counselor meant by seeing my father through God's eyes. Unconditional love. Then, another impression enters my mind, saying *you're set free, Izzy.*

Counselor, is that you? Are you there?

Yes.

I press my heart as the thought hits me. *Are you the Holy Spirit?*

I Am. I've been with you all along, Izzy, and I'll never leave you. This time, we did it together.

THE END

Acknowledgments

God——Thank you for inspiring this book and for guiding my steps. With you, all things are possible. You are the reason for sharing this story.

Keith Devine——To my favorite person, greatest love, and remarkable husband, thank you for loving me despite my flaws and for being my most loyal supporter. Without your encouragement and advice, this book would not exist.

Mike Meyer——Dad, thank you for always loving and supporting me. You taught me to work hard and deliver excellence. As my horse riding coach, I learned that achieving success requires extra effort. Without your love and life lessons, this book would not exist.

Judith Mullett——Thank you, Mom, for introducing me to Jesus. Thank you for always loving and supporting me. Among the many things, you taught me to rely on God and put others first. Without your role modeling, this book would not exist.

Tina Lorenz——To my big sister, thank you for always listening, laughing, and crying with me at any hour. You are the most courageous person I know and I've admired you since the day we met. Thank you for encouraging me in all endeavors, including this book.

DiAnn Mills——Thank you for believing in me when I didn't and for molding me into a better writer. Without your mentorship and valuable input, this book would not exist.

Jerry B. Jenkins——Thank you for sharing your vast writing knowledge through YNB and equipping me to write a book. Without your course, this book would not exist.

About the Author

TERESA DEVINE did not imagine a second career writing about Christian transformation. Her love for helping others overcome mindset limitations through God's healing power inspired this book.

Prior to writing, Teresa served as a transformational Chief Information Officer and reached the Fortune 500 company level. She studied at Indiana University and attended MIT Sloan and Carnegie Mellon's CIO Institute for executive education.

Teresa authors the column, *Fabric of Faith* on Patheos and her articles have appeared on The Christian Post, Oprah's Angel Network, and Beliefnet.

In addition, Teresa is the founder and CEO of Teresa Devine Co. LLC and brand creator of 24/7 Purpose® which is a social enterprise on a mission to help people love God and love others through writing, workshops, and wearables. Teresa's work is devoted to Jesus's greatest command found in Mark 12:28-31, where He explains our ultimate purpose as believers.

Teresa is certified with training, speaking, and coaching programs including Gallup/Clifton Strengths, John Maxwell Team, 6-Seconds Emotional Intelligence, and Marriage Today®.

Teresa lives with her husband in Ormond-by-the-Sea, Florida. She and her husband enjoy walks on the beach and coffee talks.

Thank You

FOR READING!

To show my gratitude, I invite you to visit...

facingthemindtrap.com

 Take a FREE Quiz! "Are you aligned with God?"

 Get the Mind Trap Workbook

 Join *Devine Insider* for sneak peeks, new book releases, merch & more.

Connect with Teresa online at

teresadevine.com

or follow her on

@teresasdevine

@teresadevineco

@teresa_devine

teresadevine.tv

@teresadevine

@teresasdevine